IF
I SEE
YOU AGAIN
TOMORROW

ALSO *by* ROBBIE COUCH

The Sky Blues

Blaine for the Win

IF
I SEE
YOU AGAIN
TOMORROW

IF
I SEE
YOU AGAIN
TOMORROW

ROBBIE COUCH

SIMON & SCHUSTER BFYR

NEW YORK LONDON TORONTO SYDNEY NEW DELHI

SIMON & SCHUSTER BFYR

An imprint of Simon & Schuster Children's Publishing Division
1230 Avenue of the Americas, New York, New York 10020

Text © 2023 by Robbie Couch
Jacket illustration © 2023 by Louise Pomeroy
Jacket design by Krista Vossen © 2023 by Simon & Schuster, Inc.

SIMON & SCHUSTER BOOKS FOR YOUNG READERS
and related marks are trademarks of Simon & Schuster, Inc.
For information about special discounts for bulk purchases, please contact Simon & Schuster
Special Sales at 1-866-506-1949 or business@simonandschuster.com.
The Simon & Schuster Speakers Bureau can bring authors to your live event.
For more information or to book an event, contact the Simon & Schuster Speakers Bureau at
1-866-248-3049 or visit our website at www.simonspeakers.com.
Interior design by Hilary Zarycky
The text for this book was set in Baskerville.
Manufactured in the United States of America
First Edition
2 4 6 8 10 9 7 5 3 1
CIP data for this book is available from the Library of Congress.
ISBN 9781534497498
ISBN 9781534497511 (ebook)

For the lonely ones

'M ABOUT TO TELL MY THERAPIST SOMETHING THAT I've never told anyone before. I shouldn't be nervous because it's Ms. Hazel (she's heard it all by now), and nothing matters anymore anyway. But still, it's going to be strange admitting this out loud for the first time.

"Can I tell you something?" I ask.

Ms. Hazel pauses from unwrapping her caramel hard candy to offer her full attention.

I clear my throat. "I think . . . I'm lonely."

She pops the candy into her mouth, smiling. "It's terrific to hear you say that."

My forehead crinkles with confusion. "I don't know if I'd consider it terrific."

"It's not terrific that you're lonely," she clarifies, shattering the caramel between her teeth. "It's terrific that you *told me*."

I like Ms. Hazel. I knew I would on day one. Oddly enough, it started with her office. You know how they say people look like their dogs? I think therapists look like their offices, and a therapist's office can tell you a lot.

Take Dr. Oregon. He had deep wrinkles carved into his face, like the cracked hardwood floor he insisted I sit on cross-legged and shoeless. I quit after our first session, not because I don't want my therapist to have wrinkles, but because I appreciate chairs. Mr.

Ramplewood had chronically bloodshot eyes and only wore gray, which matched the vibes of his dreary, water-damaged basement clinic. If he ever quits being a therapist—and he really should— I'd suggest Mr. Ramplewood follow his true calling and become a haunted house tour guide.

But Ms. Hazel's has a real Museum Collector Meets Amateur Hoarder energy, and for whatever reason, I dig it. We're sitting in identical brown-leather chairs separated by a coffee table covered in ancient psychology magazines, candy dishes to feed her self-diagnosed sugar addiction, and discolored rings from decades of coaster-less drinks. Faded floral wallpaper is hardly visible between rows and rows of shelves housing worn books and broken trinkets, and there are enough crookedly hung photos to sufficiently fill the interior of an office ten times larger than the one we're in. It may be a minimalist's nightmare, but I could tell, even during our first session, that the room's noisiness strangely helps in quieting my mind.

And Ms. Hazel, dwarfed in a waffle-knit sweater and yellow scarf despite the late-summer heat, is an extension of the elaborate room she's spent decades curating. An immovable gray crown of hair rests atop her head, and sparkly earrings shaped like ice cream cones dangle on the outside of her gargantuan glasses, which look like they were custom made for a beach ball with eyes—not a shrinking sixtysomething-year-old (though, somehow, they suit her.)

Sure enough, unlike Dr. Oregon and Mr. Ramplewood, I've enjoyed my visits with Ms. Hazel. Not necessarily because she's a better therapist than they are—although I think she is—or because her office is more comforting than theirs—although I know it is. I like Ms. Hazel because she gives it to me straight. Like I'm sure she will right now. So I ask, "Why did you suspect that I'm lonely? What gave it away?"

Without a moment of hesitation, Ms. Hazel breathes, "Everything."

My eyes pop at her bluntness, but Ms. Hazel doesn't seem to care as she springs up and starts busying herself around the room yet again.

During our first few sessions, I got a bit irritated having a therapist who apparently couldn't focus on me longer than thirty seconds at a time before bouncing off to a different task. But I grew to appreciate this eccentricity as I realized Ms. Hazel could be tinkering with a lampshade or pulling apart nesting dolls and still absorb my every word. She's not interested in performing the part of Good Therapist just to make me happy. And come to think of it, I sort of despised how intently the other two would stare into my eyes while pretending to care about the words coming out of my mouth. In their offices, I felt like I was on display, but in Ms. Hazel's, I feel like I'm just a part of it. And I like that.

She stops at her desk and starts rifling through paperwork before finding my session notes. "Here they are," she sighs. "Clark, I first suspected that you're lonely because you've mentioned that you've been feeling down since Sadie moved across the country, and that developing new friendships has been tough for an introvert like yourself—understandably so. It doesn't help that Sadie appears to be, as you once put it, *living her best life* without you in Texas." She emphasizes *living her best life* like it's an important clinical specification.

"But then your mom and dad are in the middle of a divorce, which, as we've discussed before, can bring about feelings of abandonment," she continues. "And, as I noted last week, it seems as though you've been succumbing to staying within an increasingly small comfort zone, which, I've found, ironically leads to *more* discomfort, like loneliness." She looks up at me with a sad smile. "All of that is to say, it sounds lonely in that head of yours, Clark."

She's entirely correct, but Ms. Hazel doesn't even know the half of it.

The *half of it* being the biggest source of my loneliness.

It's not worth bringing that up to her now, though. Believe me, I've tried. Three times. The first resulted in a concerned phone call to my mom, the second sparked a surprisingly hearty laugh—immediately followed by her choking on a caramel—and the third concluded with Ms. Hazel gently suggesting I watch fewer sci-fi movies. And since I'm actually hoping for some clarity today, I'll pass on an attempt four right now.

"How do I beat loneliness?" I ask. Her answer won't change my predicament, but knowing Ms. Hazel, it'll at least be interesting.

"Aha!" she squeals, pointing at me from across the office with a stiff finger.

I jump. Ms. Hazel *never* squeals.

Strange.

"That's a great question," she says. "I *love* that question, Clark. Because it shows you understand that loneliness can be a somewhat fleeting, fluid feeling, and not a chronic, immovable state of being. Many people aren't so convinced."

I'm not as convinced as Ms. Hazel seems to think I am (but I keep my mouth shut).

"Clark, I know what I want your homework to be this week," she says, returning to her chair with a pen and notepad, scribbling away excitedly as she sits. "It's a four-part challenge that I've found can work really well if the patient commits."

I tilt my head, thinking I misheard. "Did you say a four-part challenge?"

"That's correct, yes," she says.

That's . . . strange, too.

Ms. Hazel's homework for me is always simple and straightforward.

"Here's how I think you can beat loneliness, Clark—or, at the very least, begin to make progress," she says. "Number one: try to make a new friend, rather than just looking forward to graduating high school soon, and—"

"Hold on," I cut in.

She pauses.

My heart thuds. "Did you just say 'try to make a new friend'?"

She nods.

"Are you sure?" I triple check. "*That's* my homework?"

She nods again, but slower.

That's not right. She wasn't supposed to say that. That's not my homework.

That's *never* been my homework today, no matter what we've talked about.

She waits for me to explain my confusion, but I don't. "Did I say something to upset you, Clark?" she asks.

"No, it's just . . ." I trail off. "Never mind. Sorry. Okay, so, *try to make a new friend.* What's the second part?"

She clears her throat and looks back down at her notes. "The second part is . . ."

Gratitude journal. Of course that's what it's going to be, just like every today.

"*. . . help someone who could use it,*" she says. "Research shows that helping others can not only be incredibly gratifying, but it often connects us to others in meaningful ways."

What the hell is going on?

Ms. Hazel really has gone completely off script.

Sure, *I* go off script all the time. I deviate in just about every therapy session, asking off-the-wall questions and playing devil's advocate. But my deviations have never once forced Ms. Hazel to change her homework assignment for me.

So, I repeat: *What the hell is going on?*

I stand, circle the coffee table, and hunch over her side. Her handwriting reads, to my complete shock:

Clark's 4 tips to beating loneliness:

Try to make a new friend.

Help someone who could use it.

Be vulnerable so others can be too.

Do the thing that scares you.

"Are you serious?" I say, stepping back.

"Clark." She laughs. "Why are you so aghast? Does this feel like too much homework for one week? Is that it?" She nods supportively. "To be clear: you don't have to try all four tips this week. How about we start with just one?"

"What about the gratitude journal?" I ask, feeling sweat collect on my brow.

Her eyes widen, appearing even larger and more distorted than usual through the lenses of her glasses. Ms. Hazel flips back a page in her notes, showing me what's on the other side. It reads, as I expected it would:

Clark's homework assignment: start a gratitude journal.

"Now, how in the world did you know that I wanted you to start a gratitude journal?" she asks, bewildered. "That had been your homework—until you mentioned your loneliness."

Until you mentioned your loneliness.

I've said way more wackier things to Ms. Hazel in this office. Why would telling her that I'm lonely make any bit of difference?

I'm silent, weighing my options.

Should I lean into Ms. Hazel's unprecedented deviation in search of an answer and probably confuse the hell out of her? Or should I give it up and just go with the flow?

Before I can make up my mind, Ms. Hazel leans in, deciding for me. "You sneaked into my office before our session and peeked at my notes, didn't you?" she asks with a smirk. "That's how you knew about my gratitude journal idea? I won't be angry if you did, Clark."

I return to my seat, perplexed. "You caught me."

Ms. Hazel smiles, proud of herself for seemingly figuring it out.

But she doesn't get it. And how could she?

"Let's talk about my third and fourth tips to beating loneliness," she carries on. "Vulnerability. It's contagious, as we discussed last month, and opening up to others is often the catalyst for them to feel comfortable opening up to you. That's exactly how we build meaningful bonds. And then tip number four: *do the thing that scares you.*" Ms. Hazel pauses dramatically before continuing.

"We all have a thing that scares us, right? A terrifying thing we know we should do, or say, or try, because it's the right thing to do, or say, or try? It may not be intuitive, but I've found that it's often doing the scary things that reap the biggest rewards in terms of nurturing relationships with the ones we love—and nurturing relationships with ourselves. And . . ." She pauses, this time sensing that I'm distracted. "Clark?"

It's incredibly difficult for me to focus because, for some inexplicable reason, one of the unbreakable laws in the rulebook I've been forced to abide by just got broken, and I have no idea how or why that could have happened.

So here's the thing, in case it isn't clear: I've been stuck in a time loop. That sounds ridiculous, I know, but I'm not sure what else to call it. A temporal loop? A causal loop? The internet has lots of names for it (and none of them truly reflect how terrible they are). Basically, the same day is repeating itself. Nonstop. Presumably until the end of the Earth, because nothing I do has seemed to stop it.

To the best of my knowledge, I'm the only one aware that this is happening—or the only one that it's happening to. Everyone else wakes up and takes on the day as if they haven't already experienced it several times before. But in my world? Yesterday was today, just like today is today, and tomorrow will be today, too. Three weeks from yesterday? September 19. Four months ago? September 19.

And around and around *and around* we go.

Like I said, I've already told Ms. Hazel three times about the time loop to no avail. Even if I could find someone who'd believe me, they'd forget about it by the next today anyway. That's the main reason why I'm lonely. *That's* why I'm depressed. *That's* why my life—if you can even call it that anymore—is pretty much meaningless at this point. Sure, Ms. Hazel's new homework assignment is a bit baffling (to say the least). But as much as I want to hope that a broken time loop rule could be a clue in my effort to escape, I've been let down far too many times in this today to be fooled once again.

Still, I'll give Ms. Hazel some credit. She may be right in that Mom and Dad parting ways and Sadie moving to Austin haven't exactly helped when it comes to my loneliness. But life goes on after your parents separate and your best friend suddenly lives three states away.

It just can't when you're stuck in a time loop for the rest of eternity.

CHAPTER 2

SWING MY BOOKBAG OVER MY SHOULDERS, SAY BYE to Ms. Hazel, and push through the glass doors of her office building.

If you enjoy seasons like I do, you better pray to whatever divine being you believe in that you never get stuck in a time loop. Because as a person who appreciates snowmen and hearing the crunch of red leaves beneath my boots, leaving air-conditioned therapy and entering the same ninety-degree heat on my muggy walk home in every one of my todays is the absolute worst. As always, I'm drenched in sweat a block later.

You start noticing the most mundane things when you relive the same day over and over again—things that would fly completely under your radar under normal circumstances. Like the squirrel fight that breaks out on the corner of Eighth and North streets; the yappy Yorkshire terrier that barks at me three times from behind his human's front window, pauses, and then lets out a fourth; the old tree branch that exhales a rumbling creak in the breeze as you move beneath it.

Look, I get that adorable dogs and swaying trees are cute at face value. But after experiencing them exactly the same way over three hundred times, like I have? Not so much. By Day 309—the today I'm in now—the squirrel brawl and the terrier's four barks and the maple's creaks have lost their charm. Their predictability gnaws at my sanity, and I dread each one of the inevitable moments that remind me tomorrow will never come.

I could walk a different route home every now and then, I know. That'd probably help in keeping each today's gnawing predictability at bay. Going left on North Street to avoid the squirrel brawl would only add a minute to my commute (and what's a minute lost in my world, anyway?), and cutting across the park to stay clear of the terrorizing terrier would absolutely be worth the temporary grass stains on my shoes.

But even without knowing the half of it, Ms. Hazel wasn't wrong in suspecting my comfort zone has gotten increasingly small—and it's gotten *way* worse since being stuck in September 19. As much as I despise each today's inevitability, I'm even more overwhelmed at the thought of veering off the beaten path.

I get that this might not make much sense to someone who hasn't been stuck in a time loop. I'm bubble-wrapped in a riskless world with no lasting consequences, after all—what's there to fear? I wish it worked this way. But it's difficult for me to forget the bad things I've witnessed when I went off course in my earlier todays. Like, the car wreck I watched in real time during a spontaneous road trip to Wisconsin, or the terrified puppies living at the Rosedore animal shelter that I decided to drop into on a whim. And then there was the old man, all by himself, sitting on a city park bench, silent tears rolling down his cheeks. I hate that I know he's there, in every one of my todays, reliving whatever heartache brought tears to his eyes—just like the caged dogs will always be caged, and those car passengers will always crash. Some people might crave whatever adventure awaits them off the beaten path, but I see more opportunity for today's sadness to sear itself into my memory for good.

So it's the same exact route I always take that leads me through the front door of Mom's new, but very old, apartment. As always, it smells like pizza and stale cigarettes (thank you, previous renters). Judge Judy is on TV yelling at a man over unpaid parking tickets. All of our beige walls remain empty, their uneven paint jobs exposed. And half-empty cardboard boxes are scattered across the mint-green carpet, which Mom theorizes is older than she is, housing the random items we haven't found a place for yet. There are my younger sister Blair's old gymnastics outfits, for example, which sprinkle golden glitter wherever they go, and a giant ziplock bag of paper clips that Mom refuses to part with, even though they'll never get used.

My laptop is in one of the boxes, too, basically unusable with a badly cracked screen because it mistakenly got packed into a box without a FRAGILE label. You know what's worse than breaking your laptop? Breaking it right before you get stuck in a time loop, forcing you to use your mom's dinosaur computer for the rest of eternity instead. Yeah, I could get it fixed, which I did in a few of my early todays. But that task is not quick and gets very annoying very fast when you have to do it all over again the very next today.

We left Dad and our real house behind a couple weeks ago for this apartment and its legally ambiguous month-to-month lease. I thought it made more sense for us to stay in the house with Dad, considering Mom was the one who wanted the divorce anyway, but his sixty-hour-week work schedule made it too difficult for us to live with him on our own. So here we are.

The day we packed our bags, Mom promised that she'd find us a bigger, nicer, permanent place by the new year, claiming we'll be putting up a Christmas tree in a house with a backyard and more than one bathroom. Blair was generous in calling her timeline optimistic. I called it naive.

"Clark?" I hear Mom's voice from the kitchen.

"Hey." I toss my bag onto the sofa before finding the remote and cutting Judge Judy's volume in half.

"You're right on time," she says. "We're having—"

"Pizza."

"Huh?"

"Nothing."

"What toppings did you get, Mom?" Blair bellows from her bedroom down the hallway. "Please don't say pineapple again, because I might barf. . . ."

"Mushroom and ham for me and pepperoni and sausage for you," I answer, slipping off my shoes. "Mom will steal a couple slices from each of us but pick off a lot of the toppings because, as of this morning, she's trying to avoid red meat."

Mom leans sideways so she can see me through the kitchen doorway, her long dark hair dropping toward the pink tile. "When did I tell you I'm giving up red meat?"

I shrug.

She holds a suspicious stare before straightening back up, unsure what to make of my apparent fortune-telling abilities. "Wash your hands before we eat, okay?"

I zigzag my way between boxes of books and old photo albums before turning right into the apartment's one tiny hallway, then left into the apartment's even tinier bathroom. I close the door behind me and stare at the mirror above the sink, preparing myself for the exact same Mom Questions I've fielded hundreds of times before. ("How was school today?" is an infinitely more annoying question when you're stuck in a time loop.) I inhale, long and deep, and watch my chest expand in the reflection.

You know what's a strange thing no one prepares you for, on the off chance you get stuck in a time loop? The surrealness of seeing your body stop changing.

I'd been in the middle of a growth spurt over the summer, shooting up to nearly six feet tall (six foot one, if you count the untamable curls sprouting from my head). But as Permanently Seventeen-Year-Old Me confirms in the mirror, time loops don't allow normal biology to do its thing. So I'll probably never get to see my narrow face fill out, or get to watch the stubble scattered across my jaw grow into a legit beard like Dad's (even though I haven't shaved in what feels like almost a year). I'd be cool with some of my features staying with me forever, though, like the deep dimples that plunge into my cheeks when I grin, or my bright blue eyes, which, according to Sadie, "pair perfectly with olive skin," like mine.

Still, I wish I knew what Eighteen-Year-Old Me would have looked like by now.

I don't wash my hands—I know it sounds gross, but trust me, killing everyday germs is way less relevant in a time loop—and head back to the dining room.

"How was school today?" Mom asks me right on cue as I take a seat across from the two of them.

"Fine." I reluctantly slide a slice of my pie onto a paper plate. (And, yes, I began getting sick of mushroom-ham pizza by Day 10 or so.)

"What about you?" She glances at Blair.

Blair laughs and ignores Mom, too distracted with the video playing on her phone to hear the question.

"I *said*," Mom repeats, "how was your day, Blair?"

Still, nothing.

"What are you watching, anyway?" Mom asks her.

Derek Dopamine.

"Derek Dopamine," Blair answers, letting out another giggle.

Mom rolls her eyes. "I thought I told you not to watch his stuff anymore? His videos will make you stupider. Turn it off."

"Stupider isn't a word, Mom," Blair counters.

"Turn it *off.*"

Blair tosses the phone onto the empty chair next to her.

"Did you get a final head count for your birthday party tomorrow?" Mom asks her.

Blair, whose freckles nearly match the marinara sauce smudged around her lips, takes a moment to swallow before answering. "Fifteen."

Sounds like a party.

"Sounds like a party," Mom says.

At this point, Mom's and Blair's lines bubble up in my brain as if I'm rewatching the same sitcom episode for the 309th time.

Mom hands pieces of paper towel to us. "I know you both aren't fans of this apartment complex, but—"

"Understatement of the year," Blair interjects with a smirk.

"—*but,*" Mom soldiers on. "We won't be here all that long, so we might as well take advantage of the pool while it's still roasting outside, don't you think?" She glances at Blair, who gifts her a reluctant smile, and then at me, who does not gift her with anything.

We're not on the best of terms right now, me and Mom. You'd think I wouldn't be resentful anymore, 309 todays in, but emotions aren't that simple, I guess. Every morning, I wake up in this shoebox of an apartment and remember that she's the one who got us here because *she* wanted the divorce. She deserted Dad.

Mom, glistening in her purple spaghetti-strap shirt, clears her throat and moves on to the next subject, knowing as well as I do that my bitterness toward her won't be solved over just one dinner, even if, unbeknownst to her, we've had it hundreds of times. "What did you decide to bake for the party?" she asks me instead.

Blair, who despises cake—and especially ones associated with birthdays—perks up. "Yeah, what are you making for me and my friends?"

I pause to think. What *did* I decide on for Day 309?

Normally, I plan Blair's bakes while zoning out in class and during my walks home from therapy. But Ms. Hazel's homework deviation earlier was so disorienting, I've barely given Day 309's bake any thought.

Making treats ahead of time for the party is the only thing I enjoy now because I get to create something different each night after pizza. It's the only thing that helps keep me grounded in some sense of reality. Well, that, and obsessively tracking the number of todays I've been stuck in. Keeping a running tally helps my anxious self feel like I'm in control, even though I know that couldn't be any less true.

I've baked every kind of cookie, brownie, pie, and doughnut you can imagine, I swear. You name it, I've blended, scooped, or frosted it into culinary life. Sure, I'll probably never get to see how my birthday bakes land with Blair's friends, which is a bummer I've had to get over. But sometimes, when I daydream, I imagine all of my tomorrows existing somewhere out there in hundreds of parallel universes, a bunch of middle schoolers enjoying my bakes in all of them (minus the day I failed miserably at oatmeal raisin cookies; no one's enjoying those in that September 20, wherever it exists). And who knows, maybe my daydreams aren't that far off; maybe my baking skills *are* being appreciated by Blair and her friends somewhere in the infinite abyss. Especially those vanilla shortbreads I baked way back at the start.

Oh, that's right.

"Shortbread cookies with yellow icing," I say, remembering what I'd decided during third period earlier.

Blair licks her lips. "Will you make more than you *think* you need to make? My friends will come hungry. And it won't be the worst if we have extra."

She always asks. And I always say yes. "Yup."

We exchange quick, subtle grins, just like in every today. The bar may be below sea level at this point, but this is still one of the few highlights of my today.

Even if it can feel meaningless, I try to be there for Blair. She can be a twerp, for sure—and her twerpiness has definitely gotten worse since the divorce and ensuing move—but I know that she's feeling the same heartache over Mom and Dad's split that I am. It just manifests differently. Instead of holding a grudge, like I do, Blair finds solace in being a little brat. I can be the bigger brother and take it (most todays). That's why getting a genuine grin out of her can feel like a win.

"Can I be your baking assistant?" Mom asks me hesitantly. "We haven't spent much time together lately. I'd love to help out."

Just as Blair always asks if I can bake an excessive number of treats for her party, Mom always offers to help me pull it off. Unlike Blair's request, however, I decline.

"I'm okay," I say. "Thanks."

Mom tries and fails at masking her disappointment with a smile.

The room falls quiet, except for Judge Judy delivering her verdict in the adjacent room and the fizzing on the surface of Blair's glass of Coke.

After Mom's questions about therapy, and my confirmation that, yes, Ms. Hazel's cat, Oreo, *is*, in fact, feeling better, I start collecting our dirty paper towels and dinner plates to put the final nail in the dinner coffin.

Blair heads to the family room and balls up on the couch to sneakily watch the vlogger she loves that our parents despise, but Mom hangs back with me in the kitchen. She stays silent as she always does, watching me pull out the butter and powdered sugar, wanting so desperately to make this a mother-son thing.

I know what she's going to ask me.

You doing okay, Clark?

A time loop dinner has not gone by without concluding with this question. My answer, of course, is no. Not even a little bit. But what good would it do to tell her that? To confess that I'm lonely, that I can't get to tomorrow, and that I'm suffocating in an inescapable new normal with no end in sight? Telling the truth would ruin the night for both of us—and not make a bit of difference in Day 310.

Mom takes a step forward, about to pose her question, so I cut in.

"Could I have the kitchen to myself?" I say.

Her mouth closes.

"Sorry," I follow up. "It's just, it gets tight in here when I need all the counter space for a recipe."

She nods with a small, reluctant smile and disappears.

I preheat the oven, pull out the remaining ingredients, and try to get into a groove. But it's more difficult than normal for me to do so.

If only Ms. Hazel's wild homework deviation could work in my situation. *Meet a new friend. Help someone. Be vulnerable. Try something scary.* They seem like simple-enough tips and I'm sure her homework assignment benefited the lonely patients who had the privilege of living in a normal, linear space-time continuum. But if 309 consecutive todays have taught me anything, it's that, whatever world I've found myself in, it's far from the ordinary one.

Why would Ms. Hazel's four-part challenge make Day 310 any different?

CHAPTER 3

I HAVE A WHITE, WOODEN NIGHTSTAND THAT I DETEST. Not for any good reason, really—it's a regular piece of furniture that does not deserve to be on the receiving end of my rage. But as the very first thing I see every morning when I open my eyes to the blasting alarm on my phone at 7:15 a.m, that's what it gets.

Most people don't remember the first thing they see when they wake up in the morning. Maybe it's a ceiling fan. Or a blank wall. Maybe, if you're a stomach sleeper like Sadie, you wake up in a mound of pillows to an eyeful of cotton. Why would you remember any of that?

When you're stuck in a time loop and wake up to the same view every day, though? You remember. You can't *not* remember. The first thing you see haunts your dreams, confirming to you right away that the spell hasn't been broken and you'll be wasting away in yet another today. Thanks for being a dick, white, wooden nightstand.

I roll onto my back, turn off my alarm, and let out an involuntary yawn.

Another September 19. Day 310.

Here we go again.

Besides baking after dinner, mornings before school are my least-terrible time of today. Mom's already left to take Blair to an early volunteer project repainting old lockers at the middle school. So, this is the longest stretch of my Monday I get to be completely alone. It's only for a half hour, but still. I get to eat whatever I want for breakfast (today it's Girl Scout cookies), hang out in my underwear (something I would never do in ordinary times, knowing there's a chance Mom could walk back into the apartment at any moment), and blast whatever music or show I want to listen to as I get ready (right now, it's a podcast episode about UFO sightings).

I bet I know what you're thinking. Why go to school at all? Why do anything I don't feel like doing, if there are no consequences awaiting me in tomorrow's today? With Blair at school and Mom working at the bank, I could dance around in my underwear eating Thin Mints and avoiding responsibilities forever.

Here's how being stuck in a time loop actually works, though.

Days one through ten, you're pretty much in a constant state of horror that it's happening, convinced you're either dead, in a coma, stuck in a simulation gone wrong, waiting it out in purgatory, or some odd combination of the four. (And who knows—maybe one of those things is actually the real deal?)

Then, once the initial terror subsides, sure, you might have a honeymoon phase. That's when you skip school, eat all the junk food you want, and feel liberated to say whatever you want to say to whomever you want to say it, knowing none of it will matter in the next day's today. If you're extra fearless (unlike me), maybe you strike up a conversation with the crush you've been too intimidated to speak to, go streaking across the fifty-yard line during your school's football game, or dance around in the background of a local meterologist's sidewalk report. (I could see Sadie doing all of those things—even if she *wasn't* in a time loop, actually.) Maybe you head straight to the airport and fulfill your wildest, most expensive wanderlust fantasies since saving money doesn't matter—although you'd only have a few hours until you're back in your own bed again.

My honeymoon phase was brief—and relatively tame com-pared to what most people would be capable of in a world with no consequences—but still, it was freeing. I visited bougie bakeries that I couldn't justify going to in normal times, seeing as one muffin should never cost eight dollars, and spent another today wandering around the off-limits parts of botanical gardens that me and Sadie visited in ninth grade, taking selfies with the most bizarre-looking plants I could find. I wish my comfort zone were still as big as it had been then.

But believe me: your honeymoon phase will get old. The perks will fade, replaced with the soul-crushing reality that this is . . . *it*. This one day is now your entire life. You'll get sick of skipping school, and the insatiable wanderlust, and the endless junk food, I promise.

Around Day 50 is when the panic truly sets in.

You'll start desperately looking for answers (and I mean, *really* looking). Your internet browser history will fill up with off-the-wall sites like TheTruthReallyIsOutThere.Net. And the search terms you've pursued would have a loved one concerned for your sanity: *how to escape a time loop; are time loops scientifically possible?; extreme side effects of intense déjà vu; am I crazy or am I actually repeating the same day over and over again?* I'm not an expert on much, but during this next phase, I absolutely became an expert on all things time loops.

So, here's the time loop scoop.

Between sci-fi films, legitimate quantum physics research, and a million bloggers with too much time on their hands, you could probably guess that there are countless theories floating around. You could also probably guess that the majority of them are . . . absolute bullshit. Truly. I'm talking, dreamed up by an aimless forty-year-old typing away in his parents' basement—level bonkers.

The sad part is, even the few theories that seem to be somewhat informed by actual science have led me nowhere when I tested them out.

The even sadder part is, I resorted to trying a number of the obviously bullshit theories, too. Because, as they say, desperate times call for desperate measures.

And I was definitely desperate.

In one of my todays, I howled at the moon from Mom's apartment rooftop the exact moment the sun set because a blogger in Norway said that that tactic had worked for her. For me, all it did was prompt a neighbor to yell, "Shut the hell up, kid!" In a different today, I ate nothing until 11:11 a.m., then swallowed a cup of poppy seeds because a man in Minnesota swore it got him to his tomorrow. (I puked across Mom's family room.) And in what had to be the most pathetic attempt at escaping, I drove south into the cornfields of central Illinois around Day 90 until I found a farm horse to get into a staring contest with because a self-proclaimed "expert on time-bending"—who, spoiler alert, turned out *not* to be an "expert on time-bending"—responded to my email with said advice.

It would be really nice to talk directly to someone who knows what I'm going through, others who, at one point or another, have supposedly gotten stuck in their todays, too—like the Norwegian blogger and the poppy-seeds guy.

But those two never got back to me, and neither did five others I messaged. Two other alleged fellow time loopers did not speak English and my messages got *very* lost in translation (describing my predicament to someone is difficult enough when you both understand the same language, so can you imagine me—Clark Huckleton, monolingual seventeen-year-old from Rosedore, Illinois—trying to explain myself to a seventy-two-year-old grandma in Tokyo?). The one man who actually responded in English said he'd written his post about his experience reliving the same day when he was, quote, "shitfaced drunk," after the Patriots lost the Super Bowl. He then stalked my profile and, upon seeing a pic of my mom in a bathing suit from a family vacation three years ago in Ohio, asked me if she was single.

Not a single attempt to connect with someone claiming to have been in my boat has led me anywhere helpful.

So my desperation eventually led to apathy. And by about Day 150, I decided to give up as my existential dread went from running on fumes to running on empty. I realized that the bad things I'd noticed in my todays—the car crash, the puppies in need of rescuing, the sad man by himself in the park—were taking up far more room in my memories than the fun things I'd experienced during my honeymoon phase. I didn't want to remember them. I'd had enough. So then what?

This is the phase of the time loop where you'll devolve into an empty shell of the human you once were. For me, that meant reverting back to the painfully monotonous—but predictable and safe—routine of school, therapy, pizza, and birthday bakes until 11:16 p.m. every night.

Yes, 11:16 p.m.—the most cursed minute of my night.

That's the exact time when my today always ends. Not midnight, like you might think. Or 7:15 a.m. on September 20, which would give me a complete twenty-four hours. Nope, those two options would be at least a little bit rational.

But for some inexplicable reason, the time loop shoots me back to 7:15 a.m. right as the clock hits 11:16 p.m. It wouldn't matter if

I'm wide-awake riding a roller coaster or in the middle of a REM cycle; as a quarter past turns to sixteen past eleven, *boom*. I'm staring at my white, wooden nightstand again. I haven't seen a clock at 11:16 p.m. in a very long time.

So, yeah, that's the stage I've been in ever since, and my entire existence has been shrunken down into the same repeating sixteen hours and one minute on a smoldering, mid-September Monday in the bland Chicago suburbs.

Jealous? (Didn't think so.)

I crunch down on a Girl Scout cookie while glancing at my phone and notice that I'm running behind. Not that it'd make any bit of lasting difference, but I'm not in the mood to be lectured about tardiness in first period. So I throw on a shirt and shorts, shape my Albert Einstein hair into something resembling an acceptable style, snag my bookbag, and head out.

Just like the route from Ms. Hazel's office to home, my half-mile walk to school is filled with the torturously predictable elements: the school-bus driver who loves hearing the sound of his own honking, the stressed-out dad who spills a full drink carrier of coffees while stepping into his car, the well-meaning crossing guard who mistakenly greets me with, "Good morning, Clay," as I pass. There are two redeeming qualities my morning walk has that my afternoon walk from therapy does not, however: one, it's not a hundred degrees outside yet, like it is by 5:00 p.m., and two, I get to FaceTime with Sadie.

"Hey, babe," she says, just like in every today, as her round face lights up the screen of my phone. "G'morning."

Sadie has blond hair with streaks of teal, dark-gray eyes, and an immovable smile. She's on her own walk to school, where she'll hang out with her cool new friends in the Podcast Club. Even though Sadie moved to Texas roughly five seconds ago, she already has more friends in Austin than my introverted self has in all of Illinois after living here my entire life. Honestly, I wouldn't be surprised if she were crowned prom queen in the spring. (It's a bummer I'll never know if that happens—or maybe it already has.)

I miss Sadie so much I could cry. And on some todays, like Day 306, I do.

"Do you think I can get better at meeting new friends?" I cut to the chase.

Sadie laughs, eyebrows crinkling as she looks both ways at an intersection. "Where is this coming from?"

This morning, recalling all my failures to find others who've been stuck in a time loop—and the loneliness that has ensued after each—brings Ms. Hazel's homework deviation even more top of mind. The first tip in her four-part challenge has especially stuck with me.

"Yesterday Ms. Hazel called me an outcast who needs more friends."

She rolls her eyes. "She did not call you an outcast."

"Maybe not in those exact words, but that was the gist."

"Why were you with Ms. Hazel yesterday?" she says, her lips finding a straw. Milky iced coffee shoots up into her mouth. "You don't have therapy on Sundays."

Oh right. "It was in an email."

I try not to lie all that much on the off chance that moral behavior is somehow connected to my prospects of escaping today. But a fib here and there wouldn't hurt my chances, right?

"Speaking of yesterday," Sadie says, lighting up. "So? How was it?"

I stare at the screen.

"The *concert?*"

"Oh," I say, remembering. "Right."

This deviation is really messing with my head.

"I texted Truman this morning and it sounds like you had fun, Mr. Lightweight," she says, smirking. "I'm so jealous! Tell me everything."

It's hard to do that since I've noticed it's getting more and more difficult for me to remember much from the real yesterday. I drank too much booze in the back of Truman's dad's minivan before seeing The Wrinkles concert—*that*, I'm absolutely sure of (mostly because Sadie never fails to call me Mr. Lightweight during our morning FaceTimes). So the rest of the night is hazy. But earlier that afternoon, Mom sat me down to tell me she'd been the one who wanted the divorce without providing a valid excuse why, sparking a fiery argument between the two of us that never got resolved. Ironically, it's the conversation most seared into my memory from that Sunday despite it being the interaction I wish I could forget the most.

I mean, wanting a divorce is one thing when there's a justifiable reason. But who decides to tear up their family overnight for no good reason?

Anyway. Sadie's not interested in my family drama right now.

"The Wrinkles were great, but hold on." I don't even pretend to care about filling her in on the show this time. "Do you?"

Sadie's confused. "Do I . . . what?"

"Do you think I need to make more friends?"

She shrugs, taking another sip of her drink. "I mean, I don't know. You have friends. Don't let Ms. Hazel get in your head."

"Isn't that the whole goal, though?" I ask. "Shouldn't my therapist be in my head?"

Sadie ignores this. "What about Truman and the crew you went with last night? They're your friends."

"They're *your* friends," I correct her. "I just wound up going to the show with them."

"You're too picky. Besides," she says, "we should all be open to making new friends."

"It sounds like you've already made plenty down in Austin."

She gives me a look. "Why do you say it like that?"

Damn it.

"I didn't mean to say it like anything," I say. "Sorry."

She's quiet for a moment. "It's not like friends grow on trees down here, Clark."

"I know."

"This school is twice as big as Rosedore. It was overwhelming at first."

"I bet."

"And it's been tricky to find my people."

I try not to roll my eyes (because of course it hasn't been tricky for her), but I don't want to spoil our FaceTime.

"Please just ignore me," I follow up. "Ms. Hazel has me in a funk today with this 'make a friend' homework. You know how anxious I get around new people. If you look up 'introvert' in the dictionary, it'd be my awkward freshman-year photo staring back at you."

Sadie's lips crack into a grin. "How could I forget the photo that caught you on the verge of sneezing."

"Seriously," I continue, seeing that I'm winning her back. "I am the human embodiment of the Venn diagram overlap between 'bodily functions happening at the worst time' and 'awkwardly quiet around new people'—"

"Okay, stop it with the pity party." Her grin grows. "You can make friends. That should be obvious coming from your best one. Who cares if you're not the most outgoing?" She shrugs. "Besides, remember the promise we made each other the night before I moved to Austin?"

I pause to think.

"C'mon," she laughs. "We were in the same spot that we first agreed to be friends in middle school. The swings—"

"—in the Rosedore City Park," I finish her sentence, remembering. "Duh, of course. We promised that we'd still have great senior years, even if they couldn't be spent together."

"Exactly," Sadie says. "So let's at least try, okay?"

I nod and stare at the sidewalk in front of me, angry that the time loop has made upholding my end of the promise virtually impossible.

"Hey," she says, drawing my attention back to her and lowering her voice. "Even if you don't make a single new friend this year, you've got me. I'll be back for Christmas. We'll see each other."

"By, 'we'll see each other,' I hope you mean, 'we're going to spend every waking second that I'm in Illinois together.'"

"Correct."

I know better, of course. Christmas will never come for me, and I'll only see Sadie's face on my phone's screen from now on. But sometimes faking hopefulness makes me feel better, even if for just a split second.

"I have to run to Podcast Club before my first class," Sadie says. "But I want to hear more about how the show went at some point today! Oh, and good luck baking for Blair's birthday tonight. What did you decide to make her?"

I think. "Baked churros, maybe?"

"Whoa." Sadie's eyes double in size. "Churros? You're really going for it, huh?"

By Day 310, long gone are my evenings of chocolate-chip-cookie bakes. I've got to think outside the basic recipe box or risk my mind turning to complete mush, after all. "I'll send you a pic of the finished products later tonight."

"Mmm, can't wait," Sadie says with a wink. "Deal."

I hang up and reflect on our chat as I climb my school's concrete steps.

I value Sadie's friendship more than I can put into words, of course, and I genuinely appreciate her encouraging me after learning about Ms. Hazel's first tip. It's just difficult having to hear advice about making new friends from your social butterfly BFF when you're an anxious introvert like me.

From there, Day 310 creeps by more tortuously than normal, with every domino falling in an even more annoyingly predictable fashion. In second period, Sara Marino argues that changing Columbus Day to Indigenous Peoples Day is an attack on her Italian heritage—a stance that's somehow gotten even more offensive (and I say that as someone with Sicilian roots). Greg Shumaker trips and spills chocolate milk down his shirt at lunch, which had been funny for a while, but even seeing a total douchebag completely embarrass himself loses its luster by Day 30 or so. By the time last period rolls around, I'm in full zombie mode, floating through the halls with glazed eyes and unmistakable indifference.

The tardy bell has already finished ringing by the time my classmate Thom dashes into the room and drops into the seat next to mine in the back row. "Do you think Mr. Zebb noticed?" he whispers.

I'm shaking my head before he even finishes asking. "You're fine."

The nervousness in Thom's freckled face melts away at once, as it always does. "Thank God," he says, scratching at the red hair atop his head in relief. "I hate trig but one more tardy and I'm—"

"Screwed?"

"Exactly."

Thom is a nice enough dude now. But he was the boy on the playground who tormented the girls he had crushes on when we were kids—he pushed Sadie off the monkey bars in fourth grade, resulting in many tears and bloody Band-Aids—and I'm still a little bitter about it, not gonna lie.

"Who hated the homework?" Mr. Zebb asks from the front of the class. He's squeezed into a slim-fitting red polo and seated on a tiny stool half the size of his butt, which truly could not look less comfortable. "Don't be ashamed to speak up. I know cosines aren't for everyone."

With the inevitable mention of cosines, my mind drifts away once again.

First, it goes to the baked churros I may make for Blair's birthday (I don't think Mom has all the necessary ingredients in her pantry, so I'll probably need to walk to the grocery store after pizza). Then it's back to Sadie and her Podcast Club, which sounds pretty fun. I wish we had one at Rosedore, honestly. If only I could work up the nerve to speak to an audience, I bet I wouldn't be the worst host for a series about amateur baking—

"Oh." Mr. Zebb's surprised voice yanks me back into math class.

Oh?

The word ricochets throughout my brain. Because Mr. Zebb never mutters a surprised "oh" at this point in the day. I look up. A boy, taller than me, is standing in the doorway. I . . . don't know who he is. He's never been in the time loop before.

My stomach shoots up into my chest.

"Can I help you?" Mr. Zebb asks him.

The boy takes a step into the room. "I'm Beau."

"Beau," Mr. Zebb repeats, confused. "What can I do for you, Beau?"

Now Beau is the one who appears confused, even as his face breaks into a smile. "You weren't expecting me?"

Mr. Zebb glances around the room as if he's being pranked. "Should I've been?"

"I'm a transfer student," Beau says. "Beau Dupont." His eyes bounce around the classroom before spotting the empty chair between me and Zach.

Without waiting for permission, Beau glides down the rows of desks like a steak knife through butter, instantly captivating every eye in the room—*especially* mine. His arms, long and chiseled, are left exposed by the bright-green tank top that barely covers his brown midriff. A silver bracelet hangs near a discreet tattoo on his right wrist, and his stormy, amber eyes send the best kinds of chills down my spine.

What in the . . . ?

A disoriented Mr. Zebb glances toward his desk in search of paperwork he may have missed. "I wasn't expecting a new student today."

Same.

Beau slides behind the desk next to mine in his acid-washed

shorts. "The secretary—Ms. Knotts I think is her name?—told me I should just head here. Is that not okay?"

Mr. Zebb seems increasingly perplexed, just like I am. "Well, sure. I guess so. But before class tomorrow, I'm going to need your paperwork, all right?"

"Sure thing, Mister . . ." Beau trails off, unsure.

"Zebb."

"Right. Sorry."

Holy shit. How can this be happening?

Ms. Hazel changing up her homework assignment for me was unprecedented. But an entirely new person popping into the time loop? My mind can't compute what my eyes are seeing.

Mr. Zebb carries on about cosines, but all I hear is my heartbeat thundering away in my eardrums while my anxiety shoots through the roof. I'm pretending to direct my attention at the board and not at Beau, whoever he is, but I want to learn more about him. *So* badly.

Who is he? Where did he transfer from?

And why the hell is he suddenly in Mr. Zebb's 310th last period?

"Mr. Dupont," Mr. Zebb scolds.

I glance in Beau's direction and realize he's whispering something to Thom.

"Sorry, Mr. Zed," he says.

"Zebb."

"Zebb. Right. With a *B*—as in, banana," Beau says as if he's running through a memory exercise. Sara Marino giggles a few rows away. "I was just asking Thom for a pencil so that I can take notes."

"You can do so quietly, so you don't distract the rest of the class," Mr. Zebb says.

"Won't happen again, Mr. Z."

Mr. Zebb opens his mouth to correct him.

"Zebb," Beau clarifies. "Sorry."

Mr. Zebb clears his throat. "As I was saying—"

"Real quick, while I have you," Beau interrupts. "I have to ask, when will any of us ever use this stuff after high school?"

Every student, stunned, turns toward Beau.

Mr. Zebb, equally shocked, runs his tongue across the fronts of his teeth. "First of all, you should raise your hand if you have a question."

"Will do, sorry."

"And secondly, there are many careers that use trigonometry."

"Not any cool ones."

A few kids gasp.

Mr. Zebb, flustered, laughs awkwardly. "I disagree."

"Shouldn't we be learning about math in more practical and important ways?" Beau asks. "Like, how to run numbers while filing our taxes. That seems useful. Or how redlining in banking screwed over Black Americans for generations. That lesson should be a priority"—he glances around the classroom—"especially in a suburb as white as a jar of mayonnaise."

I snort out a laugh and quickly cover my mouth.

Mr. Zebb's eyes widen, unsure how to react. "Well—"

"When you think about it," Beau says, standing up. "Trig is probably pretty close to last on the list, in terms of relevant subjects in a teen's life, don't you think?"

I gulp, not having a clue where this interaction could possibly be headed.

"Please sit down," Mr. Zebb says.

But Beau does the exact opposite of sitting down. He jumps up onto my desk, his gray sneakers inches from my face.

Several more students gasp this time.

"Get down!" Mr. Zebb bellows.

Beau jumps onto Thom's desk from mine, ruffles Thom's red hair with a devilish grin, and then springs over to Greg Shumaker's. Then Cynthia Rubric's. And on *and on* he goes. The class erupts into mayhem.

"Can't we all admit that trig sucks?" Beau booms, his feet bouncing from desktop to desktop.

In a final act of WTF, Beau leaps from Sara Marino's desk . . . onto Mr. Zebb's.

Oh my God.

Mr. Zebb is stunned into silence.

"What the hell is happening?" Thom says over my shoulder. I turn to see him; he's wide-eyed, almost pained, at the spectacle unraveling in front of us. "I'm getting out of here before things get even more nuts."

Thom darts out of the room.

"Why is everyone so worked up?" Beau asks no one in particular, absolutely delighted. He taps his phone and a song starts blaring. Sticky notes, staplers, and framed photos slide off the edges of Mr. Zebb's desk and crash into the floor as Beau begins dancing to the beat. "I'm just trying to spice up your Monday. That's all."

"I'm calling security," Mr. Zebb announces, his phone already held firmly against his cheek.

Immediately, Beau leaps off the desk and scurries out of the classroom.

A red-faced Mr. Zebb collapses onto his tiny stool and almost topples over by doing so. Every student I see appears to be in a state of shock, glancing around the room with open mouths, unsure of what exactly they just witnessed. As I watch a rattled Mr. Zebb attempt to make sense of what happened, I hear Ms. Hazel's voice loudly and clearly in my head: *Try to make a new friend.*

I can see the first homework tip in my therapy notes, written in her extra-curvy handwriting, too.

It's rare that I come across a person who I've never met before, especially when I haven't deviated from my normal routine. And Beau certainly seemed to barge into my today with purpose (although what the purpose *was*, exactly, isn't so clear). Could Beau Dupont be a potential new friend? Thom, Mr. Zebb, and everyone else in class are unsettled by Beau's outburst, which means that I, of *all* people, should have been downright terrified. But I'm . . . not? The adrenaline pumping through my veins isn't the same nerves I feel when I deviate off course or leave my comfort zone behind. It's not dread that I'm feeling, I realize. It's excitement.

Is the universe trying to tell me something?

I take off out of the classroom and swivel my head left and right looking for him, but instead I find an overwhelmed Thom down the hall. His hands are on either side of his forehead, mouth hanging open like a suffocating fish. "Can you believe that?" he breathes as I approach.

"Where did he go?" I ask. Thom squints, confused why I would ask, before pointing farther down the hall. "Why? Are you going to follow him?"

I take off without giving an answer.

I hit an intersection and glance down each hallway before spotting Beau's back jogging away in the distance.

"Wait!" I call after him.

Either he doesn't hear me or he doesn't care, but Beau remains on the move. So I run as fast as I possibly can, straying *far* off the beaten path of my day. I can't get in my own head about that now, though.

"Please, hold on!" I yell again after gaining on him. "I want to talk to you!"

He rounds a corner, bursts through the building doors and into the teacher parking lot before finally stopping to turn back and face me.

"Hi," he says, casually. "What's up?"

"What are you doing?" I say, hunched over, completely out of breath.

"What do you mean?"

I arch my brows, then gesture back toward the building. "Why did you do all that?"

"Do what?"

I gesture again. *"That."*

He laughs but ignores my question and looks me up and down. After a few moments of quiet tension—Beau is assessing if I'm worth talking to, I imagine as I try to catch my breath—he asks, "Do you want to run a few errands with me?"

Errands?

Errands?

Who is this guy?

"You want me to run *errands* with you," I repeat, standing up straight again, my breath finally caught. "Like . . . to the Laundromat? That kind of errand?"

"Not quite. No detergent will be required."

"I mean, I—"

"You better decide fast . . . what's your name?"

"Clark."

"You better decide fast, Clark. Because I'd guess that they're coming for me."

My mind is spinning. "Would we be walking? Driving?"

Beau, his smile shifting into a devilish grin, raises his hand to show that keys are dangling from his fingertips. "I don't have a car, but Mr. Zebb does."

He snatched Mr. Zebb's keys off his desk?

Beau turns toward the parking lot and presses down on the fob. Somewhere in the distance, Mr. Zebb's car beeps its location at us. Beau circles back to me, pleased with himself. "So, what do you say, Clark?"

I pause, feeling beads of sweat begin to trickle down my face. My knees are about to buckle, my heart is on the verge of exploding through my chest, and the risk-averse voice in my head is screaming at me that this is a terrible, horrible, absolutely bonkers idea—even in my world of no consequences. And yet, for some reason, Ms. Hazel's first tip is screaming louder.

Try to make a new friend.

As he predicted, the front doors of the school burst open and a group of school officials, led by an irate Mr. Zebb, spread out onto the sidewalk, presumably on the hunt for the new transfer student gone wild.

So, before I overthink it, I nod at Beau and swallow hard. "Sure, I'll run errands with you."

CHAPTER 4

BEAU CRANKS THE IGNITION. "YOU BETTER BUCKLE up," he says, grinning at me in the passenger seat.

How do I feel stealing a teacher's car? It's a question I never thought I'd be asking myself, but here we are. I would've guessed I'd be horrified, considering committing grand theft auto is light years outside my comfort zone. And, to be crystal clear, I am. But I'm also equal parts exhilarated, like that split second of terror you feel at the top of a roller coaster, times a hundred.

The engine roars, propelling Mr. Zebb's car out of its spot. We speed through the parking lot, tires squealing against the asphalt as the group of school officials wave at us to abandon the heist. For obvious reasons, Mr. Zebb appears the most determined of the bunch. Despite being a mathematician who should know about the inconvenience that an accelerating vehicle can cause a two-hundred-pound body, Rosedore's trigonometry teacher stands directly in his own car's path.

"Uh, hey . . . ," I warn as the alarm of what's about to happen sinks in. In the blink of an eye, the gap between Mr. Zebb's car and Mr. Zebb shrinks from about fifty feet to fifty inches. I start to scream, but Beau starts to laugh.

A moment before what would have been the time loop's first homicide, Mr. Zebb launches himself to the right, avoiding death (or, at the bare minimum, a very long day in the hospital).

"Are you crazy?" I yell, clutching at my seat belt, hardly able to breathe.

Beau considers the question. "It depends on your definition of crazy."

We peel out of the school parking lot, blast through a red light, and beeline toward the expressway going three times the speed limit. Other cars honk at us as we zigzag through traffic, and as I spot in the rearview mirror, Beau's driving is the root cause of at least one fender bender.

"Question," he says calmly, fiddling with the side of his seat. It jets back from the steering wheel, making room for his long legs. "How do I know you?"

My throat is so swollen with shock that I can't find the words to respond.

"You look familiar," he continues, eyebrows crinkled. "You *feel* familiar, too—"

"Look out!" My brain finds my vocal cords again right before we obliterate a man on a motorcycle.

Beau seamlessly shifts lanes, avoiding a second deadly disaster. "Relax, Clark. I drive for NASCAR."

"You do?"

"No."

I glance in all the mirrors, expecting to see police tailing us. "If you don't kill us first, we're going to get pulled over."

"I'm a Black kid." Without looking down, his hand finds a fast-food cup in the drink holders between us. "There's a good chance that'll happen, no matter how fast or slow we're going."

I watch as he raises Mr. Zebb's drink to his lips. "Really?" I say, disgusted.

He takes a sip and grimaces. "*Oof.* Warm, stale root beer. C'mon, Mr. Zed, you're better than that."

"It's Zebb—*hey!*" We nearly take off a parked minivan's side mirror.

"Clark, I'm going to ask you one more time." Our eyes lock like magnets; I couldn't look away, even if I wanted to. "Will you please chill?"

I try to steady my breath.

"Do you trust me?" he asks.

"Do I *trust* you?"

"Yes."

"I just met you."

"But do you?"

"Uh . . ." I go silent for a moment. "No? Not really?"

He smirks with a nod, seemingly surprised by my honesty as we drift across three lanes. "That's fair."

Beau unrolls his window. The humid, hot air pulsates throughout the car as he nudges the volume up on Mr. Zebb's radio. An old disco song blares over the wind beating on my eardrums. I don't know the words, but Beau has every one memorized.

Who is this boy?

"So, have we?" Beau asks over the music.

"Have we what?"

"Have we met before?"

"No," I say, cringing as we zoom dangerously close to a Jeep. "I don't think we have."

I know we haven't. Even with the time loop messing with my memory, I know I would remember Beau; his ease, his energy, his voice—warm, deep, and a touch raspy, like a bonfire crackling on its last log. Nothing about him is subtle, and even less is forgettable.

"Well, I think you're wrong." His eyes dart between me and the road. His lips, pink and full, curl up into a grin. "Maybe we met in another life."

We veer onto an expressway ramp toward Chicago and my heartbeat rises faster than the speedometer on Mr. Zebb's car. I haven't deviated this far from my beaten path in a long time, and I couldn't tell you the last today that I ventured into the city.

"Why are we going to Chicago?" I ask, trying to sound less nervous than I am.

"Brownies," Beau answers.

"Brownies," I repeat. I . . . wasn't expecting brownies. "As in, the things you eat?"

He looks at me. "Is there another kind?" Beau cranks the radio volume even higher and begins belting along to the lyrics once again.

With Rosedore bordering Chicago, we only drive a few minutes before the views outside our windows evolve from strip malls and fast-food joints to towering office buildings and reflective high-rise condos. (Beau driving twenty miles per hour over the speed limit also doesn't hurt the commute time.) We dash off an exit somewhere downtown, where Beau begins driving slightly more carefully, presumably due to the hordes of pedestrians and cars sharing the road. Finally, he glides into a parking spot on the street and turns the ignition off.

I'm not sure if I've ever felt this level of relief to have made it to a destination. I've never died in the time loop—by accident *or* choice—and I don't want to start in Day 310.

"Here," he announces, hopping out onto the sidewalk in a flash.

"Where's here?"

"Ben's Everything Blue Bakery," he says as if it should mean something to me. He bends in half to see me in the passenger seat and realizes that it does not, in fact, mean anything to me. "You're telling me you've never been to Ben's Everything Blue Bakery?"

I shake my head.

"Are you even a real Chicagoan?"

I think. "Technically, I've never lived in the city, so . . ."

He rolls his eyes with a smirk. "I'm about to blow your mind, suburbanite."

I step out of Mr. Zebb's car and close the door behind me.

There's no question why the bakery has its name. Amid a block of beiges, browns, and grays, the storefront of Ben's Everything Blue Bakery sparkles like sapphire, its brick exterior painted a vivid, metallic blue.

"Are you, uh . . . ?" I gesture at Mr. Zebb's car.

"Am I what?" Beau asks.

"Aren't you worried about getting caught with a stolen vehicle?"

He shrugs, taps the key fob with a *beep*, locking Mr. Zebb's car, and heads toward the entrance, unbothered by my hesitation.

I take another glance around, still expecting to hear sirens chasing after us or spot my enraged mom racing down the sidewalk on foot. But we blend in seamlessly with the city's hectic hustle and bustle, at least for now.

What's the worst that could happen anyway? I spend the rest of Day 310 in jail? That'd be a time loop first, but certainly not the end of the world.

I jog after Beau—I sense that if I don't keep up, he'll easily slip away from me—and into the bakery.

Unsurprisingly, the all-blue theme continues inside. The tile on the floor? Navy. The ceiling fans? Turquoise. The guest tables scattered throughout the room? Royal blue. Even a few customers (clearly tourists) are wearing the color, seemingly in celebration of their visit.

I follow Beau to the other end of the bakery, where a long display case stretches the width of the space. Inside, an assortment of treats rest on decorative trays and tiered serving stands, and every last baked good is—yep, you guessed it—blue. Blue cookies, blue cakes, blue icings, blue macarons. There must be a massive tub of food coloring in the kitchen, because not one item is the color nature intended it to be. And here I was, thinking I was clever putting yellow icing on the shortbread cookies for Blair.

"Ben's really not messing around with this blue theme, huh?" I mutter in Beau's direction.

"He takes his blues seriously," he answers. "And the owner's name is Otto, not Ben. Here he comes now."

The swinging doors to the kitchen blast open and one of the largest men I've ever seen comes bouncing out with a basket of blue rolls and a smile that takes up half the real estate on his face. "I'll be right with you," he assures the couple ahead of us in line.

Otto is round, bald, and the height of two Ms. Hazels stacked on top of each other. His jaw makes up for what his head lacks, housing a bristly, blondish-red beard that I'd guess is a foot long (it's difficult to tell as it's contained in a hairnet). Otto's apron is dusted in shades of blue that match his periwinkle eyes, and his arms, thick and freckled, are plastered with faded tattoos and the occasional stretch mark.

The couple in front of us order two coffees and a piece of (blue) carrot cake to split. Otto dashes around behind the display case with the agility of an Olympic gymnast and rings them up at the register before returning to us, small beads of sweat dotting his forehead.

When he sees who I'm with, Otto's face bursts with elation. "Beau!"

Beau grins, offering a bashful wave. "Hey, Otto."

"It's been too long," Otto says. "*Way* too long, if you ask me."

"I know," Beau says, maybe a bit ashamed.

"How have you been?"

"As good as I can be. How about you?"

"I'm holding up okay."

The two stare at each other in silence.

There's something unspoken between them, I can tell, a heaviness that hasn't been dealt with. But my being here or the bakery's busyness—probably both—are keeping them from addressing it head-on.

Beau shift gears and turns toward me. "This is Clark."

I feel the heat rise in my cheeks, which happens just about every time my existence is acknowledged publicly. "Hi," I say, clearing my throat.

"Clark!" Otto says. "What a great name. How'd you get it?"

I scrunch my face in thought, the redness expanding into my neck. As my awkwardness begins teetering on the edge of agonizing, I decide admitting that I don't know is better than making something up on the fly to avoid embarrassment.

I shrug sheepishly. "I'm not sure."

Otto shakes his head, smile widening. "Now, see, that's a real missed opportunity." He leans forward, resting his elbows on the display case. "You could have told me your mom has an addiction to Clark Bars, or that your dad was obsessed with Superman. Any answer, and I would have believed you."

"Superman?" Beau reacts, confused but amused.

"Clark Kent?" Otto says, his eyes bouncing between me and Beau. "No?"

I let out a small laugh and nod.

Otto sighs, straightening back up behind the counter. "The usual today, Beau?"

"Yep, blue velv—"

"You think you need to tell me what your usual is?" Otto says, pretending to be offended. "I know it's been a while, but once a regular at Ben's, always a regular at Ben's." Otto looks to me. "And for you, Superman?"

I hesitate and glance across the display case, overwhelmed by my options.

"He'll have the same," Beau answers, then turns to me. "Trust me. You want the same."

"Two blue velvet brownies, coming right up," Otto announces to the entire bakery. He bends in half, digs around among his desserts, and reappears with a plastic container that's housing two enormous blue brownies inside, both topped with a thin layer of what I assume is cream-cheese frosting.

"Thanks, Otto." Beau hands him some cash and takes the container.

I expect us to turn and leave, but Beau lingers, questioning if he should say whatever's been waiting on the tip of his tongue. He clears his throat and leans toward the counter. He struggles to find the right words and finally says in a low voice, "Today must be tough."

Otto's smile stays bright, but the sparkle in his eyes dims a bit.

"Even though I haven't been around much, I'm always thinking about you," Beau adds, "and today, I'm thinking about Ben, too."

Otto drops his head appreciatively before reaching over the counter and patting Beau's shoulder. "Don't wait so long next time, okay? I like having you around, kid. And *you*"—he turns to me—"nice to meet you, Superman."

I smile and wave goodbye.

We maneuver our way back across the bakery, slowed by a group of elementary school kids on a field trip, and disappear out the blue wooden door.

"You won't meet a nicer guy than Otto," Beau says, "and that's not an exaggeration."

"He seems like it," I say, making a mental note to try blue velvet brownies for one of Blair's birthday bakes as I head to the passenger side of Mr. Zebb's car.

I have questions. Why did Beau stop coming into the bakery? And why would today be hard for Otto? But I bite my tongue and decide not to pry.

I'm just along for the incredibly fast ride, anyway.

I catch Beau staring at me from the sidewalk, looking amused.

I feel my cheeks getting pink, if they ever even returned to normal after Otto asked about my name. "What?" I look down at my outfit, expecting to see a stain on my shirt or discover that my fly is down.

"You're funny, is all," he says, grinning. "We're not driving. We're walking."

"Where to?"

"It's a surprise detour." Beau turns and strides away. "Don't worry, Superman," he adds, his voice fading down the sidewalk. "It's basically around the block."

I hustle to catch him, which isn't easy with Beau's legs being as long as they are. Now I have newfound sympathy for all the times Sadie struggled to keep up with me wandering around Rosedore Mall.

I can't get too distracted by his legs, the brownies in his hands, or wherever he's leading me to next, though, because my focus should stay on why Beau ended up as a deviation in last period—and why that feels like a sign he's the friend I should meet.

"You never answered my question in the school parking lot," I say, subtly trying to lead our conversation back to where it started.

His attention stays forward. "What was the question?"

"Why did you lose it in last period?"

"I wouldn't say I *lost* it. I was just having a bit of fun."

"A bit of fun? You barged in late—on your first day at a new school—jumped around on the desks like you were possessed, and then sprinted off to steal our teacher's car." I pop my eyes at him, even though he's still not looking my way. "Or is that a typical Monday for you?"

"Rosedore High School needs some excitement, don't you think?" he asks, taking a sharp left and picking up the pace. "Besides, I already know that I'm not graduating. Why care about doing well at something as irrelevant as trigonometry?"

I follow, struggling to keep up. "Why wouldn't you graduate?"

"It's complicated. What about you?" he asks. "You must not care about school, either, judging by how determined you were to skip with me."

School is meaningless because I'm stuck in September 19 forever, is the most honest answer. But I stick with simply, "I needed a break from my routine—a break from the boring."

"Boring is not something you have to worry about with me," Beau says, finding my eyes out of the corners of his.

We make another turn and I spot the waves of Lake Michigan crashing against the shoreline straight ahead. At the horizon, its choppy surface expands into the sky and we're met with a breeze coasting inland—a welcomed relief from the heat radiating off all the concrete surrounding us. Beau leads us through an underpass beneath Lake Shore Drive and we emerge to soft sand at our toes, the roaring buzz of the city quieting to a pleasant hum.

I close my eyes for a moment, letting the day's surrealness wash over me.

"You needed a break, all right, but from more than the boring," Beau says, dropping down onto his butt. "I can tell."

I join him, popping off my shoes and socks. "Is that so?"

"Yes."

I'm not sure I've met someone as presumptuous as Beau. Part of me is offended—how can he pretend to know me after spending an hour together?—but the other part is impressed by his confidence.

"What do I need a break from?" I ask.

He thinks, his attention on the horizon ahead, before turning to me. His gaze is focused, and, yet again, I feel trapped in some kind of warped staring contest that neither of us can win or lose. "Your loneliness."

His answer hits me like a freight train slamming into my chest. "My loneliness?" I repeat, even though we both know I heard him loud and clear. "Why would you say that?"

"Am I right?"

I'm speechless.

"I'll take that as a yes," he says. "You don't seem like someone who'd cut class with a stranger just for the thrill of it. You seem more like someone who could just"—he shrugs, trying to find the right words—"use a friend."

I shoot up onto my feet and let out a startled laugh. How could he sense that?

How could he *know*?

"Whoa, don't be offended," he says, sensing my shock. He gestures for me to sit down again, but I don't. "I didn't mean it as an insult. Look, I'm lonely, too. Aren't we all?"

He cracks open the plastic container holding our brownies. "Have the one on the right. It's bigger." He offers it to me.

But I'm still standing a few feet away, rattled by his spot-on analysis. Is Beau Dupont some kind of wizard? Has he been talking to Ms. Hazel?

Or maybe I'm just *way* more obvious than I think.

Beau extends his hand a bit farther toward me and grins. "You know you want it."

I hold out another moment before giving in. I take the brownie and shove a quarter of it into my mouth, hoping I can chew my way through the shock of Beau reading me like a book. But I'm immediately swept away by how delicious it is. "Holy shit," I say through a mouthful.

"I'm telling you," Beau says, taking a bite of his own. "Otto's the best baker in Chicago."

"I believe it."

I look down at the dyed dessert, coated in a perfectly light, not-too-sweet cream-cheese frosting. Brownies may be a relatively simple bake, but I always find a way to drop the ball. If I'm not forgetting that the eggs need to be at room temperature prior to mixing, I'm screwing up the chocolate-to-butter ratio (as Mr. Zebb can attest, numbers aren't my strong suit).

But *these*? They're perfection.

"If I could, I would get one of these every day," I say.

"That's exactly what I used to do, actually," he says. "But I won't let these brownies get you off the hook. Are you?"

"Am I what?"

"Lonely."

I give him a look, and then force myself to laugh because the line of questioning is too intense not to.

He doesn't think it's funny. "What?"

"It's just . . . *am I lonely*?" I search for words. "We just met. We're strangers. It feels a bit . . . much?"

Beau ignores me, finishes the rest of his brownie, and stands. I blink, and suddenly his tank top is off, exposing his chiseled chest.

I can feel my face turning red again.

"It's okay," he says, tossing his shirt aside. "We don't have to talk about it if you don't want to."

He unzips his shorts and lets them fall to the ground—along with his underwear.

I immediately look away and shield my eyes. "What are you doing?" I say, stunned, as my skin tingles.

"Taking a dip," he says casually. After I stay silent, he follows up with, "What? It's too hot not to."

I glance around the beach, careful where my eyes linger. "People are going to see you."

"What people?" he asks. "It's a Monday and everyone's still at work or school."

I let my hands dip low enough in front of my face that I can see him from the belly button up—and nothing farther south. "I can't believe you're doing this."

He grins. "You should come in the water, too."

"No."

"You sure?"

"Very."

"You don't have to take anything off," he says. "Go in fully clothed, for all I care."

I consider it, but shake my head.

"Okay," he says, turning to leave. "I'll be back in a bit."

My hands stay outstretched, fingers shifting as he walks away, to keep myself from seeing too much. But I can spot his long legs floating across the sand, and it's making me feel . . . things.

I expect him to give me an encouraging wave to join him, but he never turns back. He goes straight in, unflinching, like swimming at a public city beach bare naked is how he kicks off every week.

A minute goes by. Then five. And he's still out there, popping above and below the surface, letting the tide push him closer and farther away from me.

I'm getting antsy. And hot.

Should I go out there?

I've never swum in anything less than a bathing suit, let alone on the Chicago coast completely naked. Maybe Day 310 should be my first. Besides, no spectator will even remember it happening come Day 311.

Hell, I've already stolen a teacher's car today. Skinny-dipping can't be more illegal than that.

Screw it.

Before I can talk myself out of it, I swallow the last bite of my brownie, slip off my clothes, and race down to the water, anxious to avoid any prying eyes. I run into the waves and bury my head beneath the surface as quickly as possible. The cold shocks my system with a jolt as I spring up through the surface.

"Welcome," Beau says from a few feet away. He splashes me.

I splash back. "Carpe diem, I guess."

"Carpe the damn diem."

We bob around for a bit, letting the water wash away that sticky, late-summer feeling. I try an underwater handstand, but am reminded by the strong tide and my several failed attempts that this isn't the stagnant pool at Mom's apartment complex. Beau splashes at me, I splash at him, and then we float around on our backs for a few minutes, debating how many blue velvet brownies we'd be able to enjoy before our stomachs would rebel and force us to throw them up (I land on five; Beau says seven).

Something pinches my ankle and I let out a panicked yelp at the thought of some Lake Michigan sea creature wanting my legs for dinner before realizing it's only Beau. He springs up through the water and lets out a hearty laugh, eyes glowing spectacularly in the sunlight, and I suddenly realize that I haven't felt this carefree and light since hanging out with—

"Sadie," I word vomit out, surprising even myself.

Beau looks at me, confused.

"She's the reason why you're sensing that I'm lonely," I explain, pushing my wet hair off my forehead. "*One* of the reasons, anyway."

"Who is she?"

"My best friend." My *only* friend, I don't say. "She just moved to Texas."

He nods. "I'm sorry."

"It's okay." I shrug. "So . . . yeah. I guess you weren't wrong earlier. I could use a friend."

Beau extends his arm toward me above the surface. "I'm Beau." He grins.

I grin, too, taking his hand in mine, and give it a shake. Our palms stay locked a few seconds longer than any ordinary handshake would. "Hi, Beau," I say. "Clark here."

Try to make a new friend.

I did it. I completed Ms. Hazel's first tip to beating loneliness. It's a bummer that our friendship will expire in a matter of hours, when I'll be nothing but a stranger in Beau's eyes. But it still feels nice to know I can meet new people—especially when it's someone like Beau.

"C'mon," he says, moving toward the shoreline. "Let's go."

"Where now?" I ask, because for the first today in many todays, I have no idea what's coming next—and, incredibly, I'm kind of okay with that.

Beau's grin grows into a smile. "Errand number two."

CHAPTER 5

ONE PERK TO THE SUFFOCATING HEAT IS THAT we're both bone dry after a couple minutes standing in the breeze (looking *away* from each other, our hands conveniently placed in front of us, for what it's worth). I'm still pulling my shoes on as Beau leaves without me.

"Can you hold on, please?" I say, tripping on my laces as I try to keep pace.

I'm shocked to discover Mr. Zebb's car is still there without a gaggle of police surrounding it. I'm not, however, surprised to see an explosion of missed calls and texts on my phone from Mom, Dad, Blair, and Sadie after I buckle up in the passenger seat. Scrolling down the locked screen, which is lined with increasingly panicked messages, takes me back to my honeymoon phase of the time loop—when I'd deviate from that routine so often that seeing my family's texts spiraling into hysteria became an everyday occurrence.

The first text, from Mom, reads:

Where are u? The school called and said you STOLE YOUR MATH TEACHER'S CAR???? Tell me there's been a mistake

The second text, from Blair:

??!!??!! dude . . . . . what is going on

The third text, from Dad:

Ms. Hazel said she hasn't heard from you - C, will you call one of us? Please??

The fourth text, from Sadie:

okay so there's a rumor going around that you stole zebb's car which is honestly the most hilarious thing I've heard all year

The fifth text, from Sadie—ten minutes after she sent her first one:

WAIT I'M HEARING FROM YOUR MOM THAT IT'S TRUE? CLARK???

There's a sixth, and a seventh, and an eighth, and so on. I type out a new group text message assuring them it's not as bad as they think and that I'll be home soon to bake for the birthday party, but pause before hitting send. Because why should I put my own curfew on the best today that I've had in a very long time?

I tap out of my messages and set my phone down in the cupholder next to Mr. Zebb's stale root beer and notice that Beau, too, is distracted by his own texting saga. I see that his frantic messages are followed by typing bubbles from a recipient, who—judging by the rushed pace of their conversation—also seems to be concerned about our new roles as car thieves.

"Everything all right?" I ask. "Are your parents losing their mind, like mine are?"

He shoots off a final message before pocketing his phone with a stressed sigh. "It's fine."

"You sure?"

"It's just boy problems." Using his fingertips, Beau pushes the corners of his lips into a smile. "But I'm not letting it ruin our day."

Boy problems.

Ouch.

Boy problems could mean a million different things. But it confirms two traits I suspected we shared—that Beau is into boys and has problems—and a third that stings more than I expected it to: Beau is into someone else.

That shouldn't matter. We're new *friends*, after all—friends whose friendship won't last beyond 11:16 p.m. today, anyway.

But still.

We pull into traffic and follow Lake Shore Drive north along the coast. As I watch the crests of the waves turn white, glittery in the sun's rays that drop lower in the sky, I feel a bittersweetness that I haven't experienced in a long time: the bliss of enjoying my today coupled with the grief that it'll end soon. Because, as strange and confusing as Day 310 has been, the fact that it'll end with Beau's forgetting me is the part of Ms. Hazel's challenge that doesn't seem to have a solution.

Beau pulls off the expressway in Uptown and drives inland until we're right outside the Aragon Ballroom, one of the city's most famous concert venues. Unlike Ben's Everything Blue Bakery, I've definitely heard of the Aragon. He parks near the hall's towering black sign, which has Aragon's name spelled in bold, all-caps white letters for the entire north side to see, and sends a curious smirk my way before hopping out of Mr. Zebb's car without another word. He's really enjoying being a tease with these errands, I can tell.

I jump out, too and, yet again, scurry after him to keep up.

"Ever heard of the Aragon?" Beau yells backward.

"Of course," I say coolly, hoping to win back some Real Chicagoan points. "Sadie went to an event here last year—she wouldn't stop talking about it—but I haven't been myself."

"Good," Beau says. "This will be even cooler if it's your first time."

We walk up to the main entrance to the lobby, which, to my surprise, is dark and lifeless inside. A big sign is taped on the inside of a front door proclaiming that THE BALLROOM IS TEMPORARILY CLOSED FOR MAINTENANCE THRU 9/23.

"Did you know this?" I say to Beau, pointing at the sign.

"It's why we're here," he answers.

Beau pulls out his phone again and fires off a text, a pleasant grin stuck on his face. At first, I wonder if he's responding to the boy who's responsible for his boy problems, but when his phone buzzes with a response a moment later, he says, "She's on her way."

"Who's on her way?"

"My friend Dee," he says. "She works here."

Dee's small silhouette appears in the lobby darkness and her features materialize as she approaches us. She unlocks the door and swings it open. "You actually came!" she exclaims, apparently surprised that he decided to show up.

Her arms, wiry but strong, wrap Beau up and pull him into one of the most aggressively cute hugs I've ever witnessed. She starts murmuring something, but I can't hear what from where I stand because her face is so compressed into his chest.

They break apart.

"You're feeling better?" Beau whispers to her.

I look away, not wanting to seem like an eavesdropper tuning in to someone else's private moment.

"Yeah," she replies, smiling.

Beau says, "Okay," although he doesn't seem convinced, and raises his voice to a normal level again. "You seem surprised to see me. I told you that I'd come by."

"Hey, I've been flaked on by boys before." Dee laughs, pivots on her heels, and looks up at me. "Clark!" Before I can ask how she knows my name, she pulls me in for a hug that feels too strong to have come at the hands of someone of her stature. My intestines might just explode out of my mouth. "Beau texted that you'd be coming, too."

Dee, who looks a couple years older than us, is a pack of Starbursts personified. Her face is anchored by magnetic round eyes on either side of a button nose. Thin dreads, parted perfectly down the middle, hang beneath her shoulders, and the few dark freckles dotting her brown skin feel like they were placed there thoughtfully by a renowned makeup artist.

"You're pretty," I say, the words just spilling out. My stomach does a backflip, as I realize in horror that I've actually said the compliment out loud.

See? *This* is why it's been hard for me to make new friends.

But Dee's expression suggests she appreciates my accidental bluntness. "I like this guy," she says to Beau, pointing my way.

"Sorry if that came across as creepy," I say, sucking my teeth. I look at Beau and lower my voice. "Was that creepy to say?"

Beau's hand finds my lower back and guides me inside after Dee. "Let's go, Creepy."

The lobby of the Aragon is impressive, even blanketed in shadows. Mosaic tiles line the floors of a cavernous hall, where archways direct us farther into the venue. It's quiet, cool, and still in here—

almost unsettlingly so—and I sense these walls would have a million stories to tell if they could.

"I told Beau yesterday that he should drop in," Dee explains to me, her voice echoing off the walls. She leads us to the other end of the space with the ease and confidence of a seasoned tour guide. "We're closed for renovations this week, so you're both in luck."

I glance between the two of them. "Why does that mean we're in luck?"

"You've got the place to yourselves," she says. "Except for a few construction workers who you might spot wandering around. If they talk to you, act like you work here."

Beau and I exchange looks, both unsure what acting like we work here would entail.

We arrive at the end of the hallway, where a set of wide stairs, guided by bougie-looking bannisters, direct us upward. Beau and I follow Dee to wherever they go.

And when we get there, my jaw promptly drops to the floor.

"Wow," I mutter.

Beau nudges my side playfully. "I told you this would be even better if you've never been here before."

It looks like we've been dropped into the courtyard of a seaside Mediterranean village—or a movie set version of one. Straight ahead, on the opposite end of the ballroom, is your standard concert stage, but on the exterior walls on either side of us are decorated pillars, Spanish-style balconies, and fanciful circular towers that wrap around the empty, hardwood dance floor. Warm yellow lights bask the room in a cozy glow, but they've got nothing on the hues glistening down on us.

"Isn't it wild?" Beau whispers, neck tilted back so he can take in the view.

The Aragon's ceiling high above us is painted the colors of a radiant cosmos. Streaks of purples, pinks, and blues cut through a black universe, and twinkling stars, scattered every few feet, are pulling me into a galaxy light-years away from Illinois.

"I need to get some paperwork done before my shift ends at six," Dee says. "But you two enjoy! Roam around, take pics, do whatever you want, but please don't break anything—"

"Wait," Beau interjects. "You're leaving us?"

Dee nods.

"But I thought you wanted to"—he lowers his voice like he had outside—"talk about last night?"

Dee lets out a laugh. It feels like she's trying to counter Beau's serious tone. "I was being dramatic. I'm fine now. Don't sweat it."

I look up at the painted night sky again to seem as though I'm uninterested in whatever their back-and-forth is about.

Beau waits a moment to speak. "Are you sure?"

"Yes."

"Positive?"

"*Yes.*" Dee playfully nudges him farther into the ballroom. "Go enjoy this place while you still have it to yourselves."

"Okay. Thanks, Dee."

I nod and smile her way before Dee disappears back down the stairs.

"Is everything all right?" I ask him.

"I hope so," Beau says. "She had a rough night but never wants to talk about it."

"Because I'm here?" I ask. "I don't mind hanging out in the lobby for a bit so you two can have some privacy."

Beau brushes off my concern. "I wouldn't worry about it," he says, although it seems like he isn't listening to his own advice. "Dee is tough. She'll open up about it when she wants to."

He wanders toward the middle of the room, leaving me hungry for answers.

In the same way that it felt like Beau and Otto left things unsaid at the bakery, I get a similar sense that there's more to his story with Dee. Part of me wants to pry, knowing I only have hours left with him, and any stone left unturned could be holding important information related to Ms. Hazel's tips or how Beau randomly showed up as a Day 310 deviation in the first place. But I also realize that Beau's friendships with Dee and Otto are none of my business and pressing him too hard about either of them could scare off the only friend I've made in 310 todays.

I follow Beau into the heart of the ballroom.

"This is incredible," I say, gazing around some more.

"I thought you'd like it," Beau says. "You'd think being surrounded by infinity would feel lonely, but here?" He shakes his head. "It has the opposite effect. I wish I had a place like this to escape to out where we live."

We stop walking beneath a small, glistening disco ball hanging near the stage. "Why did you move to Rosedore, anyway?" I ask.

"Technically, I didn't," he says. "I live one town over, in West Edgemont, but it just . . ." He seems to contemplate how much to disclose. "It made more sense for me to be at Rosedore."

"Oof, West Edgemont." I shake my head. "I'm sorry. Even worse than Rosedore."

He exhales. "Moving out of the city to live with my boring white grandparents in their backward white town since freshman year hasn't exactly been a recipe for happiness." I'm not sure what my expression implies but he must feel the need to clarify. "My dad was Black and my mom is white. I live with my grandparents on my mom's side."

Was. So I guess it's safe to assume Beau's dad died? If his mom is still around, though, I wonder why he wouldn't live with her.

"You don't want to hear about my fucked-up backstory," he says, apparently reading my mind. "Trust me."

Actually, I do. But it's probably smart to change gears to something more lighthearted, anyway, and avoid ruining the moment with talks of our dysfunctional families.

I glance around, thinking about how wild it is that we were sneaked into Aragon Ballroom and have the place entirely to ourselves. Even when I'd deviate in my honeymoon phase, I'd never do something like this.

"You can't possibly consider hanging out in *here*"—gesture around the room—"an errand."

He steps closer to me, but his eyes go back up to the sky. "Why wouldn't this be an errand?"

Beau sure does like to play coy.

I exhale, willing to play along. "When I think *errand*, I think, like, running to the store for last-minute baking ingredients. When I think *errand*, I think tasks that need to get done."

He drops his chin to see into my eyes. "You're a baker?"

I feel my cheeks getting warm. Not because baking is embarrassing, but because being a complete amateur at the thing I'm most passionate about is. "Yeah. Well, I'm *sort* of a baker."

Beau grins. "Sort of?"

"I don't have any official training," I explain. "I mostly get recipes off the internet and just mess around in my mom's kitchen."

"Wow," Beau says, appearing impressed. "You must've really been blown away inside Ben's, huh?"

"You could say so, yeah."

We hold each other's gaze.

"Well," Beau says. "It's a good thing you don't need a master's degree in pastry arts to call yourself a baker." He turns his eyes toward the ceiling again. "Like it or not, you're a baker, Clark."

My flushed cheeks get a whole lot warmer.

"And to answer your question," he continues, "I agree with you on the definition of errand. But I consider eating brownies on the beach and loitering in empty ballrooms with you things that absolutely needed to get done today."

Beau drops down onto his back and bends his elbows, palms cushioning his head against the hardwood. I do the same, hopeful that the dim lighting is hiding how rosy my cheeks have become. The room is so calm, and the fake night sky so captivating, that it feels like we could both float away into the Milky Way and be gone without a trace.

"Thanks for coming along for the ride today," he says softly. "Most people don't appreciate my impulsivity. Or, as my mom once called it, my impul*stupidity*." He shakes his head. "My grandparents loved that phrase so much they still use it to describe me to this day."

I glance at him out of the corners of my eyes. "Why don't most people appreciate that about you?"

"It's gotten me into trouble before."

"How so?"

He clears his throat. "Let's see. There was the time I blew two whole paychecks from my Froyo job on this dope reclining chair to play video games in my room without giving it a second thought.

But the delivery guys couldn't fit it through my grandparents' front doorway. It was too big. Let's see . . . oh, in seventh grade, I flicked a kid named Mark really hard between his eyes for stealing my last chicken nugget and got detention."

I laugh. "Sounds like Mark deserved it."

"You're not wrong," he says, laughing, too. "But I probably should have told Ms. Winfords instead of resorting to violence without thinking it through. You need more examples? I've got plenty."

I grin. "Your mom might see impul*stupidity*, but I see spontaneity. And I don't think that's a bad thing," I say. "Impromptu beach trips on a Monday? Having badass concert venues all to yourself? I wish I was more like you. Spontaneity pays off."

I glance at him again, just quickly enough to catch him grinning, too, before I look away.

I'm torn. Because a part of me wants to lie back, relax, and soak up this moment. But the part that remembers why I ended up running errands with him in the first place is determined to make sense of Ms. Hazel's homework deviation and Beau's sudden appearance. My time to do it before today restarts and Beau forgets who I am is ticking away.

"Can I ask you a personal question?" I say, breaking our silence.

He moves onto his side, propping his head up with the palm of his hand. "Of course."

I do the same, facing him.

The ballroom's purple and pink lights dance across his cheeks, and his eyes—just as distracting as the universe above—sparkle like the brightest stars in the room.

Focus, Clark.

"Why are you lonely?" I say, trying to connect any dots between

Ms. Hazel's first tip and the two of us. "You don't also have a best friend who moved to Texas, do you?"

"Not quite." He sits up and faces the stage, elbows resting on his knees. "Remember the boy problems I mentioned earlier?"

I nod.

"The boy causing the problems has something to do with it."

"Oh yeah?"

"Without getting into the messy details, let's just say it's . . ." He pauses again. "It's important that I win him back."

I knew Beau's boy problems likely meant one of two things: Beau is in a relationship, or he is hoping that to be the case. Being stuck in a time loop means I could never be anyone's boyfriend anyway, and by Day 310, I should know better than to start falling for someone. But still, hearing Beau confirm with his own lips that he wants another boy doesn't feel great. "Did he break up with you?" I ask.

"Yeah."

"Then why are you trying to win him back?"

He grins as if I wouldn't understand. "It's complicated."

"Well . . ." I hesitate, questioning if I should go there or not. "If I'm being honest, I'm not sure a boy who's causing you problems is a boy worth fighting for."

He studies my face in silence. I've never wanted the ability to read minds more than right now.

"You might be right about that," he finally says, "but again, it's complicated."

"How so?"

"It's a long, sad story, Clark," he says, "and one that's not deserving to be told under such a pretty night sky—even one that's just a painted wall."

A booming voice shatters the ballroom's stillness. "Hey!" The two of us look up to the stage, where a gargantuan, mustached man wearing a construction hat is staring at us suspiciously. "What are you two doing in here?"

"We work for the Aragon," Beau lies.

"No you don't," he answers immediately.

"Yes, we do," I back Beau up confidently, surprising myself.

"*No,*" the man says slower, stepping toward us. "You don't."

Beau and I glance at each other, deciding, without exchanging a word, that that's our cue. We spring up and dash toward the exit as the man keeps shouting at us from the stage.

"Do you have time to run one more errand with me?" Beau asks as we barrel down the stairs toward the lobby.

"Yeah," I say, feet pounding the tile floor. "Where to?"

He looks back at me with a smirk.

I should have known I wouldn't be getting an answer.

CHAPTER 6

WE HOP INTO MR. ZEBB'S CAR AND BLAST AWAY down Lawrence Avenue.

"Do you think we got Dee in trouble for sneaking us into the venue?" I ask.

"I wouldn't worry about her," Beau answers calmly. "I'd guess one pissed off construction worker is the least of her worries today."

Even though the construction guy doesn't appear to be chasing us, Beau hangs a sharp right, takes a quick left, and zigzags farther into the city as if we're on the run in a video game. Rows of restaurants, stores, and brick apartments blur into streaks of color outside my window, and I'm reminded just how much of a suburban boy I am, completely lost in a sprawling city. Unlike the drive from Rosedore to Ben's bakery, though, I trust Beau will get us to our next destination.

"Hold tight," he says smoothly, tapping my left thigh with his right hand. It lingers for a moment, prompting an eruption of goose bumps up and down my arms. "We're almost there."

I learn a minute later, as Beau parallel parks the car, that there is a place called Splendid Cinemas.

"If you like old movies—especially nineties rom-coms that don't hold up well—this place is for you," he explains, opening a door to the front entrance. "It's stuck in the last century and never busy. I might be the only person who realizes it's still open."

"How does it stay in business, then?" I ask.

Beau shrugs. "I'm not asking questions."

The lobby carpet, retro themed and soda stained, carries a whiff of mildew that's pungent enough to spoil the scent of buttery popcorn. A small concession stand greets us as we walk in, with only a few candy and soda offerings on display—hardly the array of options you see at the big chain cinemas—and plastic-framed movie posters from past decades line the walls, most of them bumped crookedly out of place.

No one is here except a worker with white-blond surfer hair and vivid green eyes, who looks our age, if not slightly older. He's so consumed by whatever's playing in his earbuds and the papers in his hands that he doesn't notice me and Beau until we're a foot away.

His eyes pop open upon seeing us, like he's shocked to see an actual customer in the flesh. He snags out his earbuds and sets the papers aside. "Welcome to Splendid Cinemas."

"Hey, Emery," Beau says to him. "What's playing today?"

Emery seems confused as to how Beau would know his name until Beau nods at the large name tag on Emery's chest.

"Oh," Emery says with a sheepish smile. "Right." He scans the computer screen in front of him, which presumably holds the answers to Beau's question. "*When Harry Met Sally* starts in theater one in a few minutes and *The Princess Bride* starts in theater one in . . ." He squints. "Two-ish hours."

I wait for him to continue. But he doesn't.

"Is there not a theater two?" I mutter in Beau's direction.

"No," Emery and Beau answer at the same time.

At first, I think they're joking. But the look on Emery's face confirms that's not the case.

Beau considers our one option, with intrigue. "*When Harry Met Sally*," he says, looking to me. "Ever seen it?"

I shake my head.

"Do you want to?" he asks.

I smile. "Sure."

"Two tickets, please," Beau requests from Emery, who's immediately overwhelmed with the responsibility of exchanging money for tickets. "And we'll take a large popcorn and two pops."

Beau pushes cash onto the counter.

I reach into my pockets. "Wait, I can pay for mine."

Beau shakes his head. "I got it."

"No really," I say, pulling out my wallet. "I—"

But Beau gently pushes my hand away. "It's no big deal."

Emery looks amused. "First date struggles?"

An awkward silence hangs in the air between the three of us.

"This isn't a date," I say.

Beau jerks his head toward me, surprised. "Oh, really?"

I freeze up. What about the boy he wants to win back, though? And didn't we just agree to be friends?

Beau's face shifts into a grin. "I'm just messing with you," he says, pushing his cash farther across the counter to pay for both of us.

Five minutes and one popcorn spill by Emery later, me and Beau are in the back row of dark and empty theater one as previews promoting movies that are twice my age crackle on the big screen in front of us. The theater chairs may be small and rickety, their joints squeaking at us with every breath we take, but the cinema's air-conditioning miraculously still works, and that in itself makes errand number three worth it.

"Can I tell you something?" I ask Beau.

He nods.

"This has been one of the most interesting todays that I've had," I say, throwing a kernel of popcorn onto my tongue.

"Todays?"

"I just mean, I've had an interesting time with you, is all."

Beau considers my take. "Is interesting a good thing?" he whispers to me as the movie begins (although he hardly needs to be quiet, considering we're the only ones in here).

"Yes," I say. "Interesting is a very good thing."

After the opening credits, the movie begins with an old couple in an interview explaining how they fell in love. I know *When Harry Met Sally* is a classic rom-com—I can remember my mom quoting its funniest lines to my dad in our old kitchen, which feels like a dream from a previous life at this point—and me and Beau are getting exactly what we signed up for. But it still feels a bit too . . . cheesy, I guess? I don't know. It could be Mom and Dad's divorce or the impossibility of having a boyfriend in my predicament—maybe both—but it's difficult for me to buy into a predictable premise that surely comes with a fairy-tale ending.

I lean toward Beau. "Have you seen this movie before?"

"Yeah."

"And you like it?"

"Yeah."

I pause. "Really?"

He looks at me out of the corner of his eyes. "Why, you don't?"

I shrug.

"It *just* started," he argues, grinning. "Give it a chance."

"I will."

And I do. But thirty minutes into it, I still feel the same way.

"So?" Beau says, leaning my way. "Is it growing on you?"

I bite down on my lower lip hesitantly.

He shakes his head, disappointed in me. "I guess we can't all have great taste."

My eyes widen, a little bit offended (but not *really*). "Look, I know this is an unpopular opinion, and it's not a bad movie," I clarify. "It's funny. And it's cute, I guess. It's just . . ."

"Stupid?"

"No."

"Boring?"

"I wouldn't say that."

"Then what?"

I try to figure out the simplest way to articulate my take. "This movie is going to have a fairy-tale ending."

"And . . . that's a bad thing?"

No, not necessarily. It's just, happy endings are more satisfying when they're believable," I argue. "And this love story is not a believable one."

"So you don't think that could be you and your someone someday?" Beau asks, nodding at Billy Crystal's and Meg Ryan's characters on the screen.

I let out a laugh. "No, I don't."

"Why not?"

I stare at the screen in thought. "Not to sound cynical, but I don't think everybody's meant to have a person."

"Like, a soul mate?"

"Sure, I guess." I take a handful of popcorn. "I think it's naive to think two people can match like it's magic—like they're two perfect pieces of the same puzzle."

"I don't think soul mates have to be perfect fits," he says, stealing popcorn out of my palm, even though he still has plenty of his own. "Take the boy giving me boy problems. We definitely weren't perfect. Far from it."

I scrunch my face, confused by his rationale. "So, let me get this straight," I say. "He's the one who broke up with you, you think the two of you are, quote-unquote, *far* from a good fit, and now you're trying to win him back?"

"Far from *perfect*," he corrects me. "There's a big difference. And yes."

I shake my head at him. "I don't get it."

"You don't have to," he explains. "Relationships are about compromise. I might need to bend a little of myself in order for us not to break. And that's okay."

"I thought you already *did* break, though," I say. "As in . . . break *up*."

"Yeah," he says. "And I learned my lesson. I can try to be more like the person he wishes I were, and hopefully it'll go the other way, too."

I brush some runaway kernels off my lap, not exactly sold on Beau's approach to love. "So does this mystery boy have a name?"

Beau opens his mouth, chuckles, and then closes it again. "Yeah."

"So . . . what is it?"

"It doesn't matter."

I narrow my eyes on his. "Why don't you want to tell me?"

"Because I don't want to spoil our night."

I laugh. "Hey, *you're* the one who told Emery that this isn't a date."

"Because it's not," he counters.

"We're just *friends*."

"I know."

My eyes narrow even more. "Then why would telling me your ex's name spoil our night?"

He sighs. "Because then *I* would be thinking about him more than I am right now, and to *you* he'd become more of a real-life person."

"As opposed to a . . . *not* real person?"

"I can try to win him back tomorrow," he continues. "But, tonight, I'd rather just have a fun, *friendly* night with you."

I keep my eyes on him a moment longer. "I think it bears repeating, though," I say. "I don't know if a boy who's causing you boy problems is a boy worth fighting for."

Beau purses his lips, both charmed and frustrated with me, I can tell. "And I *also* have something to say that's worth repeating," he retorts. "It's complicated."

I grin. "Touché."

"Anyway." He shakes his bag of popcorn to spread out the butter. "I want to hear more about your ridiculously wrong opinion on soul mates. Because it sounds like you're certain you'll never have one. Am I correct?"

I shrug, truthfully unsure.

"What makes you think that?" he asks.

I exhale.

Where to begin?

The fact that I've not only never had a boyfriend, but never been on a legitimate date? The fact that I'm a product of my parents—two people who were madly in love for decades, only to have their marriage blow up like a dumpster fire sprayed with gasoline? Oh, and the fact that it'll be a miracle if I ever make it past 11:16 p.m. tonight?

I find the simplest way to tell the truth. "A soul mate may not be in my cards, and I'm okay with that."

Beau cracks a smile before turning back to the movie. "Hm."

I nudge his shoulder with mine. "What's *hm* supposed to mean?"

He clears his throat. "I'll just say this. For a soul-mate skeptic like yourself, I get why these sorts of movies aren't the best, if you need them to be believable."

"All right. I'm following . . ."

"But, for me, the brilliance of a timeless rom-com has nothing to do with its believability. The best ones do great jobs at allowing the audience to escape."

"And what is the audience trying to escape from, exactly?"

Beau takes a sip of his pop. "Reality."

"Why do you want to escape your reality?"

"A deadbeat mom and an *actual* dead dad?" Beau's eyes glance at me before returning back to Meg Ryan. "I used to come to this place all the time after school by myself. Theater one, believe it or not, would always be empty"—he smirks—"and I'd come in here and just . . . be okay. It's a luxury to be able to get lost in another world." He sinks lower into his seat and closer to me. "And it's a luxury to be able to escape the real one."

Our arms brush up against each other atop our shared armrest, and I feel the heat rise in my neck and my face and my chest and . . . just about everywhere else, really.

"I'm sorry you needed to escape your reality," I say. "I get that."

And I really do. Because that's what I'm trying to do *right now*.

We both direct our attention back to the screen. But instead of following Harry and Sally's story, I start connecting the dots in Beau's. His apparently awful mom and his dead dad, living with his boring white grandparents in their backward white town, the need to escape into a fictional world in order to leave his real one. That's what I know about Beau Dupont.

What I *don't* know is what was left unsaid during our visits with Otto and Dee. What happened to his dad, and why his mom is long gone. And, most critically of all, why did he show up as a deviation in Day 310?

I have no idea what about Beau, if anything, is relevant to me, why the universe may have wanted him to be my new friend, or if any of these questions' answers could lead me to tomorrow. But, at least for now, I'm happy to have escaped my today with Beau.

"For the record," he whispers, "I think you're wrong."

I look at him. "About what?"

"You have a soul mate," he says. "You just have to find him."

CHAPTER 7

THE CAMERA FLOATS AWAY FROM HARRY AND SALLY as the two embrace in a confetti-covered New Year's Eve kiss. Soon after, the credits begin to scroll.

"See?" Beau says, tapping the side of my knee with his. "A classic, right?"

I tilt my head from side to side. "Not bad."

"You're a tough critic, Clark."

Truth be told, I enjoyed the movie much more than I thought I would when it first started. But I think that has more to do with hearing Beau crack up at Sally's one-liners and stealing peeks at him grinning dreamily during the most heartfelt scenes.

The dim lights above us begin to brighten.

Beau leans back in his chair to stretch, his long arms expanding outward. "You must need to get home, huh?" he asks with a yawn.

I check my phone, which now has three times the number of missed texts and phone calls than it had when I last checked after the beach. At a glance, they're all pretty much the same panicked notifications that I expect when I go off course.

But one of them stands out.

It's from Sadie, sent about an hour ago:

I need you.

That . . . doesn't seem like her.

She *needs* me?

Every other message from Mom, Dad, and Blair is pleading with me to come home or, at the very least, let them know I'm all right. I rack my brain for anything that's happened in my previous todays that would give context to Sadie's text, helping it make sense. But she always has great September 19ths hanging out with her new friends and ending the night at home with her favorite food (Mr. Green's homemade spaghetti dinner). Why would she need me right now?

"Your family must be losing their minds," Beau says, watching me stare at my phone. "Do you need to call someone?"

I contemplate FaceTiming her. But I know my time with Beau in Day 310 is limited, and the idea of spending any of it with someone who I know I'll see again in Day 311 feels wrong. It's an odd text to get from Sadie, sure, but weirder things have happened when I've deviated.

"I can stay out," I say, pocketing my phone and assuring him with a smile. "What about you?"

Beau looks pleasantly surprised at my answer. "Emery did say *The Princess Bride* would be starting soon. Double feature?"

I nod, and we both stay put.

A few minutes later, the lights dim again.

"No one comes to check the theater and clean up any messes between movies?" I ask Beau, glancing around as the same old previews begin playing.

"If by *no one* you mean Emery, no—no one does," he says, finishing the final bites of his popcorn.

I settle into my seat. I'm a bit distracted from the movie because of Sadie's text, but the cozy, dark theater and the comfort of having Beau at my side lull me back into the bliss of Day 310.

I come to, my eyes blinking away the sleepiness, and see the end credits of *The Princess Bride* scrolling up the big screen.

Damn it. I fell asleep about halfway through the movie.

I glance around, anxious, because Beau is gone.

I spring up and run out of empty theater one to find Emery alone in the lobby. He is, once again, consumed by the sheets of paper in his hands and whatever he's listening to on his phone.

"Hi," I say, startling him. He pulls out his earbuds; I recognize The Wrinkles song he's listening to. "Have you seen the guy I came here with?"

"Oh, yeah." Emery points to the ceiling. "He went up."

I'm relieved Beau didn't abandon me in theater one but confused as to where *up* is. My face crinkles in confusion.

"The rooftop," Emery clarifies, now gesturing toward a stairwell. "He told me to send you up there, too, whenever you woke up."

"Okay," I say, still a bit confused. "Are customers allowed on the roof?"

He shrugs. "I'm new here. But sometimes people do it and, I mean, who am I to tell them no?"

I enter the concrete stairwell, climb a few flights to the top, and swing open the rooftop exit. The heat isn't inviting, but the views are.

With the sun completely set, Chicago has transformed into a sparkly urban forest, sprawling into the distance as far as I can see. The lake isn't too far east, its black edges clearly visible against the jagged rows of glowing apartments, while downtown Chicago's skyscrapers shoot into the clouds, breaking up the flatness to the south.

There, standing near the dazzling Splendid Cinemas marquee, is Beau.

"Right on time," he says, turning to me. "I was about to go wake you up, sleepy."

I head his way, embarrassed that I zonked out inside.

"Sorry about that," I say, rubbing my eyes.

"You must have been tired," he replies.

"I was."

And I mean it. In my predicament, sleep is practically pointless. I was up late on September 18, after The Wrinkles show, which means that I will forever be tired on September 19 no matter how early I go to bed—*wait a minute.*

I pull out my phone. It's 11:10 p.m. *Shit.*

We have under six minutes left before Day 310 ends.

My stomach tumbles into my feet and I start to panic. Part of me wants to tell Beau about everything—the time loop, Ms. Hazel's tips, why his showing up in Mr. Zebb's class truly was extraordinary. There are so many unanswered questions about our today together. Maybe if I tell him the truth—the *whole* truth—he'd be able to help me make it all make sense. But if I do that, I risk spoiling what may be our final moments together with confusing talks of time-loop nonsense.

I will find him in Day 311, I promise myself.

I take a deep breath, calm my anxious thoughts, and lean against the railing by his side. "How was the end of *The Princess Bride*?"

He considers the question. "Pretty much perfect. A ten-out-of-ten."

I think about what I want to say to him before our day together disappears into nothingness. How can I articulate how much this afternoon meant to me without seeming pathetic? Without crossing a line?

"So," Beau fills the void before I can, "can I tell you something?"

"Of course."

"I didn't feel lonely today."

My heart skips a beat. "No?"

He shakes his head, the marquee lights twinkling behind him.

"I didn't either," I reply. "Not after I met you."

We hear police sirens approaching from the distance. Beau closes his eyes and drops his chin with a sigh. "That can't be good."

I scan the surrounding neighborhood to see where the sirens are coming from and spot swirling red and blue lights bouncing off the brick buildings a few blocks away. They turn a corner, and a police car comes into view—headed directly toward Splendid Cinemas. My chest feels heavy as I remember that me and Beau haven't just gone missing, we've broken the law—and broken it *badly*.

"Should we run for it?" I ask.

"Nah," Beau says, surprisingly unbothered by the big trouble we're about to be in. "I'd rather just wait it out with you."

The police car comes to a screeching halt outside the movie theater and its sirens go silent. An officer jumps out from behind the wheel and races up to the stolen car as we stare over the edge of the rooftop. A ragged Mr. Zebb, his polo shirt untucked and hair disheveled, pops out of the cop car's back seat—followed by my mom.

"Oh my God," I sigh.

"What?" Beau asks. "Who is she?"

I scratch at my forehead, beyond embarrassed. "My mom."

Beau chuckles. "You're in deep, huh?"

Only for the next couple minutes, I want to say.

"Sorry about today, Mr. Zebb!" Beau calls down cheerily,

waving his arms at our dismayed math teacher. The three of them spot our location on the roof. "I promise," Beau continues to shout, "I don't really hate trig as much as I led on, and I'm sure it *is* important to learn for many career fields—"

"What the hell is wrong with you two?" Mr. Zebb doesn't scream it as much as he allows an entire day's worth of rage to blast from his vocal cords. He runs to his car and slides his fingers across the doors, checking for any damages.

"Clark!" my mom bellows, looking more upset than I've ever seen before. "What are you doing up there?"

"Everything's cool," I call down to her. "Don't worry."

The police officer races into the movie theater lobby, surely on his way to drag us both downstairs (hopefully not in handcuffs).

"Poor Emery," I mutter, imagining how terrified he must be behind the concession stand. If *our* entrance surprised him earlier, I can only imagine how he's reacting to a police raid.

Beau glances at his phone and sees that it's 11:15 p.m.

His face falls into regret—as if he knows the day, *our day*, is about to end.

His hands land on my hips and pull me close. "Is this okay?" he asks.

I nod as fireworks erupt through my core.

"I think I . . . kind of like you?" he says.

I try to play it cool. "Yeah?"

"Yeah."

"I thought you want your ex-boyfriend back, though?" I say.

Beau's eyes stay glued on mine. "After tonight, I'm not so sure."

My knees almost buckle. "That's good," I say. "Because I absolutely think that I kind of like you too."

His playful smile fades into something much more serious. "Can you promise me something?"

I inhale deep. "I can try."

"Can you promise that you won't forget me?" he asks. "No matter what?"

The rooftop door blasts open, and the officer comes running toward us.

"Forget you?" I say, surprised. "Of course not, but—" Beau leans in, his warm lips landing on mine. I close my eyes and try to soak in every last microsecond before it's ripped away. I feel like I'm floating, like a bunch of balloons were let go in my chest, lifting my feet off the roof. Beau's lips move against my own, slowly and confidently as a burst of adrenaline jets through my veins. I'd give anything—*anything*—to live past 11:16 p.m. tonight.

The moment I feel the police officer slam into my side, my eyes pop open. And there, staring back at me, is my white wooden nightstand.

CHAPTER 8

NEVER, IN 311 DAYS OF BEING STUCK IN THIS NIGHT-mare, have I ever wanted to see that nightstand less than right now.

Beau Dupont. I have to find him. *Right now.*

I spring out of bed in my underwear but freeze in the morning sun, unsure where to begin. Should I beeline to Ben's Everything Blue Bakery? Head back to Splendid Cinemas and wait for Beau on the rooftop? If only I had gotten his number, this would be a lot easier. Well, actually my phone wouldn't have saved a new contact entry made in Day 310, but I could have memorized it. Why the hell hadn't I thought to do that?

No, it'd be stupid of me to try looking for him at one of his errand spots first. Beau said he's a new student at Rosedore, after all, so heading to the high school is my safest bet.

But, then again, why hadn't I seen him in my prior 309 todays? Why did he show up as a deviation? If his first day as a new student is September 19, he should have been in Mr. Zebb's last period 309 times before the today he decided to jump around on desks, prompting pure chaos. This feels like something . . . different. *He* feels different.

Why did I have such an urge to listen to Ms. Hazel's first tip and befriend him in the first place? And why did he ask me not to forget him in our final moments together?

Wait a minute.

I inhale sharply, remembering our last moments together.

The somber look he had realizing it was nearly 11:16 p.m. was not a normal response to someone checking the time. The way he asked, in earnest, that I won't forget him? The way he kissed me calmly, right as a police officer was about to smash us to smithereens? Only a person who knows he has mere seconds left could pull off a kiss like that in the moment.

Beau Dupont is stuck in my today. Or, I'm stuck in his.

That has to be the case.

I should have suspected it sooner, really. Someone who fearlessly steals cars, races down expressways at a hundred miles an hour, and skinny-dips on public beaches in broad daylight is the exact kind of someone who knows there won't be repercussions for their actions awaiting them in the morning. I, of all people, should have known as soon as I saw Mr. Zebb's car keys in Beau's hand.

But if he's stuck in today, too . . . why haven't I seen him before? And if we're in this together, can we figure out how to escape together too?

I *have* to find him now.

I pace the carpet like an electron gone mad as a tidal wave of options crash in my brain. Whenever I go into anxiety overdrive like this, having no idea where to begin, I try to remember Ms. Hazel's advice from one of our first sessions together.

Make a to-do list, I recall her saying. *Either on paper, on a screen, or in your head. And start with the easiest one first.*

"Clothes," I say aloud. "Put on clothes."

That, I can do.

Once I'm dressed, I sprint to school—actually, literally sprint. I have never run faster or arrived there earlier.

I barge through the office doorway.

"Whoa, whoa, *whoa*," the secretary exclaims, rolling away in her desk chair as if she's under attack.

"Hi, Ms. Knotts," I say, face doused in sweat. "I have a question. Do you know—"

"I'm going to need you to take a moment," she advises, hands held in the air, demanding that I slow down. "It is a Monday morning before first period, Clark, and I do *not* have enough caffeine in my system to catch whatever you're about to throw at me."

"Sorry," I say, exhaling. "I'll chill."

She waits another few moments to let my energy fizzle, staring at me, both suspicious and concerned. "Are you doing all right, Clark?"

I clear my throat. "No. Well, yeah. Sort of."

She blinks, unsure what to make of me.

"I'm just wondering," I continue, "what's Beau Dupont's first period?"

"Whose first period?"

"Beau Dupont."

"Why do you need to know?"

"I just . . . I need to drop something off to him," I (white) lie. "It's important."

She shakes her head like I'm being ridiculous. "I can't give that info out to another student, but even if I could, I've never heard that name anyway. Beau Du-what?"

"Pont. Beau Dupont."

She takes a sip of her coffee, thin lips pursed. "Not ringing a bell."

"That might be because he's a transfer student who starts today."

She shakes her head. "No."

"No?"

"We don't have any transfer students starting today."

"Are you sure?"

She seems offended at the mere suggestion she could be wrong. "Yes, I am sure."

"He's a senior, I think. And he has Mr. Zebb for trig last period with me—"

"Clark," she interrupts. "Beau Dupont is not a student here. What has gotten into you?"

"But I—"

"Here." Her fingers dance across her keyboard for a moment before she swivels her computer monitor so I can see the screen. The search for Beau's first and last name in what appears to be some student directory show zero results.

"See?" she says. "Beau Dupont does not exist. Well, at least not at Rosedore High."

My mind is racing. This *can't* be happening.

"Now," she continues. "Can I help you with anything else—"

Before I get the tail end of her question, I'm dashing out of the office and whipping out my phone, moving on to my plan B. A second later, Sadie answers my FaceTime.

"Why are you calling so early?" she asks groggily through the purple toothbrush in her mouth, a bathroom shower curtain behind her. She leans toward her screen, squinting at me and my background. "Wait, are you already at school? Our FaceTime wasn't supposed to be until—"

"Beau Dupont." I cut her off. "Do you know him?"

"Beau Dupont?" she repeats, pausing her brushing. "No. I don't think so. Why?"

"You're sure?"

She starts to brush again. "The name kind of sounds familiar, maybe, but I'm not sure. Should I know this person?"

I describe what he looks like; his smoldering eyes, brawny build, broad shoulders.

She spits a mouthful of white, foamy toothpaste into the bathroom sink. "He sounds, um . . . incredibly hot? But sorry, I don't know who you're talking about. What's going on? Who is this dude?"

"Someone I need to track down."

"Track *down*?" She props her phone next to the faucet so I can see her getting ready. "Is everything okay?"

"Yes . . . and also, no. But don't worry, I'll fill you in later—" I freeze, remembering the text I got from her at Splendid Cinemas.

I need you.

"Wait," I say.

She splashes her face with water before looking back at me in the screen. "Yeah?"

Is it even worth asking what that could have been about, though? Sure, that text didn't seem like Sadie, and it's even stranger knowing she's never expressed a similar sentiment in my previous todays. But all bets are off when it comes to predicting others' actions after I deviate as dramatically as I did in Day 310. Who knows? She could've been trying a new tactic just to get my attention after I'd ignored all the texts and phone calls that afternoon.

"Never mind; it's nothing," I say, shaking my head. "I'll call you later."

"You swear you're okay?" she asks, as if not so sure that I am.

"Yes."

"Clark—"

I hang up and start tapping into every social media app on my phone, one after the other. In each platform, I search for his name and scroll endlessly through hundreds of Beaus and unfamiliar profile pictures. But I can't find him on any of them. Googling comes up empty, too. I attempt to find Dee on Instagram, hoping Beau would be tagged in her photos, but—without knowing her last name or if "Dee" is short for something else—my sleuthing comes up empty.

Finally I stand in the middle of the school's spacious main entryway in hopes that I'll spot Beau coming through the front doors. But as the initial wave of students starts pouring in, I start to feel like an underwater rock trying to chat with salmon swimming upstream. It becomes apparent how easy it'd be for someone to slip by without me seeing them, and vice versa, so I decide to just start asking people about him.

Normally, I don't start conversations with people I don't know at school. But if I can steal a car and go skinny-dipping, I know I can force myself to talk to students who won't remember our chat in my next today anyway.

I start asking every student who's willing to listen if they know Beau.

Nobody does.

"Hey," Thom calls out to me from across the entryway. He bounces forward, taking one earbud out. "Did you do our trig homework? I am terrible at cosines . . ." He reads the anxious expression on my face. "Are you okay?"

"Does the name Beau Dupont mean anything to you?" I ask.

His eyes narrow and he bites his lower lip. "Should it?"

"Not necessarily."

The rest of the school day is agonizing. I crane my neck between classes hoping to spot Beau's head bobbing above the rest down the hall (I don't). I pester the student council kids who know all the hot gossip, asking if they've heard any rumors about a new transfer from West Edgemont (they haven't). I even check back with Ms. Knotts at lunch, in case she has any updates since this morning ("You've got to knock this off, Clark," she scolds between bites of a tuna sub).

My entire body is buzzing from head to toe by the time last period rolls around. I sprint to Mr. Zebb's class, take my seat uncharacteristically early, and stare at the entrance as students trickle in one by one. My stomach flips with anticipation every time a figure appears in the doorway, only to drop in disappointment a half second later when I realize it's Sara Marino, Greg Shumaker, or Thom once again sliding in late.

In my heart—which is pounding so hard, I'm pretty sure it'd show up on the Richter scale—I know that this is the best shot I have at reconnecting with Beau in Day 311. If Beau is stuck in today and really wants to see me again, he'd come back to the place we first met. Right?

"Who hated the homework?" Mr. Zebb asks cheerily from the front of the class, oblivious to the torment me and Beau put him through in Day 310. "Don't be ashamed to speak up. I know cosines aren't for everyone."

One minute goes by. Then two. Then three. I realize in a slow-moving punch to the gut that it's not happening. Beau's not coming to class.

Could Ms. Knotts be right? Does Beau Dupont not exist? Could I be so devastatingly lonely—and so out of touch with any sense of reality—that I invented someone to befriend?

No, he has to.

Beau Dupont has to exist.

After Mr. Zebb gives us an assignment, I approach him at his desk.

"Hey, Clark." He glances up. "What problem's giving you trouble?"

"It's not that," I say nervously. "You weren't expecting a new transfer student in class today, right?"

He frowns in thought. "I don't believe so."

"Beau Dupont?"

He thinks some more. "No. Why?"

The car keys.

They're just sitting there.

"Clark?" he follows up as I stand completely frozen at his side. "You okay?"

"Yeah."

"You seem on edge."

"I'm fine. Just a weird afternoon, is all."

"Well if you *do* have a math question, feel free to—"

"Who's that?" I ask, pointing at a framed photo next to his computer.

As Mr. Zebb turns, I snatch the keys off his desk at a speed I did not think my hand was capable of moving. I glance at the class; nobody seems to have noticed.

"That's my wife, Mary." Mr. Zebb nods. "And our dog, Russell."

"Can I go to the bathroom?"

He turns back to me, increasingly suspicious. "You sure you're okay, Clark?"

I swallow hard. "Yes."

We lock eyes awkwardly. Painfully, excruciatingly awkwardly.

"Okay," he gives in, nodding at the exit. "Go ahead."

I slip out of the classroom and beeline to the parking lot before Mr. Zebb realizes what happened. I find his car—the stale soda in the middle cupholder confirms that I'm in the right place—and speed out of the lot. Unlike Day 310, I've successfully avoided having a mob of angry teachers waving me down. But still. It doesn't stop an adrenaline rush from seizing my entire nervous system.

"Oh my God," I mumble to myself, flying down the street toward the expressway, a far less skilled and much less confident driver than Beau had been.

Where to first?

Dee is probably my best bet in finding him, seeing as Emery had never met Beau before today, and Otto and Beau's relationship, though sincere, seemed a bit strained at the bakery. She'll be unreachable deep within the walls of the closed Aragon until this evening, though, and the map on my phone is telling me that Splendid Cinemas is the closest drive from Rosedore. So I take a deep breath, steady my hands at ten and two, and hope a random movie theater worker can point me in the right direction. (Or *any* direction.)

Unsurprisingly, Emery is all alone in the lobby when I arrive— the same sheets of paper in hand, earbuds planted firmly on either side of his head—as I storm through the front entrance. He gasps, jumps back from the concession stand, and throws his palms into the air.

"There's only, like, eight bucks in the register, dude," he breathes, the color draining from his face. "Please, take it all—"

"What? No, I'm not . . . do you think I'm robbing you, Emery?"

He looks even more aghast. "How'd you know my name?"

"It doesn't matter. Do you know a guy my age named Beau Dupont?"

"Beau?"

"Yes."

"Like, a thing you'd put on top of a gift?"

"Yes."

Emery thinks. "No."

"You're sure? He comes in here a lot . . . I think."

"I just got hired last week. I probably haven't met him yet."

I resist the urge to keep interrogating him. I'm sure Emery isn't lying—and why would he anyway?—which means he probably won't be much help.

"Thanks," I say, dashing away.

I hear Emery ask, "So you don't want a ticket for *Beetlejuice*?," as the door closes behind me.

I drive to Ben's Everything Blue Bakery next since it's just about the time we were there in the last today now.

A van is parked in the spot Beau took in Day 310, so I peel into a nearby alleyway and put my emergency flashers on.

"Are you kidding me?" an offended pedestrian says, gaping at my dangerously bad parking job (and with good reason).

"Sorry!" I assure them. "I'll be right back!"

The store is bustling and full, hordes of hungry customers jostling for their place in line. When it's finally my turn to order, Otto can tell I'm pining for something other than his blue brownies.

"Hey, there," he says, both curious about, and maybe concerned for, me. "You look like you could use a helping hand."

"I'm looking for Beau Dupont," I say. "Please tell me you know who he is."

But Otto's distracted by another customer trying to snag a napkin from behind the counter and doesn't seem to have heard me. "There you go," he says, pushing the stack closer to her. "Sorry," he says, turning back to me. "What was that now?"

I raise my voice a bit. "Do you know who B—"

A bakery employee appears over Otto's shoulder and asks a question into his ear.

"I'd make at *least* another two dozen," he answers, "because we sell out of them quickly—especially on Mondays."

By now, the anticipation of Otto's answer has sufficiently gripped my heart and is refusing to let go.

Otto's eyes find mine again. "My apologies," he says. "Clearly, it's a bit rowdy in here today. Now, ask me your question one more time?"

I clear my voice, take a deep breath, and ask for a third time: "Do you know Beau Dupont?"

Otto stares expressionless for a moment before his face lights up like a Christmas tree. "Of course I do!"

I nearly melt into the floor with relief, savoring the realization that Ms. Knotts is wrong; Beau Dupont *does* exist—even if he's not in the school directory.

He must have been lying about being a transfer student, though. How much of Beau's story was factual, and how much of it was fiction?

"I haven't seen him in a long while," Otto says. "He used to come in every day."

"Why'd he stop?" I ask.

Otto pauses, suddenly questioning my motives. "Pardon, but who are you again?"

"I'm Beau's friend," I say. "My name is Clark. I'm trying to find him."

His eyes fill with worry. "He's missing?"

"No, no, sorry—not *missing* missing," I say. "I just haven't been able to find him today and he's mentioned coming to this bakery before. Do you know where he lives?"

"With his grandparents," Otto says. "West Edgemont."

I feel a little lighter knowing two more details of Beau's life have been inadvertently fact-checked by the baker. At least he wasn't lying throughout our entire today together.

"You don't have his address, do you?" I ask Otto.

"His address?" He chuckles. "I can't be giving out a customer's personal information like free samples."

I pause to think through other things Otto might know about Beau that could help me. He remains silent, his periwinkle eyes soaking me in. I can tell his suspicion is growing every second I'm standing there, thinking through my next steps as the line of irritable customers grows behind me.

"Has he ever brought in family to the bakery?" I ask.

Otto gives me a look.

"What about other friends?" I follow up.

"You say he's your friend, Clark . . ."

"Yeah?"

"But you don't know where he lives, what school he goes to, or any of his friends or family?"

I open my mouth and close it again. "Okay. Long story short, I . . . like him?" I feel my cheeks turning pink. "We just met, and I didn't get his phone number, so now I'm trying to find him, and . . ." I trail off, certain that my attempt to explain away my questioning is making matters worse. "I understand this all sounds strange, and I don't blame you for being suspicious of me. I'm sorry—"

"Wait, *wait*," Otto cuts me off with a sigh and small smile. "Don't be hard on yourself, Clark." He lowers his voice. "I know what having a crush can do to a person. You don't sound strange. Look." He urges me to take a step closer. "I wish I could be more helpful, but Beau hasn't been in here for . . . gosh, it's been a long time. When you do track him down—and I know you will—can you send him a message for me?"

I nod.

"Tell him to get his butt back in here," he says, "because I miss him." He pauses. "Don't tell him that last part, though."

I smile. "Will do."

"I have blue velvet brownies with his name on them."

My stomach growls at the mention of Beau's favorite treat, and I realize I haven't eaten all day. "One of those sounds delicious right about now."

Otto holds up a finger. He disappears behind the counter and springs up again a moment later with a small paper bag housing a large blue velvet brownie.

He hands it to me. "On the house."

"Really?"

"Of course," he says, wiping his brow. "Now go find our friend."

I thank him three times before slipping out the front door and heading to the beach. Fortunately, I remember the correct rights and lefts that bring me to the exact spot me and Beau went swimming. Unfortunately, Beau's nowhere in sight.

I set down my bag with the brownie inside and look out across the glistening waves.

"Why did you disappear, Beau Dupont?" I mutter to myself. He asked me not to forget him, but judging by how this today has gone, he seems perfectly fine forgetting me.

Who knows, maybe I'm wrong. Maybe we're *not* both stuck in September 19. Or maybe Beau decided that the boy giving him boy problems was more deserving of his time, after all.

CHAPTER 9

I LOOK AT THE WATER AND IMAGINE ME AND BEAU splashing around out there. It feels like it happened a few hours ago. I remember that my last chance to find him in Day 311 is still my best one. And that chance comes in the form of a petite girl with bright eyes and arms made for shockingly strong bear hugs.

Beau texted Dee when we were outside the Aragon, so she must have his phone number, at the very least. Getting his info from her might be tricky, but if Day 310 was any indication, it turns out that I *am* willing to suspend my morals temporarily if the ends justify the means. So if I can steal a teacher's vehicle, I can absolutely steal a phone, too.

I find the ballroom's address, dash back to Mr. Zebb's car from the beach, and drive to Uptown. The only thing standing in my way now are the venue's renovations.

"Hello?" I pound on the door next to the sign announcing the Aragon's closure. I cup my hands against the glass to see inside. "Dee?" The lobby is dark and lifeless, just as it was in Day 310. I look up the venue's phone number and give it a call on the off chance she answers.

"Hello," a recorded voice that is definitely not Dee's says on the other end. "Thank you for contacting Aragon Ballroom. We are currently closed for maintenance through September twenty-third." I follow a few prompts in hopes that I'll be connected to a real human, but the succession of numbers I hit keeps me running in automated circles. I might as well wait it out for Dee to be done with her shift at 6:00 p.m., which, I realize upon checking my phone, won't be for another two hours.

I lean my back against the building's brick exterior and slide down until my butt is on the sidewalk. My skin is slick with sweat from head to toe—my shirt is nearly soaked through and through—and sand from the beach is stuck to my arms, legs, and too many places in between. A long sigh escapes my lips as I wipe my forehead with the back of my hand, wishing September 19 could've been about twenty degrees cooler. I am definitely *not* a sight for sore eyes.

I felt much cuter nestled up next to Beau in Splendid Cinemas. I'd happily watch two more not-quite-believable rom-coms if it meant being there with him again now, the air-conditioning drifting down on us from the vents above.

I hope that Beau wants to be found. But even if I never see him again—even if his offer of friendship was an empty gesture—I don't think he should keep fighting to win back the boy causing him problems. I'm certainly no relationship expert, but even *I* know that Beau shouldn't have to mold himself into the person this other guy wants him to be. Why would someone as confident and self-assured as Beau feel the need to alter who he is to appease an ex?

A businessman tosses a dollar bill at me as he hustles by, presumably because I look like a kid who could use the help.

"Oh," I say, startled. "Thank you, but I don't need—"

Help someone who could use it.

Ms. Hazel's second tip.

I've been so consumed by Beau's deviation and the chaos that's ensued that I'd forgotten about the other homework items in her four-part challenge.

I try to recall the last two.

"Something about . . . being open to others . . . ?" I mutter. Oh, *be vulnerable so others can be too.* That's right. And then, number four . . .

What was it?

Fear.

Do the thing that scares you.

I still have a good amount of time to kill. Maybe I should work on completing Ms. Hazel's tip list? I'm not sure why or how it could help me find Beau, make sense of my never-ending today, or help me get to tomorrow. But trying to make a new friend resulted in my meeting Beau. I might as well try to follow the other three tips, too, and see where it takes me.

I begin to walk around the neighborhood seeking out anyone who looks like they could use my help. I doubt I'll come across any opportunity to share my vulnerabilities—and I'd be even *more* surprised if I stumble into a situation that requires that I do a thing that scares me—but, hey, stranger things have happened.

I spot an old woman struggling to carry her bags, but she disappears into a crafts store before I can offer to carry them. I stand near the entrance of a Thai restaurant for a bit, opening the door for incoming customers before noticing the manager staring at me suspiciously through the front windows. As pure as my intentions are, she probably doesn't appreciate a random teen loitering outside.

Nothing else sticks out as an opportunity to conquer tips two, three, or four, though. No voice in my head urges me to spring into action, as it did when I chased after Beau. But I start to take note of things happening around me: small kids giggling as they hop through a sprinkler; two teary-eyed old friends reuniting near the train station; the happiest Dachshund I've ever seen eating a Puppuccino outside a cafe. I've been stuck on my beaten path for so long, reluctant to discover more sadness existing in my today, that I'd forgotten I could come across lots of good things stuck on repeat as well.

Noticing that it's 6:00 p.m., I head back to the Aragon, even more doused in sweat and exhausted from the heat than I had been before. As I turn the corner, I spot Dee striding away from the ballroom doors, head bobbing with each click of her heels. "Hey! Dee?" I say, jogging after her. "My name is Clark, and I'm—"

She stops and turns.

"Oh," I let out in surprise before I can stop myself. "Are you okay?"

Day 311 Dee is not the bubbly Starburst Dee who I met in Day 310. Tears are streaming down her face, eyes bloodshot and puffy.

"Who are you?" she asks, suspicious.

"I'm Clark," I say, wishing I had a tissue to hand her. "I'm friends with Beau, and I'm—"

"Beau?"

"Yeah."

I'm not entirely sure if she wants to slap me, kiss me, tell me to get lost, or none of the above. But the ambiguity quickly dissolves as she falls into me for a teary hug. "Why didn't he text me today?"

"He didn't?"

"No," she says. "He was supposed to."

"Is that why you're upset?"

She lets out a sharp laugh. "I *wish* that were the reason, Mark." She pulls away and steps back, suddenly aware that she's embracing a stranger. "You said that was your name, right?"

"Clark."

"And you're friends with Beau?"

"Yes."

She wipes the tears from her cheeks and glances down the sidewalk both ways before looking back at me. "Do you like BLTs, Mark?"

"As in, the sandwich?"

She nods.

"Sure?" I answer.

"Let's go."

Dee turns and darts off.

"Okay . . . ?" I mutter in her footsteps. "I'm sorry Beau didn't text you, but have you seen him today—"

"I already told you that's not the reason why I'm crying," Dee underscores, missing my point and glancing backward at me from five feet ahead. "I'm crying because I just might die."

Bubbly Day 310 Dee failed to mention an imminent death.

"What was that?" I ask, assuming I've misheard.

"I'm crying because I might die," she says before spotting the look on my face. "Oh, from *embarrassment*. Don't worry. What about milkshakes?"

"Milkshakes?"

"Yes, Mark. You like BLTs, but do you also like milkshakes?"

"Yes?"

"Great."

Dee suddenly veers left through the entrance of a diner on the corner.

I hesitate to follow her, wondering what sort of traumatizing embarrassment could have happened to Dee to spark such an abrupt change from the person I met in Day 310.

But it's clear that she'd appreciate someone to talk to right now. Not to mention, she's my best shot at contacting the one person who may be stuck in today with me. So I can't abandon my plan now. Plus, I stupidly forgot my brownie from Ben's at the beach earlier and my stomach has been growling at me for hours.

I step inside.

The diner, decorated in red and white flags, smells of bleach and sizzling red meat. Despite it being dinnertime, there are only two occupied tables aside from the one Dee has claimed near the window—one taken by an elderly couple eating large stacks of pancakes, and the other, a family of seven crammed around a table meant for four.

I slide into the booth to sit opposite Dee, who is looking into a pocket mirror and dabbing at her eyes.

"Well, hello"—the server gasps once she sees Dee's face—"what happened, hon?"

Dee laughs, snaps her mirror shut, and tosses it aside. "Hey, Sandy. Let's just say I've been better and leave it at that."

Sandy—who reminds me of my aunt Brenda if Aunt Brenda had spiky purple hair—sets laminated menus down in front of us. Those, too, are covered in the red and white flags. "You sure you don't want to talk about it?" she asks.

Dee shakes her head adamantly. "You don't need to be burdened by my dumb drama."

"Hush," Sandy says. "You know I never mind, Dee."

Dee hands the menus back to Sandy with a forced smile. "I promise, I'll be fine. We'll both take my usual."

"Two chocolate milkshakes and two BLTs coming right up."

Sandy heads back to the kitchen.

"Anyway, Mark." Dee looks at me. "How's your day going?"

How's *my* day going? "Okay, I guess?"

"Good, good."

She stays quiet for a minute, staring out the window blankly.

"So," I cut into the silence.

Dee directs her attention back to me.

"Do you want to . . . talk about it?" I ask hesitantly.

"About . . . ?"

"The embarrassment that might kill you?"

"Oh, absolutely not," she says at once, as if I'm being ridiculous.

I wait a beat. "Are you sure?"

"Yes." She nods at the salt and pepper shakers, which are also red and white. "It's the colors of the Turkish flag, by the way."

"Huh?"

"It's why there's so much red and white in here. The owners are from Turkey. The BLTs are my favorite, but the fish and chips are also great—and their baklava is to die for."

"Got it."

I may have begun to break out of my comfort zone, but not so much that this situation isn't painfully uncomfortable. I don't know Dee that well. I have no idea why she would drag me into this diner out of despair, only to refuse to talk about why she's upset. And I definitely don't know how to best navigate this conversation.

She needs her own Ms. Hazel. Or, better yet, a friend who knows her much better than I do. She needs someone like Beau.

Wait.

Beau was determined to speak to her about something private when we arrived at the Aragon, and then noted to me that Dee had had a rough night yesterday—something she clearly didn't want to discuss with him.

Could Dee's embarrassing secret have something to do with that?

Sandy returns with two chocolate milkshakes, each topped with a mountain of whipped cream, before bouncing off to seat a new customer waiting at the door.

Dee takes a long, strong sip. She moans, eyes closed, as the ice cream slowly rises through the straw and disappears into her mouth. "I already feel better."

I want to ask her if she told Beau her secret and find some natural segue into how she can help me find him, but I need to be careful. Otto grew suspicious of me right away when I started to pry at the bakery, and I imagine Dee would be even quicker to push back on someone who she thinks may be a creeper asking intrusive questions about a friend.

As I try to think of a seamless way to bring up Beau, though, Dee starts to laugh.

"I'm sorry," she says, dabbing at her lips with a napkin. "I'm realizing how absurd this must feel to you right now. A stranger holding you hostage over shakes and sandwiches? You must think I'm nuts. Feel free to go if you want, Mark."

I shake my head. "It's okay."

"Has this ever happened to you?"

"What?"

"A girl in distress scooping you off the sidewalk in her moment of need?"

"Not exactly."

She sighs. "I'm not like this. I'm fun and carefree ninety-nine percent of the time, I swear."

"I know."

Her eyes narrow on mine. "Do you?"

"I mean," I say, my face turning hot. "I don't *know*, because I just met you, but from what Beau has told me—"

"That's *right*." She claps her hands together. "That's why you were waiting for me outside the Aragon, I'm assuming? Sending a message on Beau's behalf?"

"Well—"

"Tell me," she says, smirking, "am I supposed to believe he forgot how to send a text?"

Before I can seize the opportunity, Sandy returns with a tray of food.

"Y'all are so fast," Dee says, while two plates of BLTs slide in front of us. "I'm always impressed by the speediness."

The server props her fist on her hip. "You feeling better?"

Dee nods with a smile. "Your milkshakes do the trick."

Sandy rubs Dee's shoulder, gives her a wink, and floats away.

"Anyway," Dee says, popping a fry into her mouth. "Do you have any secrets, Mark?"

Shoot. I want to stay on the topic of Beau—unless, of course, he's the root cause of her embarrassment.

I don't think I have any secrets. At least none of importance. That is, beyond existing in a day that I've already relived hundreds of times before. "Not really."

"I've held on to a big one—for *years*," Dee says. "I'd arranged to finally tell it last night, but . . ." She trails off, shaking her head in a trance. "It blew up in my face. Big-time."

I hope she continues.

But she doesn't.

"What happened?" I ask.

She closes her eyes, cringing to herself at the memory, before shielding her face with her hands. Her embarrassment looks downright painful. "It's so bad. I can't."

"Have you told anyone?"

"No. It's too fresh." She returns to her food. "I'm sorry for bringing it up again and being a tease. I don't mean to be. Let's talk about something else. *Anything* else. How did you meet Beau?"

Dee's phone starts buzzing. She holds a finger up to hit pause on our conversation.

"Hey, you," she says into the phone, putting on a fake smile. Her tone is bubblier, like it had been in Day 310. A second later, her face lights up in surprise. "Oh my God, that's right! I forgot. I'll be there in like, one minute, okay? Okay, okay, bye!" She hangs up and starts scooching out of the booth.

"You're leaving?" I ask, starting to panic.

She nods.

"But we just got our food," I say, glancing down at my sandwich.

I can't let the opportunity slip by.

"I am so sorry, Mark," she says, pulling out her wallet and throwing cash on the table. "I was so worked up, I forgot that my friend was picking me up after my shift today. Say bye to Sandy for me, will you?"

I rise to my feet. "Hold on."

She pauses, sensing my urgency.

"It's about Beau," I begin.

But what do I even say? Where do I even *begin*?

She looks worried. "Is he all right?"

"He's fine."

Her face falls into a knowing smile. "He sent you to apologize for standing me up today, huh? Is that it?" She shakes her head. "I had a feeling he would. Honestly? It's not a big deal that he flaked. Tell him I'm fine. *Clearly*, I haven't been in the best mood anyway——"

"It's not that, exactly," I say. "Do you have his phone number?"

She laughs. I wait for her to explain why that's funny, but she doesn't.

"I take that as a no?" I follow up.

"Oh, you're serious?" she asks. "Aren't you his friend? Why wouldn't you have it? Besides, no, I don't have his number."

"Really?"

She shakes her head. "Why would I?"

Why *wouldn't* she? "Aren't you two friends?"

"I mean, I guess—but brand-new ones. I just met Beau last night."

My stomach drops.

I rub my temples, trying to make sense of it. "But . . . he was texting you in Day 310."

Dee cocks her head at me. "What is Day 310?"

"I mean, I thought you said he was supposed to text you today."

"He was."

"So you must have his number, at least?"

She laughs. "You're funny, Mark. Listen." She sighs, leaning against the booth. "I'm not sure what you're digging for or what I have to do with it, but here's all I know. We met each other having a terrible time at the concert and he seemed cool, so I gave my number to him. He was supposed to text me today about stopping by the Aragon in the afternoon to check in on me, but, as you of course know by now, he didn't." She shrugs. "That's all I got for you."

"I'm confused," I say, my mind racing. "How did you see a show with Beau at the Aragon last night if it's closed for construction?"

"The show wasn't at the Aragon," she says. "It was at Lakeview Live."

I freeze. "You saw The Wrinkles? And Beau was there, too?"

"I've *really* got to go, but yes."

The prospects of Dee's secret having something to do with Beau—and possibly even the reason why we got stuck in today—just went up about a thousand percent.

Dee takes a step toward the door. "I'm friends with Mae. I had to check them out."

"Mae Monroe?" My jaw drops. "The lead singer of The Wrinkles?"

"Yeah, I met her backstage when they played the Aragon last year and we hit it off." She glances out the window and inches closer toward the exit before spotting my face. "Uh, are you okay?"

I slouch back into the booth. "Yeah."

"Are you sure? Because you're giving me looks-like-you-just-saw-a-ghost vibes."

"I'll be fine."

Dee looks for her ride outside again and then back at me, unsure what she should do.

"It's okay," I assure her. "You can go."

"You're a nice guy, Mark. Thanks for the impromptu dinner. And I don't mean to play coy with my secret, it's just . . ." She smiles.

"There's a lot happening in my head today. Hey, maybe me, you, and Beau can hang sometime?"

Before I can answer, she's swirling through the doorway on her way out, leaving me alone with my swirling thoughts.

I may not have found him yet, but Beau was at The Wrinkles show last night, too.

And that can't mean nothing.

CHAPTER 10

ACCORDING TO THE INTERNET, CHICAGO HAS almost three million people in it. Add in the suburbs, and you're pushing nine million. What are the chances that Beau happened to be in the same place, at the same time, watching the same concert the night before I got stuck in today? The night before we *both* may have gotten stuck in today?

The Wrinkles show has to have something to do with my time loop.

His time loop.

Our time loop.

After deciding against spending the rest of my night on Splendid Cinemas' rooftop, I decide to call it quits and head back to Rosedore. Because if Beau's been missing all day, what makes me think he'd want to show up at the movies now?

I turn onto the expressway in Mr. Zebb's car and head west into the sunset, the city's skyscrapers shrinking behind me in the rearview mirror. The sky ahead is striped in cotton-candy pinks and blues, and I can't remember it ever looking this spectacular, even having seen the exact same star setting the exact same way 311 times now. I wish Beau were in the passenger seat sharing this view with me.

My phone buzzes in the cupholder. I reach down and see that it's Dad calling.

My first instinct is to ignore it, just like I always do whenever my deviations cause widespread panic among my family. But seeing the screen light up with his name on it, I realize how much I miss him.

Dad manages a store that does air-conditioning installations and repairs, which means, on a day as scorching as today, he's basically working sunup to sundown. Deviating to see him late in the evening is hardly worth the trouble most of the time, as he's ornery, exhausted, and completely unaware that *that's* the only mood I get to spend time with him in now. So, I only visit when I really want to see him.

Plus, the longer I'm in the time loop, the more surreal it feels to visit what used to be our family home. To Mom and Blair, we just moved out of that place. But to me, stepping inside feels like a nostalgic trip down memory lane—a tease of what my life used to be, and what it could have been if only things went differently.

I can't even remember offhand the last today I chatted with Dad. I wouldn't mind hearing his voice. Especially right now, as I'm feeling completely dejected after failing to find Beau all afternoon. So I decide to answer. "Hi, Dad."

"C," he says, sighing in relief. "Thank God."

"He picked up?" Blair gasps in the background. "He's actually alive?"

Wait. "You're with Blair?" I ask.

"And your mom," Dad answers. "All three of us are on the line."

I hold the phone at arm's length and mouth an f-bomb in frustration. Some todays that I deviate, Mom and Dad begrudgingly sync up in their efforts to find me. And some of those todays, like this one, I forget that that could be the case.

"You're on speaker, Clark," Mom says. "Your dad started a threesome Zoom chat—"

Blair makes a loud vomiting noise. "It's a *three-way call*, Mom, not a *threesome Zoom*. Ew."

"C," Dad butts in, drowning out my sister's rant, "please confirm to us that you're safe."

"Yes," I sigh. "This is me confirming that I'm fine. I'm driving back to Rosedore now."

"In what vehicle?" Mom asks, her tone shifting from relieved to accusatory in the blink of an eye.

"Why does it matter?" I answer.

"Ms. Knotts called earlier and accused you of stealing your math teacher's car," she says. "I told her that that couldn't possibly be the case because my son isn't the type of kid who would *steal a teacher's car*." She pauses to breathe. "Please tell me the school secretary got it wrong."

I pause as I plot my next move, regretting having picked up the phone in the first place. "Everyone just chill, okay?" I say slowly. "I'm not hurt. I'm not kidnapped. And I'm, like, ten minutes from home. Can we talk about all of this when I get h—"

"It's true?" Mom booms. "You're talking to us from Mr. Zebb's car? Do you have any idea what kind of trouble you're in? Do you realize you may have just ruined your life?"

"*Melody*," Dad scolds under his breath. "Don't be dramatic."

"Dramatic?" Mom belts. I pull the phone away so that my eardrums won't be permanently damaged. "Your son stole a car and went missing, Gary, and your concern is that I'm being too dramatic?"

Blair starts giggling.

It's not funny, of course. Nothing about *any* of this is funny. But instead of feeling sad about Mom and Dad butting heads, Blair always tries to giggle away their fights. It's easier than dealing with the sad state of their relationship head-on.

"All I'm saying is that, right now, I think Clark's right; we should be focusing on the fact that he's safe," Dad rebukes. "That's the most important thing."

"Well, of course it's the most important thing," Mom says. "But now that we know he's safe, I'd like to know if our son understands that he's technically a criminal."

I roll my eyes. "Yes, Mom, I understand that—"

"You get why the police are now involved, right?" she continues.

"*Melody.*" Dad hisses at her. "Let the kid talk, for Christ's sake."

"Okay, then," she says. "Please, Ferris Bueller, start talking. Tell us why you woke up this morning and decided to commit grand theft auto. I'd really love to know about this brilliant plan of yours."

I take a deep breath.

Most todays, the idea of having to explain my predicament feels like an exhausting, completely fruitless endeavor to avoid at all costs. But every once in a while, when I'm especially drained and Mom is getting on my last nerve, I've been known to tell her exactly what's happening to me, knowing it won't make any bit of difference—other than further piss her off, as she thinks I'm messing with her. Day 311 falls under the latter.

"Well . . . okay," I say, exhaling. "Mom, Dad . . . I've been stuck in a time loop."

They don't say anything, so I take advantage of the silence to keep going.

"I've been stuck reliving September nineteenth over three hundred times. Three hundred and eleven, actually. Each one of my todays is exactly the same," I say, remembering how cathartic it can feel to tell the truth (even if telling it is pointless). "Like, Mom, I know you wanted to order pizza for us tonight, and you planned on eating only veggie toppings because you want to start cutting out red meat. And, Blair, I know you confirmed the attendance of your birthday party today: fifteen kids plan on being there."

"Wait, how would he know that?" Blair whispers. "This sounds like that one Derek Dopamine video where—"

"Dad," I continue, "I'm sorry, but it's rare that I see you in my time loop because we didn't have plans together in the original September nineteenth, and today's been one of your busiest of the year at work anyway."

"Original September nineteenth?" Dad mutters, confused.

"My point is, I can't tell you as much about your day as I can with Mom and Blair, but if I'm remembering correctly, you're wearing . . ." I close my eyes in thought for a second. ". . . a yellow tie with ducks on it. Right? At least that's what you wore to work when I saw you last, which would have been on Day . . ." I pause again, trying to remember. "I don't know, I think it probably would have been in the Day 270s or thereabouts."

Blair squeals. "What the . . . ? Dad, is he right?"

Dad waits a beat before confirming: "Shockingly, yes."

"But here's the thing," I barrel on. "I met a boy named Beau at school in Day 310. Ms. Hazel's deviated homework assignment in Day 309 inspired me to start a conversation with him because she thinks I should try to make new friends to help beat my loneliness."

"See?" Blair says. "I told you he's depressed and needs more friends."

"I really like Beau," I continue. "I really, *really* like him. You know the strangest part? He's never been at my school in the time loop. Day 310 was his first. We spent the entire day together. Actually, we stole Mr. Zebb's car in Day 310, too, and—you wouldn't remember this, Mom, but—the day ended with you screaming at me while I stood on a movie theater rooftop in Uptown, and the cop—"

"Stop with this lunacy," Mom interjects. "Right now."

"I was *just* getting to the good part, though," I say, perfectly fine with getting under Mom's skin.

"This is a stupid joke to you, huh?" she asks, reaching her boiling point. "Have you been spying on us all day?"

I laugh. "Spying? On *you*? Why would I do that?"

"How else would you know about your dad's yellow tie, or my no-red-meat goal?"

I sigh. "I'll start again. This time, try to keep up. Okay? So." I sigh. "I've been stuck in one of those time loops. You know, the things you see in the movies? And—"

"Knock it off!" Mom bellows.

"What?" I say innocently. "You asked about my day, so I'm trying to tell you about my day."

"See what divorce can do to a kid?" Blair whispers with a laugh, just loudly enough for me to hear. "He's losing his mind, you guys."

"Cool it, Blair," Dad finally speaks up. "You're not being helpful."

"And neither are you," Mom mutters.

"What's that supposed to mean?" Dad asks.

She sighs. "What do you *think* it means? I'm sick of playing the bad cop as you sit back and watch."

Now *I* let out a laugh alongside Blair.

The line goes quiet.

"What could possibly be funny?" Mom asks.

"It's just . . ." I pause.

Should I?

Hell, at this point why not? She won't remember what I'm about to say in Day 312 anyway.

"I hate to break it to you, Mom," I say, "but no one is forcing you to play bad cop. You just naturally are one."

There's finally quiet on the other end.

"You know what I think is funny?" I continue. "That you think I've ruined my own life today, when you've already done that for all of us."

"C," Dad warns. "Cut it out."

"You wanted the divorce, Mom," I say. "You tore apart our lives and forced me and Blair to move into your tiny, terrible apartment—why? For what reason? Because you just *fell out of love* with Dad, or some bullshit you won't explain?"

"*Clark.*" Dad's voice tells me he's about to pop. "Stop it—"

"You don't need Dad to make you into a bad cop, is all I'm saying." I breathe. "You destroyed this family all on your own."

There. I said it.

It isn't the first time I've told Mom how I really feel, and it may not be the last.

But it still feels great . . . for about five seconds.

Then, once again, I'm gutted with guilt.

There's only silence. Earsplitting, uncomfortable silence. The only sounds are the humming engines of cars passing me by. Not even Blair is trying to crack a joke now, which, I've learned throughout many todays, is a clear indicator that I've gone too far.

Finally, Mom speaks up. "You're headed home now, you said?" she asks. Her voice is so quiet, it's barely audible.

"Yes," I say.

"Okay," she says, and hangs up.

I don't realize that I'm crying until I feel a teardrop fall onto my chin.

Another reason why it sucks to be stuck in a time loop? Everyone else gets to forget what's happened in all of your todays. They get a fresh start at 7:15 a.m., their memories wiped clean, unaware of the pain I've caused them or the destruction I've made in all the other September nineteenths. I can't forget that pain, though. Not really.

But I can delay facing it for a little longer.

When I drive off my expressway exit, I take a right instead of a left.

I can't go home right now. I need to go back to Rosedore High.

W HEN I'M AVOIDING MOM'S APARTMENT AND can't utilize her kitchen to bake, the next best thing to help me escape the torment of the time loop is the Rosedore High School pool. It's rare that I actually take a swim. Most of the time, I just lay poolside, appreciating the calm in a place where no one would think to find me. I never go during the school day, when the shallow end is awkwardly packed like sardines with underclassmen who'd rather not tread water. I can't go in the evening, when the boys' swim team is practicing in their Speedos (I may appreciate the view, but the swimmers don't appreciate my staring). So mostly I go at night, when my thoughts can wander in peace.

I learned by trial in the earlier todays that every single door to the high school gets locked once the sun goes down, except for one. I'm not sure if a custodian always leaves it open or if the swimming coach forgot his keys this particular Monday, but someone is to blame for the exterior entrance to the boys' locker room staying unlocked all night. And I've decided to take advantage.

I park Mr. Zebb's car in the empty school lot and sneak in. Despite there being no students in sight, the locker room smells like the dirtiest socks a laundry hamper has ever seen.

Then I enter the pool area.

The air is warm and humid, as always, and thick with the scent of chlorine. The only light glows from bulbs beneath the water's surface, their beams casting fluttering reflections throughout the room. The tiles beneath my shoes are still slick from the swim team splashing around during their practice, and I know from firsthand experience (a bad fall early in the time loop) to tread especially lightly in here.

I head to the bleachers nearest the deep end and lie on my back on the first row of seats. I stare up at the ceiling and disappear into my thoughts, finally able to soak in my past two todays.

I've been numb for a while now, shrinking away inside my tightening comfort zone. I think that's why Days 310 and 311 have hit me especially hard; because I'm not used to feeling feelings anymore. So when they hit, they *really* hit.

I haven't blown up on Mom like that in at least a hundred todays or so—not because I'm over the divorce, but because I've learned that it's better for me to be indifferent toward her than be a dick over and over again. I lost my cool today. Badly. Probably because of Beau—or, more accurately, my inability to find him.

Even though it's only been hours since he kissed me on the cinema rooftop, I've never missed someone as intensely as I do right now. I don't think I'd miss him so much if I knew I'd see him again soon—or ever again, at all.

It's the most cliché of all the clichés, I know, but maybe opposites *do* attract. Beau is spontaneous, confident, unguarded when it counts. I'm an overthinker, unsure, a good problem solver when it matters most.

Before Day 310, I'd never in a million years skinny-dip at a city beach or sit through a rom-com double feature. But in a single afternoon, Beau lured me into the water and had me questioning my disdain for fairy-tale endings. On the other hand, it seems like few people have told Beau how great of a superpower his confidence and curiosity truly can be—especially if you add a drop of spontaneity. I think he appreciates that I get it. I think he appreciates that I get *him*.

But what if I'm wrong?

What if it wasn't some weird time principle that kept us apart today? What if he's not as into me as I am into him? He's got the boy giving him boy problems, after all. Maybe Beau spent his day running other errands with the ex who wants him to change who he is in order for them to be together.

That would be ironic, huh? The one guy who started to succeed in making me believe in happily ever afters stands me up hours later.

The door to the locker room closes with a *thud*. I bolt upright in shock—no one ever visits the pool this time of night—and turn toward the sound.

Beau.

I blink several times, just to make sure he's not a mirage.

He scans the surface of the pool before looking my way. "How come you're not skinny-dipping again?"

I open my mouth to respond, but the shock of seeing him standing there leaves me stunned like a fish out of water.

"Clark." He grins. "I'm just kidding."

Beau walks closer to me but stops near the deep-end ladder, a good ten feet away. He stands at the edge of the pool with the tips of his sneakers hovering above the water's surface, and he somehow looks even taller than I remember.

I realize that he's holding a small paper bag in one of his hands—a bag from Ben's Everything Blue Bakery. "You went to see Otto?"

"No," he says. "This is yours."

"What do you mean?"

"Your brownie," he says. "You left it at the beach earlier."

My eyes expand. "So . . . you've been following me?"

He nods.

"All day?"

"Yeah."

I don't know whether I should laugh, cry, or grab the nearby pool skimmer and throw it at his face. "If you were following me, then you'd know that I went on all of our errands just to find you . . ."

He nods again.

My face twists in confusion.

He's avoiding direct eye contact with me, I realize, which feels very unlike him. Instead, he's staring at my reflection through the water's still surface.

"Why?" I ask, since he doesn't seem eager to explain. "Why were you following—but also hiding—from me?"

He licks his lips in thought, trying to find the right words. "I wanted to make sure."

"Make sure of what?"

"That it was true," he says. "That you're in my repeating Monday from hell, too."

Sweet relief spreads to my fingertips. Because I knew it. Even if I had my doubts earlier this afternoon, deep down, I knew that had to be the case.

Beau can't get out of September 19, either.

I'm not alone in here.

But my euphoria quickly fades.

He's nervous, I can tell, and it throws me. *I* was the anxious one in Day 310, not him. Beau was never rattled. He never sweat it. But he's rattled and sweating it now.

"So how'd you know that I'm stuck, too?" I ask.

He rocks back and forth on his sneakers, dangerously close to falling into the pool. "I came to school this morning, and it just . . . clicked."

He's still not making eye contact. Something is up.

"Hey." I wait for him to look at me. "Is everything all right?"

He sighs. "I didn't come here just to return your brownie. I came here to . . . tell you goodbye."

My stomach drops. "Goodbye?"

He doesn't say anything.

"Why? Where are you going?" I glance around. "Where would you even . . . *go* in a time loop?"

He places the bakery bag on the tile floor. "It's best if we don't see each other again—at least not while we're still in today."

He heads toward the exit.

I follow him. "Tell me that you're joking, Beau."

He swings the locker room door open. I scoot in behind him before it closes.

"Please don't do this," I say as the stench of dirty socks hits me in the face. "I'm not lonely when I'm with you."

"And I'm not lonely when I'm with you."

"Good! Shouldn't we stay together if we're both stuck? Shouldn't we try to escape?"

"I *am* trying to escape," Beau replies. "That's exactly why we need to stay apart."

What?

He glances back at me as we reach the locker room exit. "I like you too much, Clark. And I don't trust myself around you."

"What does that even mean?"

He steps out into the parking lot.

So do I.

"You're not making any sense," I argue, trying to keep up with him, just like when we were darting between errands.

"I mean what I told you at the movies," he says, striding toward a white car that's parked near Mr. Zebb's.

"Can you be more specific?" I ask. "You told me a *lot* of things at the movies."

"You have a soul mate, Clark. You have to. Or else you wouldn't be stuck in here, like I am."

My mind might explode. Actually, *truly* explode. As if the past two todays weren't disorienting enough, now Beau is spouting utter nonsense at me and acting like it should all make sense.

"You just have to find him, whoever he is," he follows up, arriving to the car. "That's how we escape this hellhole. Trust me."

I gape at him as he unlocks the driver-side door.

"*Trust* you? You mean like I trusted you when you told Mr. Zebb that you're a new transfer student? Because, according to Ms. Knotts, there's no new student with the name Beau Dupont at Rosedore High."

He looks at me like I can't be serious. "That's hardly a white lie to get worked up over, Clark."

"Oh yeah? What about Dee?" I retort. "The girl who's not so much a friend of yours, as much as she's someone you just met yesterday—at the same concert *I was at too*?"

"Dee *is* my friend who, yes, I happen to have met on Sunday night." He drops into the car behind the wheel. "And I know you saw The Wrinkles as well."

I let out a sharp laugh, exasperated. "Then why wouldn't you tell me that? It seems like a pretty big coincidence that the two of us were at the same concert the night before we both got stuck in a time loop together."

"I only just remembered that I'd seen you at the show when I saw you again this morning." He closes the car door, stares at me through the open window, and sighs. "Remember how I thought we'd met before but I couldn't place you? That was real. I'm not trying to be a dick, I swear."

I scoff. "Well, you should try harder."

He pauses. "I wish we could still hang out."

"There's nothing stopping us from doing that!"

"But there is." He buckles up. "I like you, Clark. A little too much. And I know myself. The more that I'm with you, the more distracted I'll be."

"Distracted from what?"

He exhales. "The boy giving me boy problems." He turns the ignition and the car roars to life. "I loved our day together, but it has to be our last, okay? At least for now."

"I still don't understand why, though." My eyes fill with tears.

I can't be sure, but I think Beau's do too. "Because then maybe I'll get to see you tomorrow."

The car rolls in reverse and blasts off through the parking lot. Knowing the way Beau drives, I don't even attempt to run to my car and chase after him.

CHAPTER 12

I DON'T GO HOME IN DAY 311. I CAN'T FACE MOM, ESPE-
cially after being gutted by Beau appearing out of nowhere,
only to abandon me once again. So I ignore the barrage of new
notifications that begin blowing up my phone—my family realizes I
should have been back by now—and wait it out at the pool. I lie on
my side next to the deep end watching the stillness of the water and
hoping that my next today brings better news, until it's 11:16 p.m.

I wake up in Day 312 to my white, wooden nightstand and a
continuation of my increasingly confused thoughts. I guess all of
them can be boiled down into the same, succinct question I had
after Ms. Hazel's homework deviation in Day 309, though: *What the
hell is going on?*

I've never been more baffled before. And for someone who's
been stuck in a time loop for three-hundred-plus todays, that's saying something.

I sit up in bed and try to make sense of what I learned at the
pool. Beau said that he realized two things when he saw me at
school in Day 311: that I was stuck in today alongside him, and that
I'd also been at The Wrinkles concert. I'm not sure how he saw me
without my noticing, considering how determined I'd been to find
him first. But knowing he spent the rest of the today following me
as I dropped by our errands, I think it's safe to say Beau is a master
at spying.

Also, soul mates?

Apparently, I have one—at least according to Beau.

"Or else you wouldn't be stuck in here, like I am," I mutter his words to myself.

Beau must believe we need to find our soul mates to escape today. For him, I assume that means getting back with his ex.

I'm not sure how he pieced this theory together. I never ran across an idea like that while doing my research. That doesn't say much, though, I guess, seeing as there are countless claims floating around every weird corner of the internet.

Beau's theory sounds rational enough (or about as rational as you can be with time loops), and it's a cute concept, too—especially if you're someone who loves fairy-tale endings. There's just one problem.

"I know I don't have a fucking soul mate," I sigh.

I didn't have one prior to getting stuck. There's no one even *close*. I've had a few crushes, sure; most of them, boys on the internet whom I've never met in real life. Can you even call it a crush if they don't follow you back?

The point is, Beau's theory couldn't apply to me. Unless I can meet my soul mate in the time loop. If that's the case, then, yeah . . . maybe it'd be more believable. But then why, with the exception of Beau, have I not even come close to connecting with another guy on September 19?

Beau may not need me anymore, as a friend or otherwise, now that he's laser focused on rekindling things with his ex, but I still need him. If we both got stuck together in the same today, there has to be a way we can help each other get out. Whether or not Beau's soul-mate theory is correct, I need to know more.

I contemplate heading into school on the very slim chance that Beau will actually be there this time—and *not* spying on me again— but decide against it. I text Mom the excuse I typically use whenever I skip school (food poisoning) and roll around under my covers until I come up with another plan.

If Beau isn't a student at Rosedore, I imagine he might go to West Edgemont. So I decide to call the school's main office.

"Happy Monday, and go Raiders!" an unjustifiably cheery woman says answering the phone. "How can I help you?"

I shift my voice to sound like an old, straight grandparent. "I'm hoping to get in touch with my grandson, Beau Dupont. It's an emergency."

"Do you know what class Beau is in right now?"

"I don't."

"One moment, sir." I'm put on hold. After a minute of silence, the secretary returns. "This is odd. Our attendance records indicate that Beau never came into school today."

I hang up, unsurprised.

It's useful to confirm where he goes to school, I guess, but I shouldn't expect to find Beau there. He told me in Day 310 that he has no plans on graduating, after all, which feels even more believable now that I know he's stuck in today, too. Unlike me, I can't fathom Beau wasting away behind a desk just for the sake of sticking to a routine.

It can't hurt to try Sadie again, I decide. Maybe I called too early in Day 311. She'll be the first to tell you her brain has a difficult time functioning before 9:00 a.m., after all. Plus, I still haven't forgotten about the text I got from her at the movies telling me that she needed me. Even if it was nothing but a last-ditch effort to grab my attention because I was missing—or a very bizarre consequence of Day 310's ripple effect of deviations—I can't quite shake it. Putting everything related to Beau aside, I should check in on her.

I pull my phone out from under the covers, and text: Hey! How's it going? ☺

A few seconds later, she responds with: Uh oh. You never use that emoji. Should I be worried?

I grin. Lol no. was just thinking about you. I'm sorry I missed our Face-Time.

Yeah what's up with that?? I want to know how the show went last night! I heard you were Mr. Lightweight . . .

I respond, sorry, I'm home from school, sick af, with a puking emoji.

Hungover?

Maybe? But I think it's food poisoning. How are you doing? I ask. How's Podcast Club?

There's a long pause. I see text bubbles appear for a few moments, disappear, and then return again. This happens for another minute, convincing me that an entire novel is about to drop into my messages, but all her text ends up being is:

I'm good! But really, stop burying the lede. How were The Wrinkles?

Is she . . . not telling me something?

She *is* messaging me from class. It makes sense that she wouldn't be able to text and send her response as quickly as she would otherwise. Maybe I'm overthinking that text from Day 310.

I give her a quick rundown of the concert—the parts I can remember, at least—before moving on to a far more important topic.

Beau Dupont, I text. Does that name mean anything to you?

No clue, she responds.

Really? Nothing? He was at the concert last night, if that helps.

Is he famous or something? she asks. The name sounds like a French tennis player, and you know how I feel about French tennis players.

he's a new kid at school, I write. What about a girl named Dee? Do you know any Dees?

IDK a Dee. You're being weird. What's this about?

I sigh, respond, I'll fill you in later, and stare out the window, thinking of a plan B. Or is it plan C. . . . D?

I can't keep track at this point.

Maybe I could have better luck combing through the apps again—especially now that I know Beau was at the concert.

I scroll through a bunch of hashtags associated with The Wrinkles show—#TheWrinklesChicago, #WrinklesInTheWindyCity, #WrinklesNearWrigley—squinting at the photos on my screen. I look for Beau's distinguishable traits in the sea of faces—his long legs, triangular torso, amber eyes—but I can't find him anywhere.

Maybe one of our errands' social media accounts could hold a clue.

There wouldn't be any reason for a picture of Beau to be on the Aragon's profiles, and Splendid Cinemas has never entered the twenty-first century (I wouldn't be surprised if the theater didn't even have a website). But if Beau used to stop in and see Otto all the time, maybe there's an old post buried on the bakery's grid that could tell me something more about him.

It's a long shot, but still a shot.

"Wow," I mutter, finding @BensEverythingBlueBakery on Instagram. The store has over a hundred thousand followers, years' worth of mouthwatering photos of his blue treats, dozens of pics of tourists flocking to his store from all over the country, and cheery, all-caps captions with way too many exclamation points, matching his personality. Now I get why Beau was surprised in Day 310 to learn that I'd never heard of this place.

I notice that the bakery's most recent pic is unlike the rest, though.

It's a school photo of a young boy in a blue polo shirt, uploaded two hours ago. At first, I assume it's a throwback of Otto from his childhood—the kid's gingery complexion and light eyes look like a miniature version of the baker—but the caption corrects my thinking.

Today, you would have turned 17, it reads, followed by a heart emoji (which is, of course, blue). *Most days, I don't feel like smiling, but I do to make you proud. I hope, somewhere, you're smiling down on me too, Ben. Love you forever.*

My heart sinks as I put two and two together.

No wonder Beau and Otto had a moment in Day 310. Otto lost his son, whose birthday was today. Ben would have been just a few months younger than me if he were still alive.

I tap back to read the bakery's profile bio, wondering, and sure enough:

The tastiest blue treats in CHI! Ben's Everything Blue Bakery began in 2015 in honor of my late son and his favorite color.

I tap back, like the old photo of Ben, and notice that hundreds of commenters have responded with rows upon rows of solid blue hearts. I add my own heart-laden comment, too, and swallow hard before scrolling back through many months of posts for any evidence of Beau in the bakery.

I don't spot a single helpful thing.

I swing my legs out of bed, press my elbows into my knees, and stare at my bedroom carpet.

Where do I go from here?

I snag my phone and start listening to a playlist by The Wrinkles, hoping it will transport me back to yesterday—which is way more difficult than it sounds, considering yesterday feels like 312 days ago to me. They say music does the best job connecting you to your memories; maybe a song will spark a recollection related to Beau. One song could be the first domino to fall, making this all make sense.

I skip through a few songs that aren't my favorites before stopping on one called "Avery," which is a throwback from The Wrinkles' first album.

Why do I feel like I just heard this one?

I know I haven't played it in a really long time, but it's incredibly fresh in my head, the lyrics are rolling off my tongue seamlessly—

Emery! At Splendid Cinemas.

I jump out of bed.

He was listening to "Avery" on his earbuds during his shift in Day 310. If he's a Wrinkles fan, could he have been at the concert, too?

Rejuvenated by this glimmer of hope, I hop into the shower, put on fresh clothes, and pay way too much to rideshare into the city.

Splendid Cinemas has just opened for the day when I walk inside.

Emery, as to be expected by now, jolts at the sight of a customer but at least doesn't think I'm about to rob him. He pulls his earbuds out and sets aside the papers in his hands. "Welcome to Splendid Cinemas."

"Thanks," I say, approaching the counter. "I have an odd question for you—"

"We don't allow birds in the theater, sir," he says at once, surprisingly firm. "I'm sorry, but rules are rules."

I check my shoulder to make sure a pet parrot hadn't magically appeared there without my knowledge. "What? No, it's not . . . do people try to bring birds in?"

He nods. "I've only worked here a few days, and it's come up *multiple* times."

I stare in disbelief. "Okay, well, my question isn't bird related. I'm wondering if you like the band The Wrinkles."

His expression basically transforms into the mind-blown emoji. "They're my favorite!"

My heart thuds. "You were at their concert last night, weren't you?"

His smile collapses into a frown. "I had tickets to go with my best friend, but my little sister got sick at the last minute. I had to babysit."

I bury my face into my arms on the counter, hopes dashed.

"What's wrong?" he asks.

I contemplate how much to spill. "It's a long story," I say into my bicep.

"You mixed me up with someone else, huh?" he asks. His tone suggests it happens just as often as guests inquire about the cinema's bird policy.

I glance up at him—his big jaw, rosy cheeks, and soft skin. He *does* have that Generic Handsome White Guy look that I'm sure feels familiar to a lot of theater guests. "Yeah," I say, standing upright again. "That must have been it."

"I'm Emery," he says, holding out a hand to shake.

I comply. "Hi, Emery. I'm Clark."

"One ticket for the 1991 *Addams Family*, I take it? It starts in about"—he glances at his computer—"*oof*, twenty minutes ago. Sorry."

"It's okay, I better get going." I begin to back away. "But thank you for—"

"Hold on." He laughs. "So you don't want to see a movie?"

I shake my head.

"You walked in off the street because I looked familiar?"

I shrug. "I warned you it was an odd question."

He laughs harder. "That's a first."

I spot the papers Emery was once more studying, and my curiosity kicks in. "Can I ask what those are?" I nod at them. "Every time I've been in here, you're reading them."

"That's impossible," he says, grinning, "because I only brought these papers in this morning and we just opened. Maybe you have me confused again?"

Three-hundred-and-twelve todays in, and I *still* sometimes forget that this is everyone else's first September 19. "I just mean to say," I clarify, "it seems like you're really into whatever you're reading."

Emery leans closer and lowers his voice. "Don't tell my boss if you ever see him, but"—he holds up the papers, revealing the text of a script—"it's lines for an audition I have tomorrow. And I am seriously struggling to get these words to stick."

"You're an actor?"

"No. Well—" he catches himself. "I'm trying to get better, but I have a lot to learn." He sighs, the question an obvious source of frustration. "I'm *not* an actor who is getting paid to act, is one way to put it. But technically, I act. Sometimes. I guess."

A little laugh escapes through my lips. "You remind me of myself."

His face lights up. "You're an actor?"

"No, but I'm a baker and feel awkward referring to myself as one," I say. "I love being in the kitchen, but I'm on a learning curve, too. A steep one."

"Yeah?"

"Definitely. My main problem is multitasking. If a sheet cake needs to come out at fifteen minutes, but my mind is focused on getting the frosting's consistency right, there's a hundred percent chance that cake will stay in there too long."

"I'm sure you've baked some delicious things."

"I have, but I've baked plenty of disastrous things, too." I remember Beau's words of encouragement to me at the Aragon. "I'm still, by definition, a baker, though. Just like you're an actor."

Emery glows pinker than usual. "Thanks. I needed to hear that." He glances around the lobby—as if anyone else would be around—and lowers his voice. "Can I tell you something?"

I nod.

"This will be my first audition," he says.

"Ever?"

"*Ever.*" He inhales deeply. "I've done little gigs and short films for friends without having to audition. But this film?" He closes his eyes and shakes his head, terrified of the thought. "There's going to be craft services on set and everything."

"You seem nervous."

"Very."

Relatable.

"To be honest, I don't think I'll end up going tomorrow," he says, defeated. "It's going to be a disaster."

My leads on Beau have all fallen short, and with Mom under the impression that I'm home sick, I won't have anyone breathing down my neck if I stay out a bit longer. Plus, do I really want to go back to that apartment and stare at the wall all day? Go back to the same boring routine and accept that I'll never see Beau again?

No. Not now that I know what September 19 *could* be.

"Do you want help memorizing your lines?" I ask.

Emery assumes I'm joking until he realizes from my expression that I'm not. "For real?"

"Yeah."

"You really want to?"

"I've got time." I've got nothing *but* time.

"Well . . . yeah. I would love that." He beams as if it's the offer of a lifetime, and hands the lines over. "I think that I'll catch on much faster when I'm working with someone else."

"So I'm reading the lines for Lisa?" I ask, skimming the page. "Who is apparently learning how to do a downward-facing-dog pose?"

"Yep. And I'm the yoga instructor." He pauses, then exhales. "Let's do this."

This, I learn as we get started, is Emery showing me in real time how unprepared he is for this audition. He mumbles, stammers, and skips an entire paragraph of lines during our first run-through.

"You okay?" I ask.

Emery wipes his brow, frustrated with himself. "Yes."

"You sure?"

He breathes, staring at the countertop. "I think so."

"Hey." I draw his attention. "You, Emery, are an actor. An *actor's* actor," I say dramatically.

He snorts.

"Let's start from the top," I say.

So we do.

We go again. And again. And again.

And each time, it's . . . equally terrible. He actually may be getting worse, I think? I can tell he's in his own head, overthinking every syllable that leaves through his lips, and hardly able to remember what words come next without staring into space to retrieve the line.

After an hour of torture and enough flop sweat to fill a bucket, Emery implodes. He sighs heavily, throws an elbow onto the counter between us, and lays his chin in the palm of his hand. "There's no way I can do this tomorrow."

I cringe at him hesitantly. "Really? You don't want to at least try?"

"No way," he says, shaking his head adamantly. "I've heard of this casting guy. The dude is vicious. And if I bomb as hard as I know I will, I'm going to be laughed out of the room."

It's tough to see Emery, one of the most happy-go-lucky humans I've ever encountered, appear so defeated. I want to encourage him to follow through with it, anyway, but it seems like his mind is made up. And honestly? He's not wrong.

He probably *would* get laughed out of the room.

"How about this," I say. "You let this one go"—I push the papers off the counter and into a nearby trash can—"and just focus on improving for a while. I'll help you."

He perks up.

"I'm free anyway," I say, which isn't exactly a lie. "I can drop in and run lines with you this time every day."

His expression shifts from despair to hopeful. "You'd do that for me?"

"Of course." I fist bump his shoulder. "You have a ton of

potential, I can tell. You may just need someone to help you get there."

He sighs in relief. "I would *love* that. You're sure, though?"

I nod.

"You swear?"

I laugh. "Yes."

The bells on the door ring as a few guests wander into the lobby.

"That's my cue," I say, turning away. "I'll be back tomorrow—"

"Clark?"

I look back.

"Feel free to say no—I know this is out of left field, but—would you want to join an acting class with me?" He cringes, preparing for my response.

I almost let a laugh escape at the thought of it. "Me? In an acting class?"

"Classes are expensive," he explains, "but they're half off if you bring a friend, and it seems like you're really good at running lines. Have you ever thought about being an actor?"

That, I think, may be the funniest thing I've heard in the time loop.

I could say yes, of course, knowing that the chances of me having to follow through on a promise I made to a movie theater employee is slim to none (even if I *am* ever able to get to September 20). But before I can decide, Emery reads my expression and answers for me.

"Never mind," he says, shaking his head with a laugh. "That was such a weird thing to ask someone I met five seconds ago!"

"No, it wasn't—"

"It's okay," Emery says. "You've already done so much for me.

Really, it's fine, Clark." He smiles. "I have to help these guys"—he nods toward the customers beyond where I'm standing—"but I'll see you tomorrow, same time, same place?"

I nod, feeling a bit guilty for not saying yes, but happy I was still able to brighten his day. "Sounds like a plan."

I leave the cinemas with a grin, pop in my earbuds to listen once more to The Wrinkles, and head down the sidewalk with no destination in mind. I begin dripping with sweat at once, but, oddly enough, I don't mind the heat in this today.

As my shoes hit the pavement and I crank up the volume, I'm reminded of a craving that's been dormant for so long, I assumed it was gone for good. I'm actually yearning for the possibilities that September 20 could bring, and how important I could be to the people living in it.

I could be the friend who helps Emery with his lines. I could be Dee's confidante and learn her secret, if only I hadn't fumbled our conversation at the diner. I could be there for Blair on her first birthday since the divorce (even if she doesn't think she needs me), and I could happily run errands with Beau every afternoon—if only he'd want me along for the ride.

I could really use some friends in my tomorrow.

And I'm realizing maybe they could use me in theirs, too.

CHAPTER 13

I REALLY WANT TO VISIT DEE AGAIN AND TRY TO LEARN her secret. I'm curious to know what kind of earth-shattering embarrassment could have left her in such a frazzled state, of course, and I think she'd feel much better letting it out anyway, even if it's to a complete stranger. Plus, it sounds like her secret could involve The Wrinkles show, Beau, maybe even his supposed soul mate (if his ex was at the concert, too), and how we got stuck in this mess. Stopping by Splendid Cinemas to help a struggling Emery with his lines sounds equally tempting, as I imagine the poor guy obsessing over an audition he's bound to botch. I want to be there for him, too.

But my focus really should still be on finding Beau, I remind myself, because he still seems like the most promising person to help me (*and* himself) get to tomorrow, even if I'm unsure about all this soul-mate stuff. And if I can't escape today, what good will it do helping Emery with his lines indefinitely, or trying to sniff out a secret of Dee's that may not have anything to do with me, after all?

I'm willing to bet that, sooner or later, Beau will want another blue velvet brownie. And I'm determined to be at Ben's when the craving hits.

I use the food poisoning excuse on Mom again in Day 313 and head to the bakery with her laptop in hand, considering mine, with its cracked screen, is basically useless. I have nothing that needs to get done on it—completing homework assignments is as pointless as you'd imagine now—but I should at least appear to be busy. (No one likes a loiterer in a busy café with limited seating and even more limited electric outlets.)

The bakery is especially hectic in the morning, I learn. Overzealous tourists squeeze their way through the blue door in droves, anxious to beat the line before their visits to The Bean or the Field Museum. Add to the mix ravenous morning commuters in desperate need of caffeine and carbs, and Ben's bakery turns into a war zone. I order a blue velvet brownie from a cheery but perspiring red-cheeked Otto and snag a table in the corner to be on the lookout for Beau.

That's when the anxious thoughts kick in.

What exactly would I say to him if he walks in?

His mind was made up when he said goodbye to me in Day 311 and blasted out of the school parking lot. Will I come across as a stalker, sitting here waiting for him? Could that push him even further away?

I inhale deeply and sit up straight, reminding myself that I can't let Beau's opinion of me hinder my desire to escape today—although that's much easier said than done. If he knows more than I do about how we both got in here and why we can't get out, I deserve to know.

I think through some of the specific questions I'd like to get answers to.

Like, did anything unusual happen while he was at The Wrinkles concert that could've led to us getting stuck? Why won't he tell me more about the ex-boyfriend he needs to win back, the boy he's afraid I'd be distracting him from?

And why would Beau have even shown up in Mr. Zebb's last period anyway, if he's not a new student at Rosedore? I chew on a piece of brownie, thinking aloud: "Could his ex be a student at my school?" I've got questions for Beau, and I'm willing to wait at Ben's until I'm blue in the face to get them, and not just from eating frosting.

Which is pretty much what I do.

This isn't going to be a one-and-done operation, I have to remind myself, as hour after hour ticks by with no sign of Beau. Day 313 is just the first of what will probably be many todays that I'll need to spend at Ben's, craning my neck to see each and every customer who walks in the door.

When I finally leave as Otto begins to close down the store, I tell myself hopefully Day 314 will be the today.

I learn as Day 314 draws to a close, however, that it is not.

On the morning of Day 315, I start getting restless. A particularly obnoxious customer who complains in each today that his peanut-butter cookie isn't blue enough sends me over the edge. As I listen to him demand that a worker disclose what secret ingredient makes their cookies blue—has he never heard of food coloring?—I'm reminded of Dee's secret and its potential relevancy to the time loop.

Even though I told myself I'd stay at Ben's from open to close, fearful Beau will show up for a blue velvet brownie the one today I decide to skip out before closing time, I decide learning more from Dee is worth the risk and head Uptown.

The Red Line train stalls for nearly a half hour, though, and I show up at the Aragon way later than expected. Dee's already left work so I dart to the diner, where I see the same elderly couple eating pancakes and the family of seven who were dining in last time.

"Just you today, hon?" Sandy asks, approaching me at the entrance.

"Yeah, but I don't plan on staying," I say. "Have you seen Dee around? From the Aragon? I know she comes in sometimes after her shifts."

Sandy's welcoming expression fades, replaced with worry. "She was just in, getting some food to go. Is she okay?"

I turn around and look out the front windows, hoping to spot her.

"Don't bother; she's already gone," Sandy says. "A friend picked her up."

I turn back. "Did she seem upset?"

"She'd been crying, I could tell," Sandy says. "I asked her what's wrong, but she didn't budge. What happened?"

"I think she'll be fine," I say, hoping that I'm right. "Just a rough day."

"That girl." Sandy shakes her head and stares out the window in thought. "She's not the quickest to speak up when she should."

"You think?"

"Not at all," she says. "Dee always tries to be a ray of light, but I don't think she realizes those of us who know her well can still see the gray clouds hiding underneath."

I nod, remembering Dee's fake cheery voice when her friend called the last time we were in the diner—her attempt to hide the heartache of whatever drew her tears, I'm sure.

Sandy's eyes find mine again. "How do you know her?"

I start to back up toward the exit. "We're . . . friends from school. I've got to get going. Thank you, Sandy."

I'm out on the sidewalk before she can ask any more follow-up questions.

Not the quickest to speak up when she should. The gray clouds hiding underneath.

I guess it makes sense, then, that Dee would have a secret. I just wish I'd been better at convincing her to share it with me.

Since I've missed Dee, I make my way to Splendid Cinemas next to keep my promise to Emery, even though it's a few todays late. There's still enough time for me to run some lines with him, should he seem up for it again. So, after I reintroduce myself at the concession stand, I make a seemingly off-the-cuff remark that I think he has a real "movie star" look.

"Wow," he says, grinning from ear to ear as his face flushes into the color of a ripe tomato. "You just made my week."

The conversation flows naturally into the papers in front of him, and within a few minutes, he's back to being a yoga instructor teaching me—er, *Lisa*—how to do a downward-facing-dog pose. Fortunately, I've become a better scene partner, having remembered my lines from last time. Unfortunately, Emery is still a disaster.

I offer a few words of encouragement and then dip into the theater one in time to watch *When Harry Met Sally*. The film's starting to grow on me the second time around. Or it just reminds me of Beau. Maybe it's both? I can't tell.

I wasn't so sure about the idea of true love *before* September 19, and spending 309 todays stuck in a time loop finished the job, pretty much squashing any lingering hope that a person could be out there for me. Then Beau came along.

When you experience firsthand how many directions a single day can go in based on even the smallest, most inconsequential deviation, it illustrates how absurd it is to think there's just one *you* for every *me*. But meeting Beau turned that logic upside down. Of the thousands of choices I've made within my hundreds of todays, I know, without question, that deciding to run errands with him was the one I was meant to make.

So, after spending some much-needed time away from the bakery, I know I have to return on Day 316 so that I'll be there the next time he surrenders to a blue velvet brownie craving. At least I'm familiar with the same faces walking in at the same times, so I'm more confident that I can multitask now without letting Beau slip in and out without my noticing.

I pull out Mom's laptop.

"Okay, Clark," I sigh to myself, watching the cursor blink at me from the search field. "Here we go again."

I start mining the internet for the time-loop theory Beau believes in. I'm hopeful it'll be a quick search, now that I'm looking for a specific idea—one that involves soul mates and at least two people getting stuck together.

My hopes are dashed pretty quickly, though, because even with a more narrowed search, I discover dozens of theories in the first ten minutes of clicking around that sound vaguely similar to Beau's. Which could be the one he believes to be true? And what about it stands out as more believable than the others?

Overwhelmed by the feat of hacking the space-time continuum all day, I decide to go easy on myself in Day 317. I spend another Beau-less morning and afternoon at the bakery and then head to the lake to take a dip at our spot as the sun drops below the skyline. This time, I keep my shorts on. When I'm in the water, I can feel Beau pinching at my ankles playfully, like he did in Day 310. I wish it weren't just my imagination.

By Day 318, I may not have seen Beau again, but I've learned a lot about Ben's menu, after having tried out a different item in each today since Day 311. The blue velvet brownies are still my favorite, but the cinnamon rolls I sampled in Day 316—lightly sweetened with the perfect punch of spice—are a close runner-up, and the cheddar scone I inhaled in Day 315 lands in a respectable third (Otto got its density *just* right). With his brilliance in the kitchen and his charisma at the counter, I don't understand how Otto hasn't starred in his own baking show by now. He'd be a hit.

Pastry skills aside, I've learned a surprising amount about Otto the person while loitering around his store most of the day, too. Like the way he knows damn near every guest's name. And I don't just mean the regulars; I'm talking about Tori, a nurse from Minneapolis who notes that her last stop at Ben's was over a year ago; and Reggie, a teacher from Rogers Park, who's genuinely baffled when Otto remembers not only what grade he teaches (fifth) but also his partner's *and* pet rat's names (Fred and Bob, respectively).

I start picking up on Otto's subtleties, too. Like, how he walks with a slight limp that's probably not even noticeable to most customers but still painful enough to force a grimace on his face when he bends over too far cleaning tables, how he tends to recycle the same ten or so topics with the customers who like to chat (the unbearably muggy weather is his favorite go-to in my todays), how he happily winks at every dog who enters with their human, and, if given permission, gives them a free lick of blue whipped cream off a plastic blue spoon.

But I also see something else, because each morning, I reread Otto's Instagram post about Ben, too.

Most days, I don't feel like smiling, he writes, *but I do to make you proud*. And he *does* smile a lot. One time, when I mentioned to Ms.

Hazel that my parents seemed happy but apparently were miserable together, she told me that "sometimes the saddest people wear the biggest smiles." I get a feeling that's Otto.

But even if I wanted to ask Otto about it, another thing that begins standing out to me is how incredibly busy Ben's tends to *stay*. There's not just a morning rush, but an all-day parade of insatiable guests champing at the bit to raid the display case. For the most part, Otto and his small team keep the line flowing at a reasonable pace, but there's a nearly unwatchable period between lunch and the post-work rush where they're left floundering, one worker short.

I've come to dread this awkward train wreck, cringing as I watch the line to order grow awkwardly long. Customers get antsy—and a few downright irritated—as their plans for a quick afternoon pick-me-up turn into a frustrating ordeal. And to make matters worse, under pressure, a bubbly but stressed Otto and his three overwhelmed workers in the kitchen begin botching orders.

By Day 325, I can't handle it anymore.

I have to jump in.

"Hi," I say, approaching the side of the display case as Otto finishes a transaction. "I have an idea."

"Hello, Clark," he says, ripping off his plastic gloves to put on fresh ones. Somehow, even amid the chaos, he recalls my name from this morning without missing a beat. "I would love to hear your idea, but can it wait a few minutes? We're a little backed up here."

"My idea would help with that."

"Oh?"

"Want me to collect orders from customers waiting in line and pass them up to you?" I ask. "I think it could speed things up a bit."

Otto laughs. "Awfully kind of you to offer, Clark"—he hands

another customer a bag to go—"here's the *correct* cookie, Dotty, and sorry about the mistake!" He turns back to me, wiping his brow with his forearm. "But you're a first timer and that might overcomplicate it, pal."

"I promise that it won't," I say, confident I can't possibly make the situation worse. "If I'm wrong, I'll stop and get out of your way."

"I won't be able to pay you legally in anything except free samples."

"That's all right."

He considers my proposal with a heavy sigh. "Hell, I guess it can't hurt."

"Really?" I ask, surprised he's willing to give it a shot (although, from what I've learned about Otto watching him in action since Day 313, maybe I shouldn't be).

Otto holds up a pen and blue sticky notes near the register. "Want to use these for the orders?"

"Sure."

I take the pen and sticky notes, try to calm my nerves, and get started.

As I go, I make sure to apologize for the long wait, double-check that I'm hearing each customer correctly, and keep my handwriting big and clear for Otto to read. It makes the most sense to separate orders by sticky notes, I learn quickly, and then place each one behind the display case in corresponding sequence. Most customers are happier at once, just from finally getting acknowledged, and Otto is able to work faster and more efficiently behind the counter by seeing upcoming orders ahead of time.

"Your handwriting is beautiful, Clark," he says, passing me with a tray of the bluest blueberry buckle I've ever seen. "Keep it up."

It's clear that my strategy is working. The line is shortening fast, there hasn't been a single error with an order since I started, and the irritated sighs I noticed from impatient customers in the past several todays are being replaced with friendly hellos instead.

And actually, it's more fun than I imagined it would be, too.

A half hour later, the line is gone—something that hasn't happened since I began coming. I give myself a mental high five, realizing that I wouldn't have done something like this before Day 310. Ms. Hazel said that succumbing to an increasingly small comfort zone can lead to more discomfort, but I imagine she'd agree that the reverse of that is true, too. I didn't so much break *out* of my comfort zone today as much as relish in its recent expanse.

"Wow," Otto sighs, taking a seat in his rickety folding chair behind the register for the first time all day. "Incredible job, Clark."

"Yeah?"

"Yes. When Cassandra leaves at one, we're usually playing catch-up until five," he explains, shaking his head. "This is the first Monday in *many* Mondays that that hasn't happened."

"I enjoyed it," I say, circling the display case to be on the customer side once again, now that my help is no longer needed. "I love baking, so I guess I shouldn't be surprised to learn that I'd like working in a bakery."

Otto, finishing a cup of water, perks up. "What do you bake?"

"I'm a bit all over the place," I say. "My sister's birthday is tomorrow and she hates cake, so I've been playing around with different recipes to make for her and her friends instead. For example"—I spot the blue velvet brownies and point—"Blair would love those."

I've been meaning to try to pull off my own version in Mom's kitchen but haven't had a chance, as finding Beau has been my number one priority. When I return home from being in the city all day after saying I had food poisoning, Mom isn't usually in the mood to just let me bake.

"I'm not surprised to hear that," Otto says, nodding. "They're one of our top sellers. Hey"—he glances around, making sure no customer's been left waiting—"c'mon back." Otto stands and waves at me to follow him into the kitchen.

"Am I allowed?"

He grins. "I'm the one in charge, pal."

The kitchen is small, filled with stainless steel, and dusted with remnants from dozens of recipes. Tubs of ingredients, sheets, and pans are scattered across most of the counter spaces and, as expected, there's no shortage of blue food coloring on hand.

Otto bends beneath one of his workstations and starts rummaging around a shelf. "How'd you hear about my bakery, by the way?" he asks. "I always like to ask brand-new customers."

It's funny to hear him calling me brand-new when I'm starting to think of myself as a regular. "My friend Beau told me about it," I say. "I think you know him?"

Otto pauses and looks up at me from beneath the workstation, eyebrows arched. "You're friends with Beau?"

"Yes."

"I miss him," he says. "How'd you two meet?"

I think on the fly. "We both went to the same concert," I answer, which is technically true. "I like Beau." A lot.

He hesitates for a moment before asking: "Would you mind doing me a favor?"

I nod.

"Will you tell him that I'm sorry?" Otto says.

Sorry?

"Sure," I say, then wait a beat. I don't want to spoil the special access I've gained to his kitchen, but if it could help me understand how to reach Beau . . . "Can I ask what you're sorry for?"

Otto turns his attention back to the space underneath the workstation, which is overflowing with utensils, binders, and an assortment of spices. "You know, pal, it's a long story. I'll let Beau fill you in."

Sensing his hesitation, I back off.

"Of course," I say. "No worries."

"Here it is."

He hands me a yellow, slightly ripped notecard.

"Seriously?" I say as I read BEN'S BLUE VELVET BROWNIES across the top.

"You were a lifesaver today," Otto says, large hand landing on my shoulder. My knees buckle a bit. "I couldn't have survived the afternoon without you."

You've survived it plenty of times before, I want to say, *but it wasn't pretty.* "You're absolutely sure?" I ask.

"Of course!" He points at his temple. "I've got the recipe up here, anyhow."

I'm not sure how to express how grateful I am, so I stick with a simple "thank you."

"You're very welcome." He removes his hand, and my shoulder rebounds to its normal height. "I hope Blair enjoys them." I glance down at the recipe. It seems surprisingly simple for how delicious those brownies are, but—after three hundred-plus todays of test runs in Mom's kitchen—I've realized that seems to be the case with the best-tasting bakes.

"You must be out of school, then, huh?" Otto asks, wiping his hands off on his apron. Upon seeing my confused face, he follows up with: "Unless schools were off this Monday for some reason?"

"Oh." I nod. "Yeah, something like that."

"Well, if you're looking for part-time work, it'd be great to have your help in the afternoons."

My heart flutters. "Really?"

"Yeah."

"Can I start . . . tomorrow?"

In the same way that I can't see Emery's progress with his lines or am forced to start at square one in my quest to learn Dee's embarrassing secret, I know that I won't be waking up to a shift at Ben's bakery anytime soon. Still, even just the thought fills me with hope.

"Sounds like a plan," Otto says. "Come on in, fill out some paperwork, and we'll get an apron on ya, stat." He presents his hand to shake. "Welcome to Team Blue."

For a moment, I contemplate bringing up Ben's birthday. I'm sure Otto would appreciate my acknowledging it. Right? Or would it end our day together on a sad, low note?

I get nervous and decide against going there. "Thanks, Otto," I say, smiling, my hand enveloped in his. "I'll see you tomorrow."

Despite not seeing Beau yet again, I leave the bakery on cloud nine, having no business being this thrilled about a prospective job that will likely never come.

CHAPTER 14

T HE KITCHEN AND DINING ROOM ARE SPICK-AND-
span, not a stray pepperoni in sight, confirming how incredibly late I am for dinner.

"Where the heck have you been?" Mom asks as I walk in. I
watch in real time as the worry on her face shifts to relief, then
anger. "I was about five minutes away from filing a missing person's
report."

"They wouldn't have cared, Mom," Blair says from the couch,
scrolling through her phone. "Clark would've had to be gone for
at least a few more hours for the cops to consider him missing.
Derek Dopamine did a whole video on how messed up our missing-
persons laws are, and—"

"Sweetie, please don't cite Derek Dopamine as an official
source of information—on *anything*," Mom says to her, then turns to
me. With a softer voice, she says, "You need to get better at returning my calls, okay? Where were you?"

I throw my bag onto the sofa and glide into the kitchen, antsy
to get started on Ben's blue velvet brownies. "With a friend," I say,
setting the recipe card on the counter and reading through the
ingredient list again. Aside from the blue food coloring, I'm almost
positive we have everything I need. But I should be certain before
preheating the oven. "Don't worry," I say to Mom, one step ahead
of her, "I know you just cleaned up. I'll take care of my mess."

"You were with a friend?" Blair questions me curiously, moving from the sofa to the dining room. "But you don't have any friends."

I let the insult roll off my back because I'm in too good a mood from my day at the bakery to let Blair ruin it.

"Blair," Mom scolds, taking a seat next to her. "Don't."

"Don't what?"

"Be a brat to your brother."

"It was a *joke.*"

"I'm glad you're over the food poisoning that kept you from going to school and seeing Ms. Hazel today," Mom says, just enough suspicion in her tone to convey she's onto me. "I wonder what you could have *eaten* at the concert that made you sick."

"I'm not sure," I say, determined not to sound guilty as I dart from cabinet to cabinet.

"Well, there's leftover pizza, but that might be hard on your stomach," Mom says. "I think we have some of that noodle soup that you like in the pantry, if that sounds more appetizing."

"Thanks," I say, laser focused on the recipe. I make a mental note that faking food poisoning is one simple way to get out of eating pizza in every today.

Blair looks up from her phone. "What are you making, anyway?"

I determine we have just enough cream cheese for the frosting, then snag the butter out of the fridge. "Blue velvet brownies."

"*Blue* velvet brownies?" Mom balks. "What in the world? What's in them? And how blue are we talking?"

Blair perks up. "Are they just like red velvet, but blue?"

"Basically, yes," I say, smiling wide as I pull a bag of powdered sugar down from the top shelf, an extra spring in my step (even with

Mom's incessant questions), "and they'll probably be the best thing I've ever made."

"My friends are going to *freak*," Blair says, grinning. "Especially Josie. She loves brownies."

"Tell me about this friend of yours," Mom says. "Are they someone I know from school?"

"His name is Otto and he gave me this recipe," I explain, laying out all the ingredients in front of me. "He owns Ben's Everything Blue Bakery."

"Really?" Mom pauses. "I've heard that place is neat, but I've never been." She turns to Blair. "The name is literal. *Everything* there is blue."

Blair's eyes widen.

"Wait." Mom's eyes shift in my direction. "You went into the city?"

"Yes."

"Clark." Her tone gets serious again. "You can't do that without telling me. And I'm not sure how comfortable I am with you being *friends* with an adult who's old enough to own his own business."

"It's not like that, Mom," I say. "Otto's cool. But I know, you're right. I'll ask before I go next time."

"What prompted all of this?" she asks, brushing some straggler crumbs off the dining room table.

I rummage through our pots and pans. "Can we talk about this later? Sorry, it's just, I need to make sure I know what ingredients we have before going to the store for the food coloring. Oh"—I turn to her, unable to contain the smile on my face—"can I use your car?"

There's a long pause from Mom, who I'm pretty sure doesn't know what to do with this exhilarated version of her son jumping around her kitchen. "I guess so. Don't you want some soup first?"

"Can I eat later, too? I want to get to the ingredients quick—"

"What's gotten into you today?" Mom asks.

She and Blair are looking at me, both suspicion and intrigue etched across their faces.

"What?" I say, turning red.

"She means it as a good thing," Blair giggles, putting her phone down. "You're acting all weird and happy. It's not like you."

Mom gives her a look. "It's not *weird*, it's nice." She turns back to me. "To be clear, you *do* need to ask before going into the city next time, and I'll need to know more about this Otto fellow. But it is nice to see you with a pep in your step."

I nod and shrug, feeling my cheeks returning to a normal hue. "I guess I had a good day."

"Hey, how about I help you in there once you're back from the store?" Mom asks.

Even in a day full of my own deviations—faking sick, skipping school, and spending the afternoon at a bakery downtown—some things will never *not* happen in the time loop. Mom asking if she can bake with me every evening is one of those things.

Between the great mood I've been in since the bakery and the fact that I still feel a bit guilty after snapping at her in Day 311, I can almost see myself accepting her help in today's today.

Almost.

I rock back and forth on my toes. "Can we plan on another day?" I say softly, not wanting it to sting this time.

But it still does, I can tell. She nods. "Okay."

"It's just, I'm really excited about this recipe, and I'll need to focus if I'm going to nail these for Blair," I say.

"Of course," she says, forcing a smile. "Do your thing. My car keys are on the coffee table."

I scoop them up on my way to the front door. "Anyone need anything from the store?"

"Nope," Blair says.

"Just *text me* if you go anywhere else," Mom demands. "Okay?"

"Okay." I put on my shoes and slip outside.

Before I'm too far down the sidewalk, I hear our front door creak open and turn back, expecting it to be Mom remembering a last-minute grocery request.

But it's Blair.

"Hey," she says quietly, her face peeking out through the crack.

She wants ice cream to serve with the brownies, I bet. "I'll see if they have mint chocolate chip—"

"No, I just wanted to tell you," she begins, strangely bashful, "sorry again for saying that you don't have any friends. I didn't mean it."

I nod, a bit surprised.

"I'm happy you're making something for my party," she follows up. "You're a great big brother and I love you."

It's rare to get a moment of sincerity out of Blair, and even rarer to hear a genuine apology. I'm not sure it's ever happened before. Could my good mood in the kitchen have inspired her to reach out like this?

I make another mental note (this one, unrelated to pizza fatigue): my attitude at home makes an impact on Blair.

I open my mouth to respond to her, but she shuts the door before I can.

CHAPTER 15

I WAKE UP TO MY WHITE WOODEN NIGHTSTAND WITH a smile on my face in Day 326.

It's a bummer that Otto won't know who I am. I won't be able to report back on how the bake went (my brownies were a touch drier and a smidge flatter than Otto's, but still one of the tastiest things I've ever pulled out of an oven). I'll have to reintroduce myself, pitch my idea to speed up the line again, and hope today goes as smoothly as Day 325. Still, the bakery is feeling more and more like home, even if I'm technically a stranger in the eyes of Otto and his customers alike. It's nice feeling as though I have somewhere to be. A day I can at least pretend to share with others.

I mysteriously get food poisoning once again and take off for Ben's, thinking through ways I can make the sticky-note process even faster. But when I arrive at the bakery and step outside the rideshare I took into the city, customer orders are immediately placed on my back burner.

Beau.

My throat runs dry and my insides bottle up like a coil that's about to spring.

He's walking toward Ben's from about a block away, wearing the same bright-green tank top he had on in the today we met. His long legs push and pull him down the sidewalk as if he owns this town, his eyes as striking as the sunbeams bouncing off the city's skyline above.

My shock immediately turns to euphoria—and then straight into panic.

Breathe, Clark, I tell myself.

I've had plenty of todays to think this moment through. I got this.

Beau stops, twenty feet away, eyes frozen on mine. My lips curl up into a weak smile as sweat begins to pour down my face. I raise my hand and wave hesitantly, hoping this will go better than I think it will.

"Hey," I yell over the hustle and bustle all around us. "How've you been?"

For a moment I can't read his expression. Is he relieved to see me, or am I ruining his today?

Then he turns and disappears around the corner.

So I guess I have my answer.

I hesitate, suck my teeth, and try to think fast, as my gut churns up into my throat.

Normally, I believe in boundaries. I respect others' wishes— even if those wishes inconvenience me. (And not getting to relive the best kiss of my life is a pretty major inconvenience.) But nothing about my situation—*our* situation—is normal. And if there's even the slimmest chance that I can piece together what it'll take for me to escape this time loop, it seems like I'll need help from Beau to do it.

I exhale, close my eyes, and jump in place for a few seconds before sprinting off after him.

When I turn the same corner, I see that he's already more than a full block ahead of me. I pick up the pace.

"Beau!" I yell.

He doesn't turn around.

Thankfully, he gets held up by the orange hand warning him not to cross at a congested intersection. But he ignores the rules and walks anyway, nearly getting splattered to smithereens by a speeding car. I groan, but before I can even contemplate my odds of making it without ending up in an emergency room, I dash across the pavement behind him. A chorus of honking taxis blast their disapproval, but I get to the other side in one piece.

Beau runs into a large group of tourists being guided by a woman with a megaphone, which lets me close the gap between us even more.

"Hey!" I yell again, now that he's only a few paces in front of me. "Can't we just talk?"

"I think it's best if we don't," he says, finally acknowledging my existence.

"Because of your ex?"

"Yes."

"Why can't you tell me his name?"

He refuses to provide an answer.

"Can you stop, *please*, just for a minute?" I beg.

Shockingly, he does, freezing in place. He turns and faces me, a deep sadness in his eyes.

"I don't like not seeing you, Clark," he says, softer than I expected. "It's not fun avoiding you every day."

"Then don't!"

"I have to."

"I know that you think I'm a distraction from your ex, or whatever," I say, "but regardless of *us*—whatever we are—we're still stuck in the same time loop, and I think it's only fair that I get some answers."

"Answers to what?"

"Like, do remember anything weird happening at the concert that could've resulted in us getting stuck?"

He spins away from me and keeps walking.

I hustle after him.

"I already told you," he says, zigzagging between walkers. "You're stuck in here because the universe wants you to be with your soul mate, whoever they are. I recommend that you start looking for him."

"I don't *have* a soul mate, though."

"You have to."

Beau darts up a long flight of rusty stairs leading to a stop on the L train. I continue in his path but get bogged down in the fight upstream against a group of exiting commuters.

Sensing that I may lose him and wanting more answers, I blurt the next question that comes to mind: "Why would Otto want you to know that he's sorry?"

Beau pauses at the top of the stairs and turns back. He opens his mouth to respond before changing his mind and hopping over a turnstile on the train platform.

I'm finally able to break through the crowd, and I follow in his path. I spot Beau disappearing into a train car and hustle to get through the same doors, knowing they could close at any second.

"Okay, listen," I say, jumping in next to him, out of breath. "I want to respect your wishes and leave you alone."

"Okay, good."

"But I'm not going to." I stare at him. "I think we should work together."

He exhales. "I'd rather not."

"Only because you like me? Because I'd *distract* you from your ex? That sounds like a flimsy excuse, when I think we'd both benefit a lot from—"

"Stop!" He snaps. "What we have *isn't real*, Clark. All right?"

Other passengers glance at us curiously.

I step away from him, unsettled. "What do you mean?"

"I understand why it feels like we shared something special that day," he says. "But, knowing what we know now, doesn't it make sense *why* we would feel that way?"

I shake my head.

"You're the only person I know of who's stuck in September nineteenth."

"And you're that person for me, too."

"Exactly!" He throws his hands in the air, exasperated. "Don't you get it? You don't like me in the way that you think you do."

"But I do."

"You're *comforted* by me because we're in the same boat— because I'm the only other person who knows what it's like to live in this hell."

"That's not true."

"We only spent a few hours together, Clark. We know nothing about each other."

"I know that you love impromptu adventures and Ben's brownies and maybe-not-great rom-coms you can get lost in," I say. "I know that you're a good friend, because you went to check in on Dee after she had the most embarrassing night of her life yesterday, and that you can get lost staring up into the stars, just like me, even if those stars are made of paint and drywall. And I know that, even without your dad or your mom around, you still believe in your own happy ending."

He waits a beat, swallows hard, and lowers his voice. "You're relieved that you've found someone else stuck in your day, and you're confusing that feeling with something else. That's all. It's not *real*. Our soul mates are real."

"How do you know?" I say. "Why do you get to decide what's real and what's not?"

An automated voice comes over the speakers: "Doors closing." They begin to slide shut but pause and reopen as a straggler jumps on board.

Beau steps closer and stares, unblinking. "Please," he whispers. "It'll benefit both of us if you forget that I exist."

"You know I can't do that."

"You have to."

Shockingly, he pulls me in for a hug. I can feel his heartbeat pounding against my chest. I don't want him to let go. But I know he will, at any second, leaving me just as frustrated and hungry for answers as I was before.

"Find your soul mate and get out of here with me," he says. "It's the only way."

"But—"

"I'm sorry."

"Doors closing," the automated voice repeats.

Beau jumps through the exit. I turn to follow, but the sliding doors shut in my face. We're staring into each other's eyes through the windowpane as the train rolls away.

CHAPTER 16

THAT MAY HAVE BEEN THE LAST OPPORTUNITY I had to learn more from Beau, and it couldn't have been more of a disaster. He wasn't even slightly more open to having a conversation with me, which I guess shouldn't have been a surprise, knowing how adamantly he said goodbye in the high school parking lot. But still, I'm gutted.

I don't know anything more about the soul-mate theory he believes to be true, if The Wrinkles show could have had anything to do with it, or how we both got stuck. But even worse than that?

Beau supposedly thinks Day 310 was a fluke; that our connection wasn't real; that I've been conflating true feelings for him with simply being *comforted* by his presence in the time loop alongside me. It sounds like a bunch of BS.

But . . . could he have a point?

I mean, we only did spend a matter of hours together. And I definitely *am* comforted by knowing I'm not stuck in today by myself. I admit that, regardless if it was Beau or not, I'd probably want to see the other stuck person quite a bit, as they'd be the only one whose sense of time aligns with my own.

But . . . *no.* He's wrong.

I was drawn to Beau like a magnet *during* Day 310—before I even realized he was stuck in today, too. I know our connection was real and not a fluke. I know that I like Beau—and that I'm not just comforted by him being in here with me.

But my knowing won't change his mind.

I jinxed myself in Day 326, apparently, having allowed myself to feel excited to relive my today. Because Day 327? It's a rough one. I still skip school but I stay curled up on the sofa rewatching my comfort shows (although they hardly work in providing any comfort). By the late afternoon, I resort to scrolling through the "newly added series" section before remembering that I've already watched all of those, too. In a time loop, it's only a matter of time before the new releases become your personal classics.

Day 328 isn't much better, but I do manage to numb my emotions with a full day of baking. By the time Mom and Blair are home, the apartment looks like my own dessert catering business gone wild, as hundreds of mediocre snickerdoodle cookies line sheet pans covering every surface of the apartment.

"Um, are you . . . okay?" Blair asks, staring at me. The fact that she's even ignoring her phone to gawk at the chaos surrounding her underscores just how over-the-top I went. "Thanks, I guess? But this feels like a lot for one birthday party, bro. I'm only expecting—"

"Fifteen," I mumble, disappearing into my room. "Yeah, I know."

I can feel my world contracting again, just like it had been prior to Day 310. And with Beau abandoning me—*again*—my loneliness is worsening, too. But I refuse to keep regressing, now that I've gotten a taste of what my today could be like, now that, deep down, I have a reason to feel a little hope. So I retrace my steps, thinking through what actions I took to feel better connected to my today. What prompted this domino effect in the first place?

Try to make a new friend.

It was following Ms. Hazel's first tip, without a doubt. Should I try following her second, third, and fourth tips, too? Sure, I gave them a shot as I waited for Dee to get out of work, but it wasn't much. I could go back and try harder. Besides, I still haven't spoken with Dee since Day 311 or gotten any closer to learning her secret, so maybe a trip to the Aragon is a smart choice. I could go see Otto and Emery beforehand while she's at work— *Hold on.*

"Maybe *they're* the keys to completing my homework," I mutter to myself.

I sit up in bed, recalling each one of Ms. Hazel's tips to defeat loneliness:

Try to make a new friend.
Help someone who could use it.
Be vulnerable so others can be too.
Do the thing that scares you.

I already completed tip number one (even if the friendship blew up in my face), so that's taken care of. But Otto absolutely qualifies as someone who could use the help during the bakery's afternoon rush. I can try to be vulnerable with Dee so that she'll share her secret with me. And acting classes with Emery? I can't think of much more terrifying than that.

So, in Day 329, I decide that I won't let myself shrivel down into a depressed robot running on autopilot again just because of Beau. While he does whatever *he* thinks is going to end the loop, I'm going to relive our errands, again and again, knocking out Ms. Hazel's tips with my new friends. Even if they don't remember me.

Splendid Cinemas. Ben's Everything Blue Bakery. Aragon Ballroom. My new routine.

It won't be the same as it was on Day 310. But it'll still be better than before that.

I put on a fresh outfit and head to see Emery. As I expect, he's memorizing his lines behind the concession stand and startles when I walk in.

"Welcome," he says as I approach, popping out his earbuds.

"Hey, Emery," I say.

He looks confused.

I point at his name tag.

"Ah." He nods with a smile.

"I've got a random question that I'm hoping you can answer," I say. "And don't worry, it's not about birds."

His face deflates. "Our showing of *Titanic does*, in fact, include the topless drawing scene, so if that offends you, I—"

"No, it's not that," I say, halting a laugh. I prepare the question I already know the answer to in my head. "Do you know who that actor is?" I point at a movie poster for *Guys and Dolls* behind him. "I was in here the other day and couldn't remember. It's been bugging me ever since."

Emery glances backward briefly. "Marlon Brando."

I close my eyes. "Of course. I knew that."

"There's this thing called Google," Emery pokes fun, grin growing, as he holds up his phone, "for the next time you can't remember a famous actor's name."

I purse my lips and nod, pretending to be embarrassed.

"I'm just teasing you." Emery winks.

"I'll see whatever's playing in theater one," I say, trying to seem a little more normal.

"One ticket?"

"Yeah. I need to escape into a dark movie theater all by myself for a bit."

Emery nods. "Completely get it. I have days like yours, too."

If only that were true.

As he punches in my ticket order, I pretend to examine the *Guys and Dolls* poster again. "All the hard work it would take to become an actor, let alone an iconic one like Brando, is so admirable," I mutter, handing Emery cash for the ticket.

He takes it with a chuckle. "Funny you say that, because I am one."

I perk up. "Oh yeah?"

"Yes. Well—" He hesitates, unsure. "Maybe not *technically*. I'm not getting paid to act in anything right now, but I'm trying."

"Are those lines?" I nod down at his papers.

He holds them up. "I have an audition tomorrow. My first one, actually."

"Nervous?"

His expression collapses. "Very. I don't think I'll end up going."

I bite my lip and stare at the counter, pretending to contemplate my next move (maybe I *could* make a decent actor). My eyes shift toward him. "Do you want help running through your lines?"

He smiles, but doesn't respond, like he's unsure if I'm kidding. "Really?"

"Yeah." I shrug. "Why not?"

"Didn't you want to escape into a dark movie theater?"

I glance toward the doors of theater one, remembering being

in there with Beau. My heart thuds a bit harder. "This is a better use of my time." I extend my hand. "I'm Clark."

He shakes it, beaming, before handing over his lines.

Emery is still a complete trainwreck, of course. He can barely remember his lines, pivots back and forth between Southern and Boston accents, weirdly enough, and is just as stressed out over the prospects of bombing as the last time we did this together.

"I can't go to this audition tomorrow," he says, a look of dread draped across his face.

Do the thing that scares you.

I decide to take a different approach this time. "You have to."

"Why? So I can get booed out of the room?"

"No, so that you can get it out of the way."

He looks at me, confused.

"Hear me out," I explain. "Will you get this part? Maybe—"

He laughs. "*Very* likely, no."

"But even if you don't, it's your first audition," I continue. "*Of course* it's not going to be your best and the odds are stacked against you. But you just have to survive it. Rip that Band-Aid off and carry on."

He thinks. "Yeah?"

"Yes. And your next audition will get easier. And the next one, easier than that."

His smile returns, even if it's small. "I guess."

"You can't let fear hold you back from the thing you want," I say.

Emery thanks me for the pep talk and running lines with him. We say our goodbyes and, just as I'd hoped, he calls after me as I head toward the exit.

"This is going to be a weird question, but have you ever thought about acting?" he asks.

"I mean . . . not really," I say. "Why?"

"I want to sign up for these acting classes, but you get a good discount if you bring someone else, too. Would you be . . ." He trails off, nervous to hear my answer, ". . . open to joining with me?"

I pretend to think about it for a moment.

"Never mind," Emery says, shaking his head with a laugh. "You were such a good Lisa that I thought you might be interested, but it was stupid—"

"I'd love to." I smile wide.

He's shocked. "For real?"

"Yeah, why not?" I shrug. "It sounds scary, but I can't not take my own advice, right?"

I admit: the idea of joining an acting class tomorrow is much less terrifying when you know tomorrow will likely never come. But it's the thought that counts, right?

I float toward the door. "I'll come in tomorrow and we can talk about it."

"Sounds good, Clark," Emery says. "Thank you!"

Another tip down.

Two more to go.

Feeling lighter than I have in many todays, I head to Ben's Everything Blue Bakery right as the afternoon rush starts to spin out of control.

"Hi," I say to a sweaty Otto behind the register.

"Hello, there," he breathes, doing only a mediocre job at hiding his stress. "What's your name?"

"Clark," I say. "I—"

Otto is immediately distracted by an agitated woman who requested three maple doughnuts (not two). I attempt to chat with him again after he retrieves her missing item, but he's dashing away to refill napkins before I can get a word in. A coffee spill moments later steals him for another minute, just as the line reaches the door, and the other bakery employees are too busy playing catch-up to help.

"Screw it," I mutter under my breath.

I pop behind the counter and start taking orders using my sticky-note method. Some patrons are confused at first, suspicious of my quick role reversal from customer to employee, but don't seem to care much after realizing it means they'll be getting helped faster.

It takes a frantic Otto a few minutes putting out fires at guest tables to even notice what I'm doing. "Excuse me?" he says, jogging up to me behind the counter.

"Thanks, Marge, I'll see you next week!" I hand a retired teacher a slice of vanilla cream cake before turning to Otto. "I thought I'd jump in to help."

He looks bewildered. "You can't be back here, Clark."

"I know, but I have experience behind the counter and think I can help you out. See?" I gesture toward the much shorter line. "I can be an asset."

Otto rocks back and forth, contemplating. He seems confused as to why a random kid would want to jump in and help with no apparent ulterior motive, but he also sees the clear value in my strategy.

"If we're going to do this," he says, snagging an apron and throwing it around my neck, "we've got to do it right. Go wash your hands!"

I smile and hustle toward the sink.

I work even faster than I had on Day 325 because I can put faces with orders ahead of time. Otto is stunned at how quickly the line evaporates.

"Please tell me you're available to work afternoons," he says, shaking his head with gratitude. "Needless to say, I could use the help."

"I would love to," I say, proud that I impressed one of the best bakers in Chicago. Again. "If I did take the job, would it be okay if I get trained in the kitchen at some point down the road?"

I may not get to tomorrow, but I might as well have a little fun fantasizing about it.

"I'm an amateur baker—emphasis on the amateur," I follow up, "and I'd love to learn from the best."

Otto's gargantuan fist nudges my chest. "Absolutely."

"Yeah?"

"Of course. Would you like a quick tour of the back?"

"Right now?"

"Yes"—he glances around, lowering his voice—"before more hangry customers come barging in."

I smile.

Otto leads me into the kitchen, where he unveils a thick recipe book that looks a century old. Its pages are torn and covered in blue stains from God only knows how many different ingredients.

"I won't go into the details before you're officially on the team, but for now"—he pushes the book in front of me—"why don't you get familiar with our bakes, if you have a few minutes. On your first official day—heck, it could even be tomorrow—I'll train you on the register."

"Tomorrow?" I feel a burst of joy at the prospect. Otto has such a commanding presence that it feels like he could singlehandedly save me from the time loop with a flick of his spatula.

He pauses, puzzled by my reaction. "Does tomorrow not work?"

"Right, sorry, yes, it does." I nod, crashing back down to earth. "I can roll with that."

Otto stares at me with a twinkle in his eye. "Was that a baking pun, Clark?"

I turn red.

A half hour later, I arrive at the Aragon just in time to catch a teary-eyed Dee beelining down the sidewalk toward the diner. Instead of mentioning Beau right away like last time, I decide to keep it simple: "Are you okay?"

She stops and glares, offended that I'd ask. "Do I not *look* okay?"

I tense up, unsure how to steer the conversation forward. "No, you look . . . great?"

She laughs. "That sounded real believable."

"You *do* look great," I say. "I love your jeans. And your smile."

Her forehead crinkles. "What are you, some kind of creep?"

"No, *no*, I'm—"

"Because, although I'm never in the mood to deal with creeps, I'm *especially* not in the mood today."

"You're right, I'm sorry, I don't mean to come across as creepy."

"Good."

"It's just, you looked upset, and I wanted to make sure you're okay. That's it."

She holds my gaze for another moment before dabbing at her eyes. "You're too forward but not entirely off base," she says, her voice much softer. "I had the most disastrous night last night."

"Yeah?"

"And I had to keep it in at work all day, until now."

"Why was your night so terrible?"

"I might die."

"You might *die*?" I try to act surprised.

"Yes. Well," she clarifies, "of embarrassment."

"Oh."

She thinks. "Do you like BLTs? Also, who the hell are you?"

I fib, telling Dee that I'm killing time waiting for my mom and Blair to finish up shopping nearby. We head to the diner and Sandy seats us at the same table, double-checks to make sure Dee is okay, and takes our order.

"So, last night?" I ask Dee.

"What about it?" she asks.

"You're going to die from embarrassment?"

She sighs. "Right."

"Want to talk about it?"

She stares out the window for a moment, expressionless. "It's beyond embarrassing."

Okay, keep going. "How so?"

"Have you ever held on to a secret for years, only for it to go the absolute worst way imaginable when you finally decide to let it out?"

Yes, keep talking. "No, but it sounds rough."

She pauses, hesitant to divulge more, before turning her attention to me. "We don't need to talk about it."

Damn it. "If you need to vent to someone, I don't mind. Are you sure?"

She nods as Sandy returns with our milkshakes. I remind

myself of Ms. Hazel's third tip—*be vulnerable so others can be too*—and take a deep breath. If I can be open about my own life, maybe Dee will feel more comfortable sharing her secret with me.

"I go to therapy," I say.

Dee finishes a sip of her shake. "How come?" She looks as though she knows she crossed a line. "Sorry, that was a nosy question . . ."

"It's okay." I think. "I feel like we tend to hold a lot in, you know? Afraid of what people will think of us. Therapy's a great way to help with that."

"Okay, that sounds like why going to therapy is good, in general," she says, biting down on a fry. "But why do *you* go?"

Huh.

No one's asked so directly before.

It feels like I've been going forever, having gotten stuck in a day where I visit Ms. Hazel every afternoon. But in the normal timeline—the *real* one (if reality even exists anymore)—I've only been in therapy for a matter of months. I try to think back to the pre-loop days. Mom and Dad thought it'd be good for me to talk to someone after news of Sadie's move and the divorce hit like a double whammy.

"Mark?" Dee says, staring at me. "You said that's your name, right?"

I realize our BLTs had been delivered without me even noticing. "It's Clark."

"*Oops.* You okay, Clark?"

"Yeah."

"You don't need to tell me why you see a therapist," she says, wiping her hands off on a napkin. "It's personal. I get it."

I know that Dee's phone will buzz any minute now, reminding her of the friend who's picking her up, and I should be using this time to learn more about Dee's secret. But I'm a bit rattled after realizing the honest answer to her question isn't the one I've been telling myself for quite a while now.

What if escaping today does nothing to cure my loneliness? What if my loneliness is still waiting for me on September 20 when I can't predict what anyone else will say or do?

"Hey, you," Dee says, answering her phone. "Oh my God, that's right!" She gathers her things and starts scooting out of the booth. *I'm so sorry,* she mouths to me a moment later.

I smile and gesture toward the exit. "It's okay."

Dee holds her phone away from her mouth. "Thank you for this."

"You're welcome."

"For real, though, Mark—er, Clark." She smiles at me too. "You made me feel better after a terrible day."

Dee pivots on her heel and disappears through the door.

I didn't get her to share her secret, but I shared a bit of mine, and that at least feels like a start. This is why Ms. Hazel's homework matters. I might not master every tip on the first try, but I can use the loop to learn. I can still work on her four-part challenge, so that if tomorrow ever comes, my loneliness won't be waiting for me there.

CHAPTER 17

CREATE A NEW ROUTINE FOR MYSELF. EVERY TODAY, I wake up, make breakfast, get ready while I blast The Wrinkles, and arrive at Splendid Cinemas a few minutes after it opens. Emery is behind the concession stand like a determined Labrador puppy—earbuds in, holding his lines in his hands, and anxious for the audition.

We run through the lines, but we chat about a lot of different things, too. He gives me advice on beating high school senioritis (if he only knew how much worse senioritis is in a time loop), and I suggest a few foolproof recipes he can try to get more comfortable in the kitchen. He learns that my parents are divorcing, that I've never had a boyfriend, and that I am endlessly annoyed by—and would absolutely die for—my younger sister. I learn that he's the middle child of five, a popcorn thief who sneaks handfuls through-out every one of his shifts (even though it's against cinema policy), and head over heels for a girl he's not sure likes him back.

"Emery," I say, grinning, "you've just got to ask her out."

He laughs with a nod, his cheeks flushed.

Whether it's auditions or admissions of love, I've gathered that he tends to put off the things that intimidate him most.

He ends our time together the same way each today: asking me to take acting classes with him—an offer I happily accept—before I slip out the door.

Then I go see Otto.

Otto believes I'm starting from scratch learning my way around the bakery in each today, which explains why he's increasingly stunned at my competency behind the counter. I get faster and faster breezing through the daily afternoon rush up front, armed with my pad of sticky notes and pen. He grows suspicious of me in Day 337, I can tell, as he catches me writing down a woman's order (three black coffees and a dozen blue doughnuts) before she says it aloud. But in the moment, I think he's too busy to question my apparent sorcery.

The more time I spend with Otto, the more I sense that secret sadness simmering beneath the surface. He may be a big ball of joy to most guests who don't know better, but his melancholy becomes more apparent to me every afternoon in the time loop. Each today, I make sure to like his Instagram post about Ben's birthday and add to the rows of blue-hearted comments. But even though I contemplate mentioning something to Otto about the significance of today, I always end up deciding not to, unsure how it might land on our "first" time meeting. It's always going to be a hard day, I decide, whether I say something or not, but at least I help make the afternoon rush easier.

Then, finally, I head off to see Dee.

Winning her trust is the toughest part of my today, as you probably could have guessed, because persuading an upset person to tell you a big, embarrassing secret is no easy feat. In fact, I haven't been successful at getting it out of her. Not even once.

Some todays, I mess up before we even get to the diner. Like in Day 331. I stupidly mention the call she's expecting from the friend picking her up when we're right outside the Aragon. Needless to say, that today did not end well.

"How the hell would you know that?" Dee breathes, stiff finger pointed directly at my face, as she slowly backs away. "Leave. Me. *Alone*."

So I do.

In Day 340, I propose having BLTs and milkshakes at the diner before she offers to take me there, which sets off alarm bells.

"Have you been following me after I get out of work?" she says, disgusted. "Let me be clear: I'd rather eat a BLT covered in fire ants than drink a milkshake with you, douchebag."

Understandable.

The evenings when I'm able to get some smiles out of Dee at the diner are rewarding. But even on nights like Day 340, when I botch my approach and she puts me in my place as the intrusive stranger I appear to be, I can't help but grow fond of her. Sure, I desperately want to learn Dee's secret, but I look forward to our exchanges in each today, regardless if I get rejected on the sidewalk or not. Her quick wit always leaves me grinning, even after she reads me for filth and strides off. Whatever embarrassment Dee survived yesterday must be truly awful if someone like her feels ashamed to open up about it.

But then again, Dee's *not the quickest to speak up when she should*, as Sandy put it.

I shouldn't pretend to know her as deeply as I want to believe I do.

There's still something missing in my interactions with each person, though. Just like I can't cure Otto's blues, or help Emery nail his upcoming audition, in just one today, I can't force Dee to disclose a secret that she refuses to share.

It's an odd feeling, growing closer to friends who can't be my friends in return. I may know about the time Emery's family dog ran away when he was in sixth grade, or piece together that Ben's death slowly tore Otto and his ex-wife apart, or learn that Dee started coming to the diner long before she worked at the Aragon and Sandy is like a second mom. But when we meet again, they know nothing about me.

I like running my errands, but my attempts to accomplish Ms. Hazel's steps still haven't cured my loneliness.

Because every today I see my friends, but they only see a stranger.

On Day 345, I decide to stop in to see Ms. Hazel for the first time in a long time to figure out if I should be approaching her tips in a different, more fulfilling way. Seeing Emery, Otto, and Dee in each today has made the time loop better, without question, but the closer I feel to the three of them while remaining a nobody in their eyes, the more unsettled I feel.

Am I actually being a friend or am I just manipulating people I care about to feel a little less alone? And is it even working?

"I heard you had food poisoning this morning, Clark, and missed school." Ms. Hazel tosses her yellow scarf behind her shoulder. "I assumed our session was canceled, but I'm happy it's not. You must be feeling better?"

I nod with a shrug. "Yeah. I'm all right."

I glance around her crowded but cozy office: the candy dishes overflowing with treats, the coffee-table books and old psychology magazines piled high between us, the overworked air conditioner keeping the room nice and chilled. Somehow, even when everything familiar eventually becomes dull, I'm realizing now that I've strangely missed the reliable solace of Ms. Hazel's office—even 345 todays in.

"I have a random question," I say right away, avoiding any small talk. "Does friendship have to be a two-way street?"

She ponders. "My hunch is to say yes, but I'd love for you to elaborate first. What's on your mind?"

I think about how to explain myself in a way that won't leave her head in a tailspin. "I have these new friends—well, potential friends, I guess—who I'm feeling closer to, but I don't know if they feel the same way about me."

"How come?"

"Well, let me back up a bit," I say. "I've applied three of the tips in your loneliness challenge to these possible new friendships, but it doesn't seem to be working in defeating my loneliness."

She crosses her legs slowly, a perplexed look on her face. "My four-part loneliness challenge?"

"Yes."

"I don't recall assigning that homework to you, Clark," she says, lips protruding in thought. "I've suggested it to many people before, but not to you."

"You're right, but you did mention it a few weeks ago, when I brought up Sadie moving to Texas," I lie, hoping to avoid shifting the conversation due to a time loop technicality. "Don't you remember?"

Ms. Hazel, increasingly confused, shakes her head. "I don't, but I trust your memory more than I trust my own. And I'm glad you took it upon yourself to test out my tips without being asked first." She smiles. "So, let's hear it. How's the challenge going?"

I sigh. "Okay, I guess. But I'm not sure if I'm applying your tips in the right ways."

"What do you mean by the *right* ways?"

I stare at the coffee table for a moment before getting an idea. "So, there's this girl, Dee, who has a secret that's been eating her up." I pull a candy dish closer to me, signifying that it symbolizes her. "As tip number three encourages, I've told her that I go to therapy in hopes that my vulnerability will wear off on her and she'll feel comfortable enough letting me in on her secret."

Ms. Hazel, smiling wide like a proud parent, nods. "Terrific. And, has it worked?"

I shake my head. "Not yet. For tip number two"—I pull a blackened candle next to the candy dish to represent Otto—"there's this business owner who could really use some part-time help during the afternoon at his bakery."

Ms. Hazel lights up. "You've mentioned your interest in baking before, Clark. That seems like a wonderful opportunity."

"Yeah, I agree, but . . . I don't know," I say. "Even though I make the afternoon rush less wild, he still always seems a little sad to me. You know? And then there's this actor who I met at the movie theater"—I grab the top magazine off a pile of old issues and place it next to the candle and candy dish—"who's really nice and cool, but I've been running lines with him and—" But my line of thinking gets completely derailed by a magazine called *Psychology Now!* that had been underneath the one I used to represent Emery. One of its cover blurbs reads, "Trapped in Today." And smaller copy below that provides more context: "Is it possible to relive a day more than once? This renowned psychologist believes so—because it (allegedly) happened to them."

"What's the matter?" Ms. Hazel asks.

I bend forward and pick up the issue. It's so worn down, it feels like the paper might disintegrate between my fingertips.

"Oh, that old thing," she says. "I've been cleaning up around here at the demands of my daughter and need to throw out an embarrassing amount of, what she's so eloquently characterized as, *crap*."

I stare at the cover. "So it's been in here awhile, then?"

Ms. Hazel thinks. "Well, technically, yes." She points over her shoulder. "I found that entire stack of old magazines in a box behind my desk last week. But just this morning I pulled them out and placed them on the coffee table, only to forget to toss them during my lunch break. Here, let me trash them now—"

She reaches forward.

"No!" I pull the magazine away.

Her eyes pop open.

"Sorry." I clear my throat, trying to compose myself.

"How old is this issue?"

"Probably a couple *decades*. The year should be on there."

I find the date in tiny print. "February 1990."

A sharp laugh escapes her mouth. "My daughter would have a fit knowing I still have magazines in here older than she is." She sighs. "What can I say? It's difficult for me to part with things that I've found interesting."

"Do you know who this is about?" I point at the blurb.

Ms. Hazel squints, pushing her glasses up the bridge of her nose. "Oh," she says, nodding, "That explains why I didn't want to part ways with it. I always admired Dr. Runyon."

"Who is he?"

"*She* was an accomplished psychology researcher back in the day, whom I respected quite a bit—a smart cookie, really. But her whole . . . what did she call it again?"

"*Trapped in Today?*"

"*Trapped in Today*, that's right . . ." Ms. Hazel shakes her head gently, implying it's a waste of time. "It's a little out there. If you'd like to learn about her contributions to psychology, there are more, let's say, *legitimate* readings I could point you toward."

"What is *Trapped in Today?*"

"The title of the book she wrote. I read it."

"And?"

"And what?"

"What was it about?"

Ms. Hazel pauses, surprised at my interest. "Well," she begins, "if you must know, it had something to do with her experiences related to, how can I put it . . ." She thinks, unwrapping a caramel candy. "Extreme feelings of déjà vu, more or less. It was a bit out of left field, to put it mildly, which is unfortunate, because plenty of academics deemed her unwell after that."

Ms. Hazel carries on as I flip open the magazine and scramble to find the section featuring Dr. Runyon. It's only one page toward the back and features a photo of the psychologist smiling sweetly in a yellow suit jacket. Her hair is styled in a short, brown bob, and a thick layer of bright-red lipstick pops off the page.

There are only a few paragraphs providing more context:

As a teenager, Rebecca Runyon found herself in quite a dilemma. Every morning, she woke up and relived the same day: January 13, 1970. Or so she claims.

The researcher has shied away from discussing the surreal experience publicly for decades, fearful of how the professional world would react. Behind the scenes, however, Runyon secretly went to work, interviewing others who've also been, as she characterizes it, Trapped in Today, the title of her new book. Thousands of people have had the same agonizing experience, she believes, and many fields of study—"medicine, psychology, theology, astrology," Runyon writes, just to name a few—should start taking this phenomenon seriously.

"My data suggests that fate is fallible," Runyon writes in her book, which hits shelves on February 10. "And when the universe allows someone to veer off the path they're meant to be on, time will repeat itself—like a scratched vinyl unable to escape the chorus—until the course is corrected."

Will Dr. Runyon's research shatter our conceptions of time and fate? Or has the trailblazing psychologist, as her many new critics say, lost her way?

CHAPTER 18

'VE READ ABOUT A LOT OF TIME LOOP THEORIES coming from a lot of time loop theorists since getting stuck, and I can already tell from four short paragraphs that Dr. Runyon's is . . . different.

Unlike hundreds of anonymous profiles littering comment sections below sci-fi articles, she's not someone spouting their egregious ideas purely for the sake of getting attention or stirring the pot. And far from the dudes word vomiting their nonsensical thoughts on space-time continuum forums without ever having taken a basic physics course, Dr. Runyon appears to be an actual researcher with real data to back her up.

I need to learn more.

I grab my bag and flee Ms. Hazel's office in a near sprint.

"Clark?" she calls after me. "Has the food poisoning returned? There's bathroom on your right, if so!"

It turns out that finding a copy of an unpopular book written over three decades ago by a psychologist who everyone dismissed as "crazy" is just as difficult as it sounds. While frantically searching the title on my walk home, I discover that no bookstore on earth (or at least in the Chicago suburbs) still has it in stock, and neither do any of the major online retailers. It's almost as if *Trapped in Today* was never published at all.

Dr. Runyon is a bit of a mystery, too.

I'm able to dig up a few articles about her earlier research. She made a name for herself in the 1980s, having authored a few consequential studies related to the intersection of grief and mental health. But she seems to have not so much fell as plunged off the face of the earth the same year *Trapped in Today* was released. The next mention of her I found was her obituary when she died from a rare disease about a decade later.

What happened to her? And what happened to her book?

In Day 346, I use the food poisoning excuse on Mom for the umpteenth time and head to Splendid Cinemas earlier than usual, hoping hanging out with Emery and a big bag of buttery popcorn can temporarily pull me out of the Dr. Runyon rabbit hole I've fallen into. Even that can't prevent my thoughts from wandering back to Trapped in Today, though.

Emery clears his throat to get my attention. I glance up from my phone, which is six pages deep into the results of a search for Was Rebecca Runyon right about Trapped in Today?—and see that Emery is eyeing the page of lines in my hand.

I pop my phone into my pocket and shift my voice into character. "Hi, can you help me with the bench press?"

But Emery stops me. "Clark," he says with a little laugh. "You don't have to stick around."

"It's okay."

"You've already gone *way* above and beyond just by running through the lines a few times," Emery says. He looks at me curiously. "Your Mondays must be pretty free, huh?"

I hear the front doors opening behind me and I tense up, because no one comes into the theater this early.

I brace myself for the only possible deviation.

Emery's eyes dart away from me as a warm smile spreads into his cheeks to greet whoever entered. "Welcome to Splendid Cinemas."

I turn around.

And, sure enough, Beau is standing there.

My palms begin to sweat. We lock eyes. He's silent; his face is unreadable. As has been the case since Day 311, it's impossible to know what he's thinking.

Beau exhales in defeat. "You're not usually here this early."

"You're still following me?" I ask, surprised. After our last interaction, I assumed he wanted me as far off his radar as I could be.

"No, I'm not," he says. "But it's hard to miss that you've been stopping in here to see Emery and going on our other errands every day like clockwork."

"Huh?" Emery says, mouth ajar. "How did you . . . ? What errands?"

Beau and I both ignore him.

"I can't get into this again with you," Beau says to me softly. "Take care, Clark. You too, Emery." He turns and leaves.

Emery exhales, bewildered. "Well, that was weird."

I run out after Beau.

Neither time we spoke after Day 310 ended great for me. So instead of trying to convince Beau that he *wants* me in his time loop life, maybe I should try to convince him that he *needs* me to be.

"Dr. Runyon," I say, a few paces behind Beau. "Ever heard of her?"

"I have not," Beau replies, eyes straight ahead.

"I came across her work in Day 345. Even though I haven't found her book yet, she seems legitimate, and I think we should look into it—"

"Day 345?" Beau cuts in, glancing back at me. "What do you mean?"

"Day 345," I say, like it should be obvious. "Today is Day 346, so Day 345 was basically our yesterday—*wait*." I realize we've never talked about this. "How long have you been stuck?"

He shrugs. "I stopped counting a while ago."

"Does 346 todays seem like it could be accurate, though?"

He's silent for a moment. "Maybe."

"See?" I say, shoving his shoulder gently to convey how wild that revelation should be. My stomach flips, remembering another thing we didn't discuss yet. "I already know from the night on the rooftop that your todays end at eleven sixteen p.m., but I bet you wake up at seven fifteen a.m., too, huh?"

He pauses, folds his arms against his chest, and faces me, suspicious. "The time loop always wakes me up fifteen minutes before my alarm did before we got stuck. How did you . . . ?"

"Because," I say smugly and with a grin, "I wake up at seven fifteen a.m., too."

We stare at each other, eyes locked.

For a split second, it feels like we're back in Day 310 again.

Until Beau turns around and continues on. "You still don't know why I was in Mr. Zebb's class that day, do you?" he asks. We reach a bike that's locked up against a pole; Beau retrieves a key from his pocket.

"It's one of the many questions I haven't been able to get an answer from you on," I say, leaning against the brick wall next to the bike. "Care to share?"

"I can't."

"Shocking."

He unlocks the bike and pulls it away from the pole. "Believe me, I wish I could tell you, but it's not my information to share."

"Why bring it up, then?" I ask. "So you can taunt me about the things I don't know?"

He swings one leg over the bike seat and hops on. "Derek Dopamine."

"The vlogger?"

Beau nods.

"My sister loves that idiot," I say. "What about him?"

"Find his video on time loops," Beau says. "It has the answers. Maybe that'll prove I'm telling you the truth."

I laugh. "You mean to tell me that Derek *Dopamine*, of all people, can help us escape today?"

Beau starts pedaling away slowly.

"Cool," I mutter sarcastically. "Thanks, Beau, for being so generous with your time. Maybe see you again? Maybe not? Who cares, really?"

Beau's feet strike the pavement, stopping the bike's forward motion. He turns to face me. "I get why you do it."

"Keep trying to talk to you?" I say. "Yeah, it should be obvious by now."

"No," he says, "I understand why you keep going on our errands. And I don't fault you for it, even though it means that I can't."

I don't respond. "In here, it's nice to feel like you have somewhere to be," he continues, lips bending into a sad smile. "It's nice to feel like people need you in their day as much as you need them in yours. It's nice to feel a little less alone—even if the feeling doesn't last long."

I'm not sure what to say.

We stand there for another moment before Beau's feet find the pedals again. "Derek Dopamine," he reiterates, rolling away. "Watch the video."

CHAPTER 19

THE LAST THING I WANT TO BE THINKING ABOUT after another not-so-great run-in with Beau is pizza for dinner for the 346th time.

"Are you sure you don't want even just one small slice?" Mom asks, standing in my doorway with a plate in her hand. "I got your favorite toppings. Or would soup be better for your stomach?"

"Ham and mushroom aren't my favorite toppings," I mutter from bed.

Her eyes narrow on me. "How'd you know that's what I ordered for you?"

I roll over to face my window. "A sixth sense, I guess."

"You're still going to bake something for my birthday, right?" Blair calls from the kitchen. "Even though you've been moping around all day."

"I'll get to it when I get to it," I mumble.

"Seriously?" she yells, mouth full of food. "Clark, you *promised*—"

"I *said*, I'll get to it when I get to it."

"Whatever you make, it's not going to be as good if you wait to the last minute!"

"Hey!" Mom cuts in. "Both of you, chill out. Blair, your brother had food poisoning today and is doing a very nice thing for you for your birthday, so take it easy. And you." She pauses.

I twist just enough to see her out of the corner of my eye.

She lowers her voice. "You sure you're okay?"

"Yeah."

She lowers it even more. "You can tell me if it wasn't food poisoning. Sometimes we need a day off just to . . . you know. Breathe. I get it."

"Can I just be alone?"

The room swells with awkward silence, interrupted only by Blair's banging around in the kitchen.

"Sure thing," Mom says as she closes my bedroom door. "Love you."

I flip onto my back and stare at the ceiling.

As unfulfilling as each one of my interactions with Beau have been, at least I left this one with the most solid lead yet. I pull Mom's laptop onto my chest.

"I can't believe it's come to this," I mutter, typing *Derek Dopamine time loop* into the browser search bar.

And yet? Nothing.

Not a single mention connecting Derek Dopamine to time loop theories. Not one video, headline, or image result comes remotely close to explaining why Beau believes he needs to win back the soul mate who remains nameless.

"You've got to be kidding me," I breathe, scrolling through page after page of bogus results. Is this Beau's idea of a practical joke? Is he just straight up *mocking* me at this point in an attempt to push me further away?

As much as Beau wants me focusing on finding my nonexistent soul mate, I can't get The Wrinkles out of my head. Because that concert had to have something to do with our getting stuck together.

There's no way it was a coincidence that we were both there—with Dee, too.

Even though I've gone over yesterday again and again in my head, I've never typed out every last detail before. Maybe that'll help relevant info float to the surface of my mind.

Sunday, September 18, I think to myself, opening a blank document on the laptop. *What do I know for sure?* Well, cereal happened for breakfast (or was it bagels?). There was a lot of unpacking from the move into Mom's apartment. I know I organized framed photos on the bookshelf near the TV . . . maybe. Or was it cutlery in the kitchen? (I don't know.)

I remember talking to Mom and Blair about Blair's party on Tuesday as they cleaned the dining room and I broke down some cardboard boxes. Blair went to a friend's—or went off to watch Derek Dopamine videos in her room, or something—and the conversation shifted to the divorce. Mom admitted that she's the one who wanted it. We got into the biggest fight we've ever had, and it left me fuming.

The afternoon gets a bit fuzzier.

The house felt tense after our clash, so Mom went for a long walk around the neighborhood. I vented to Sadie about the divorce in a FaceTime (the only reason I know that for certain is my phone's call history). Then I took a cat nap, got some trig homework done, and wasted too much time scrolling through my phone.

And that's when the biggest question marks crop up.

Okay, think Clark.

Sunday night . . .

I was excited to see The Wrinkles, but less excited about the circumstances that got me there. Sadie and I had bought tickets a long time ago—before her dad got a job in Austin and abruptly moved the family there. A few days after we did, a big group of her neighborhood friends got tickets, too, and asked if she wanted to go together. Sadie jumped on board and I, not wanting to be That Friend, agreed, even though I would have preferred it be just me and her. It became a group thing—but I knew I'd end up the awkward guy tagging along.

Then Sadie moved and sold her ticket, which meant I'd had to go to the concert with a bunch of not-so-much friends as barely friendly-ish acquaintances. I contemplated selling my ticket, too, but Sadie convinced me that the concert would be a good opportunity to get closer to the group. Clearly, it didn't quite work out that way.

But what happened that night?

I keep typing out every last detail I can manage to remember:

- Sadie's neighbor Truman picked me up in his dad's minivan.
- It was crammed with Sadie's neighborhood friends.
- I felt claustrophobic.
- Cynthia Rubric was wearing orange lipstick.
- A full cup of some type of booze—tequila? vodka? I don't drink often enough to have a clue—that was mixed with (not nearly enough) pop was handed to me.
- I drank it.
- Ron Hamilton had on a metallic silver fanny pack.
- I felt buzzed.
- I didn't like the music Truman decided to play on the way there.
- We got to the city.
- We did a few shots in a grimy parking garage.
- I regretted doing the shots as fast as I did.

- I felt more than buzzed.
- They all kept drinking to heighten the show; I kept drinking to curb my shyness.
- And also because I was still angry about the argument I got in with Mom about the divorce, I think.
- I was drunk.
- We walked from the parking garage to Lakeview Live.
- I tried to look Not Drunk as they processed our tickets at the door.
- It worked (or the ticket-taker person didn't care enough to deny me entry).
- Even though I'd stopped drinking, the alcohol kept seeping in, I think.
- Of the three times I've ever been drunk, this was the drunkest.
- The Wrinkles got me out of my head. They were amazing.
- But, really, I can only recall two or three of the songs they played for sure.
- I remember realizing in a drunk haze that I needed fresh air, so I left Truman and the rest of the group and sat outside the venue for the last few songs.
- After the show wrapped, people began pouring out through the doors and Lakeview basically turned into a block party.
- Still drunk. Way, *way* drunk.
- I met up with the group and they wanted to go ... where was it again?
- Oh, yeah, I can see it in my head. That cool-looking wooden tunnel that's designed to look like a beehive, or something.
- Wait, yes. It's called The Honeycomb.
- I was in a bad mood, though. I can't remember why. But maybe it was just the alcohol wearing off.
- So I ordered a ridiculously expensive ride home as the rest of the group left for The Honeycomb.

- I got back to the apartment late and sneaked into bed without waking Mom.
- I woke up at 7:15 a.m. on Monday, September 19, and I never left. Thank God I didn't have a hangover. Can you imagine being stuck in a time loop with a terrible headache and nonstop nausea?

I have . . . no recollection of meeting Beau.

None, whatsoever. I close Mom's laptop again—this time, with a bit more elbow grease, courtesy of my increased frustration—and sink into my mattress.

What options do I have left to try to escape?

Piecing together the concert hasn't led me anywhere useful. I can't find this supposedly significant Derek Dopamine video anywhere (assuming that it even exists), leaving me even less sure that Beau's soul-mate theory has merit. So, really, I've only got one more path to pursue.

And I'm hoping Dr. Runyon can lead the way.

CHAPTER 20

ON DAY 347, I HUNKER DOWN AT BEN'S EVERYTHING Blue Bakery, brownie in hand. I need to get out of Mom's apartment in order to focus on getting out of September 19.

I claim a table in the corner of Ben's with my brownie breakfast, flip open Mom's laptop, and get to work.

"Dr. Rebecca Runyon . . . ," I say under my breath, typing her name into my browser. "What happened to you?"

I dig deeper than I've dug before, combing through the dozen or so sources cited in her (short and mostly unhelpful) Wikipedia page, tracking any living loved ones—she never married or had children, I learn—and searching out any and all information about *Trapped in Today*. Spoiler alert: I still can't find much.

How can a book by a famous psychologist just . . . disappear?

There are plenty of websites that mention Dr. Runyon's studies, but only a few explore her thoughts on getting stuck in a time loop. To make matters worse, none of those go into any detail about if she had theories on how to get *out*.

Dr. Runyon died in the pre-internet era, which seems to have reduced the digital footprint she left behind. I suspect that her reputation has been closely guarded by the institutions associated with her work, too. Dartmouth College loves sharing the credit for Runyon's groundbreaking work related to PTSD among veterans, for instance. But the school seems less thrilled about being associated with the woman who "lost her marbles with the *Groundhog Day* crap," as one random commenter quipped on an old Facebook post shared by Dartmouth that touted the researcher's findings.

Otto appears at my side and sets down a cup of water. "Hey, there. You've been working away all morning and look parched."

"Thanks, Otto," I say, chugging it.

"Have we met?" he says, confused. "My apologies if so, I'm usually great with names."

Oops.

I shake my head, thinking fast. "No, I follow the bakery on Instagram. I recognized you from your posts."

"Ah, well." He grins and bows slightly. "Glad to see my silly photos have lured another hungry person inside. Happy to meet you . . ." He holds out his hand.

"Clark," I say, shaking it.

"Nice to meet you, Clark." He smiles and walks away.

I wish it didn't sting as much as it does to be a complete stranger in his eyes.

Back to business.

Although I don't want to fall into the tinfoil-hat-land abyss, I know the time has come to revisit a few of the more outrageous time-loop-theory sites. Cringing, I begin punching away at my keyboard until I land on a conspiracy theorist's blog that I've come across before.

Here we go.

Most of the content on TheTruthReallyIsOutThere.net is as reliable as you'd expect it to be. There are photos of alleged Martians dining outside a food truck in Oregon (you can see the zipper on one guy's alien costume), an in-depth explainer filled with straw-man arguments that "proves" the moon landing photos were staged by a German billionaire, and a detailed map specifying the migratory habits of Bigfoot.

In other words, I don't believe this site has a strict fact-checking policy in place.

Although, now that I think about it, my experience in the time loop doesn't sound any less absurd than the stories featured on sites like TheTruthReallyIsOutThere.Net, I guess. What *real* journalist working for a *real* news site would take my claims seriously? I couldn't convince smart people like Ms. Hazel that what I'm experiencing is legitimate, so how am I any different from the guy who says he knows the exact cave where Bigfoot spends his summers?

Next to a listicle titled, "Five Reasons We Know The Loch Ness Monster Has Loch Ness Babies," is a short post on Dr. Runyon. Or, as its headline reads, "The Woman Who Got Trapped in Today."

Compared to the other stories on the site, the post on Runyon doesn't seem too out there—although there is a hand-drawn infographic made by the blogger that ranks which planets would be the least annoying to get stuck in a daily time loop on. (Venus, they argue, takes gold, as one of its days equals 243 Earth days.) But beyond that, the post mostly regurgitates what I already read in the magazine in Ms. Hazel's office.

It has one useful thing that the issue of *Psychology Now!* doesn't, though: several photos of Dr. Runyon with whom appear to be colleagues.

The blogger at TheTruthReallyIsOutThere.net didn't include any information about the pics, which would've been helpful in identifying others who I could try to speak to (assuming at least some of them are still alive). But one photo of a smiley blond woman about the same age as Dr. Runyon catches my eye.

It looks like the image was photocopied from an old newspaper clipping or something similar. Fortunately, it did *not* cut out the original caption, which was typed in tiny, barely legible text in the corner of the photo. I easily would have missed it, had I not been scanning every square inch of the post looking for clues.

It reads:

Dr. Rebecca Runyon (left) and Professor Cassidy Copeman (right). Although Dr. Runyon has never confirmed either way, it's rumored that Copeman was Trapped with her reliving the same day. Copeman has brushed off the hearsay. "If that's what Rebecca believes, my heart breaks for her," Copeman tells *The Journal.* "A brilliant mind, spoiled by the pursuit of fame and fortune."

"Trapped with?" I whisper to myself. I try a variety of search terms in hopes of finding the original article that the photo was featured in, but it doesn't appear to have been republished online. There has to be a thousand local newspapers that dub themselves *The Journal*—and many of them have probably gone out of business since this was published, anyway—so I don't even attempt to figure out which outlet the caption is referring to.

Instead, I open another window on my browser and search, "Professor Cassidy Copeman." The first result gives me goose bumps: a faculty page for the University of Chicago's psychology department, where Copeman is listed as a current professor.

"Holy shit," I breathe, louder than intended. I snap the laptop shut, drop it into my bag, and head for the exit.

"Hope to see you again soon, Clark!" Otto hollers at me from behind the register as I wave goodbye.

I flag down a cab and ask the driver to take me to Hyde Park. Rush-hour traffic makes what seems like the longest drive of my life even more unbearable.

"How much farther?" I ask from the back seat.

The driver gives me the stink-eye in the rearview mirror and refuses to answer (which I honestly deserve).

When I start to see sprawling brick buildings covered in ivy and twentysomethings wearing backpacks, I know we've made it to campus. Finally, the driver pulls up to the building that Professor Copeman's office is listed in.

"Thank you!" I say, tossing way too much cash into the front seat.

I spring up the steps, walk inside, and glance around like a lost puppy. Unlike Rosedore High, there are no lockers, posters on any wall, or an inkling of school spirit. The air smells like old books, number two pencils, and high IQs. No one is around and there aren't any signs directing me to professors' offices. The panic starts to set in, convincing me that I'm in over my head.

I mean, the caption made it pretty clear: Copeman was *not* on the same page as Runyon when it came to time loops. It sounds like she thought Runyon's book was nothing more than a sad attempt to attract more fame and fortune. What if she's disgusted that someone like me would drop by? What if she laughs me out of her office?

But I can do this.

I *need* to do this.

I've pushed my limits plenty of times since Day 310, I remind myself. I can't possibly stop now, with a promising theory within reach.

A smiley man with red hair and a striped tie comes striding toward me from down the hall, looking friendly enough to approach.

"Hi," I say as he draws near. "Can I ask you a question?"

He nods. "Of course."

"Do you know if Professor Copeman works in this building?"

"Copeman . . ." He stares at the floor in thought. "The college reshuffled our offices recently and I'm not sure where hers was moved to. I'd ask"—he points at down the hallway—"in there."

"Thank you."

I follow where his finger led and push open a creaky wooden door that has a MAIN OFFICE sign signifying what's on the other side.

The room is surprisingly large, drowning in harsh fluorescent light and filled with the unpleasant smell of mothballs. A woman who looks a few years older than me with dyed black hair and a horrible sunburn is sitting behind the receptionist desk, fingers dancing across the screen of her phone.

"Can I help you?" she asks without looking up.

"Yes." I step toward her. "My name is Clark Huckleton, and I'm hoping to speak to Professor Copeman."

"Hi Clark, I'm Kelly," she says, eyes still glued to her phone. "Professor Copeman is in Florida." I wait for her to provide more context, but she doesn't.

"On vacation?" I ask.

"No," Kelly replies. "For life."

I feel my chest deflate.

"She moved to Orlando with her daughter last month," Kelly says.

She finally sets down her phone—it lands on the desk with a dramatic thud—and directs her attention to me. "What do you need Copeman for?"

"I was hoping to chat with her about some psych stuff."

She grins. "Well, I could have guessed that, considering"—she gestures all around us—"we're in the psych department. What kind of psych stuff?"

I shake my head. "I don't want to bore you to death. How does she work in the psychology department if she lives in Florida, though?"

"She *doesn't* work in the psychology department."

"But the school's website lists her as a faculty member."

Kelly leans toward me and lowers her voice, even though no one else is in the room. "She's been sick for a while, dude. I'm surprised they kept her around as long as they did." She shrugs. "But now, she's retired. Like, officially. The website probably just hasn't been updated."

"Is she going to be okay?"

Kelly cringes, like she's said too much.

"I don't want to be pushy, but . . . is there any way I could get ahold of her?" I ask, knowing it's a long shot. "Did she leave an email or phone number?"

She smiles, amused. "I can't do that. Obviously."

"Well, are there any staff or students I could talk to who knew her well?"

She pauses, her face studying mine. "What did you say your name is again?"

"Clark."

"Clark, you aren't . . . shit, what was the phrase again . . . trapped in today, are you?"

I nearly let out a gasp. "Yes."

Her face lights up before breaking into a laugh. "Wait, really?"

"Yeah."

She doesn't seem convinced. "You're not messing with me?"

"No. Definitely not."

"Congrats," she says. "You're the first one."

The first one?

Kelly pops up out of her chair, walks to a large cabinet behind her desk, and swings open its doors. There, lining an interior shelf, are dozens of copies of *Trapped in Today*.

I try my hardest not to scream.

"Before Copeman moved, her daughter dropped these off with us," she says, pulling a copy off the shelf. Her fingers move across the glossy cover. "She said the professor wanted us to give a book to anyone who came in looking to speak to her about being trapped in today, regardless if they're a U.C. student or not." She looks up at me. "What does the title mean, anyway? I haven't read it."

I pause, considering how forthright to be. "It's a reference to getting stuck in a time loop."

Kelly laughs, examining the cover again. "I had no idea Copeman wrote sci-fi. And here I was, assuming she was off her rocker and I'd end up having to throw all these books out by Christmas." She hands the copy over to me. "I'll have to read it."

If what Kelly is saying is correct and the professor's parting gift to the psych department was free copies of Runyon's book, Copeman must have had a change of heart since she was quoted in the old news clip. She must believe in Runyon's theory.

And she probably was Trapped with her too.

I look down at Dr. Runyon's focused, knowing face staring back at me.

DR. REBECCA RUNYON WAS TRAPPED IN TODAY, the cover reads. My fingertips tingle against its surface.

"Please don't throw those books out by Christmas," I tell Kelly, even though I know she won't remember this conversation. "It's the type of book that'll need some time to fall into the right hands."

She smiles in return, a bit mystified. "I won't, Clark."

I head down the hallway while opening the book, and spot a handwritten note written on the title page:

To whomever sought this book,
You're not alone. You can get to tomorrow.
I believe in you.
—Cassidy Copeman

P.S. Should you need my help:
TrappedInATimeLoop@gmail.com

CHAPTER 21

'VE NEVER TYPED UP AN EMAIL FASTER IN ALL MY
life.

To: TrappedInATimeLoop@gmail.com
Subject Line: Help, I'm Trapped

Hi, professor. I hope you're well. My name is Clark Huckleton, I'm a
17-year-old from Illinois, and I'm Trapped in today (September 19).
Would it be possible for us to connect? I'd love to learn more from
you. Thanks.

I hit send before I even leave the psychology building and find
a shaded bench on campus to dive into the book.

By the second chapter, I can see why the world thought she was
full of it. But more important, I can see that she was onto something. Everything about Dr. Runyon seems credible. She wasn't just
a nobody pulling ideas out of thin air, nor was she relying solely
on her own personal experience being Trapped. Dr. Runyon spent
years seeking out and interviewing hundreds of others who reported similar experiences. There was a lot of consistency between their
stories, too—and my own.

By late afternoon, the unbearable heat forces me into air-
conditioning. I spend the rest of the evening on campus shuffling

between building lobbies as each one closes to the public, glancing at my inbox every few minutes to see if Copeman has written me back (she hasn't). As I tear through the book in the laundry room of a dorm hall that I sneaked into, a suspicious student approaches me with caution.

"Hey," he says, squinting at me. "What floor do you live on?"

I glance at my phone.

Damn. It's already 11:15 p.m.

"Uh . . ."

When my eyes open on the other side of a blink, I'm staring at my white, wooden nightstand in Day 348. The time loop may have saved me from an awkward interaction with a nosy undergrad, but now I have to start from scratch.

I shoot off a near-identical email to Copeman—but this time remember to include my phone number—text Mom that I have food poisoning, and trek back to campus to get the book from Kelly.

"Hi, I'm Trapped in today," I say at once, walking in.

"Whoa," Kelly says, looking up from her phone. "You people really exist, huh?"

I get a copy from her, find the same shaded bench where I sat the today before, and pick up right where I left off. Each page I turn feels like a glimmer of hope, as Dr. Runyon's research aligns perfectly with my experience.

Like, how she believes deviations work:

Each day would remain remarkably identical for every subject I interviewed, unless their own actions altered the behaviors of others or the world around them, the doctor wrote on page 81. *Non-Trapped persons never exhibited unprompted, modified behavior.*

Yup. I can relate.

And she validated my struggles holding on to memories before I got Trapped:

The longer Trapped individuals stayed Trapped, the faster their recollection of prior life diminished, Dr. Runyon reported on page 112. *Even remembering basic facts from what would have been their yesterday—say, what the weather was like or what they ate for dinner—grew increasingly difficult to recall.*

Check.

But it wasn't until Chapter Nine that I knew, without a doubt, that Dr. Runyon's theory was correct.

Experiences related to a repeating day's start and end times were extraordinarily inconsistent, she wrote. *Subjects reported waking up at the same time each morning, and their repeating day would stop—and then immediately restart—at a seemingly arbitrary point later in the day. TORONTO MALE #4, for example, said he woke to a honking bus outside of his apartment at 6:49 a.m., only to have his day restart again at 5:13 p.m., as he took the elevator down his office building.*

I look up from the book with a smile planted on my face and a tear collecting in my eye.

I knew it all along, deep down, but it still feels incredible to have it confirmed on the pages between my fingertips.

No, I'm *not* delusional. No, I'm *not* losing my mind. And more than ever before, I'm certain that I'm not alone in this phenomenon.

One thing I don't have an answer to, though, is what prompted Copeman to change course?

Clearly, something must have inspired her to acknowledge that she, too, was Trapped after denying it publicly. Otherwise, why would she be giving away the book—*and* her personal email address—to people like me?

My phone buzzes. I glance down, assuming it'll be another message from Mom checking to see if I'm feeling any better, but it's from an unknown number.

Hi, it reads. This is Jodie Copeman-Brown. My mom, Professor Cassidy Copeman, is feeling well enough to speak now. Are you free to connect on video?

I spring to my feet, heart racing.

Hi, Jodie, I text back at once. Yes, that would be great.

I begin pacing back and forth in front of the bench, fanning my sweaty face with the book. After 348 todays, has the moment finally arrived? Am I about to speak to someone who knows what I'm going through?

My phone lights up with the same unknown number. I take a deep breath, sit back down on the bench to calm my nerves, and answer Jodie's FaceTime.

The screen comes to life and a middle-aged woman with blond hair, rosy cheeks, and white, round glasses appears.

"Clark!" she says. "Jodie here. How's it going?"

I try to hold the phone in front of me as steady as possible, despite how terribly the adrenaline is rattling my limbs. "I'm okay. How are you?"

"Oh, just another manic Monday, as they say, which I'm sure feels *especially* true for you."

Jodie sets her phone down on a countertop and begins chopping lettuce in front of me. A sprawling kitchen with hanging copper pans and a large stainless-steel oven twice the size of Mom's fills the background behind her. I feel like I'm watching some famous internet chef starting a livestream. "You don't mind if I finish making food as we chat?"

"Not at all."

"Great. So, a few things I need to go over with you before you talk to Ma." Jodie's demeanor changes at once, as she swings up her knife and points it directly at the phone camera.

I jolt.

"You're not messing with her, right?" she asks.

"Of course not."

"Because it's happened plenty of times before," she warns, eyes searing into mine through the screen. "Teenagers think this is some kind of joke, calling up an old lady who's just trying to help. It's sick."

"I am not one of those people," I say adamantly. "I swear."

"And you're not one of those obnoxious *thunderbolts*, are you?"

I shake my head, confused by the question. "Like, a flash in the sky?"

She rolls her eyes. "It doesn't matter. So, you really are Trapped?"

I nod.

"Promise?"

"Yes."

She lowers the knife to the cutting board again as her expression shifts back to friendly. "You can talk with her."

"That would be incredible."

"But I've got tell you—she's not well." Jodie tosses the lettuce with veggies in a bowl. "She doesn't have much energy and won't be able to talk long."

"All right."

"I'd get to your most important questions first."

"Okay."

"Chad! Jon!" she shouts over her shoulder. I pull the phone away. "Come eat!" She turns back to the phone and lowers her voice. "You ready, Clark?"

I clear my throat and nod.

Jodie lifts the phone off the countertop and starts walking through the house. My stomach swells with nerves.

"Can I ask," I say, "how many people like me have called to talk to Professor Copeman?"

Jodie laughs as the shaky screen follows her through a hallway off the kitchen. "I've lost track at this point."

She leaves the house through a back screen door, and a blur of vibrant green landscaping reminds me that Copeman moved to Florida.

"Ma, ready to talk to him?" Jodie asks, her voice coming from behind the phone.

There's a moment of pause before she props the phone onto a glass table and Copeman comes into view.

"Hi," the professor says, smiling warmly.

Copeman's thin, frail frame appears even smaller in the plush red bathrobe tied around her front. Her wavy blond hair in the photo with Dr. Runyon has been replaced with thinning gray strands, and her round, bright face is now narrow and wrinkled. I'm certain a strong gust of wind could blow Copeman out of the patio chair she's resting in.

Two boys, probably a few years younger than Blair, are splashing around noisily in a pool built into the ground behind her.

"Chad, Jon, I told you to head inside," Jodie demands of them. "The taco salad is ready."

One of them advocates for "just one more minute," but Jodie doesn't budge.

The professor doesn't say anything as they towel off, and remains silent even after they've left.

So I decide to speak first. "Thank you for talking with me today. I—"

"You've got to speak up," Jodie says off camera. "Basically, shout at her, Clark."

I swallow hard and raise my voice. "Thank you for talking with me today, professor. I found Dr. Runyon's book at the University of Chicago."

Copeman nods and continues smiling.

"Are you enjoying retirement in Orlando?" I ask.

Copeman nods again. "Illinois is too cold."

Her voice is kind, soft, and strained. I turn the volume up on my phone as loud as it'll go.

Jodie addresses me out of the frame with a whisper. "Just dive into your questions, Clark," she says. "We have limited time."

My heart thuds faster.

"Professor Copeman," I say, unsure where to even begin. So I just state the obvious: "I'm, uh . . . I'm Trapped."

Her smile stays fixed. "Don't worry," she says. "We'll get you out."

My eyes immediately fill with tears.

But to hear someone respond to my truth in that way—not with confusion or skepticism, but with *hope*—feels like the warm hug I didn't know I needed. I'd been yearning to share this feeling with Beau in Day 311, I realize—and I felt something similar for a split second at the high school pool, when he confirmed he was stuck, too. But it was such a fleeting moment, I wasn't able to let the relief sink in, like I can now.

"You've read Rebecca's book?" Copeman asks, speaking slowly.

"I'm about halfway done." I wipe my eyes and hold up my copy to show her.

"And it's brought you solace, I hope?"

I nod, embarrassed by my emotions and desperate to stop my eyes from leaking even more. "Definitely."

"Then why the tears?"

I shrug. "I guess it just feels nice being believed."

Copeman's arm trembles as she lifts a glass in front of her to take a slow sip of pink juice. "I understand that feeling," she says, setting the drink back down. "I know it well."

"What was being Trapped like for you?" I ask.

Then panic grips my insides.

Did I just overstep?

Dr. Runyon may have been open to telling her story, but I have no idea if the same is true for Copeman. Clearly, she's come around to discussing the book and Dr. Runyon's theory, but who knows how she feels about sharing her own experience with a stranger.

I speak up after Copeman remains silent. "Maybe I shouldn't have asked—"

"It's okay," Jodie says. "Ma? Want to tell him?"

Copeman looks confused.

Jodie raises her voice. "He's wondering what being Trapped was like for you."

Copeman takes another sip of her drink. "It was torturous."

I nod at her in agreement.

"It may have been 1970," Copeman continues, "but I'll never forget the specific form of despair that comes with being Trapped."

"You were nineteen, huh, Ma?" Jodie asks.

Copeman nods. "Yes. And our Trapped day was January thirteenth. I'll never forget it."

I hear Jodie move closer before she whispers into the phone's speaker: "She's dreaded January my entire life, Clark. On the thirteenth, she won't look at a calendar. She won't even leave her bed. I think a part of her is scared it could happen again."

I swallow hard.

My heart breaks for Copeman. And it makes me scared for my own future in a way I've never considered before. Even if I'm lucky enough to escape today, will I be tortured by September 19 the rest of my life?

"When did she tell you that she'd been Trapped?" I ask Jodie.

"Ma," Jodie says, dragging the phone across the table. She perches it against an object that's closer to Copeman. "He's asking when you decided to tell your family that you were Trapped. Are you up for sharing?"

Copeman clears her throat. "When I got sick, I knew it was time. The biggest regret of my life was not speaking out publicly sooner—when it would have made a difference."

I sit down in the grass next to the bench. "I was hoping I'd get to ask you about that," I say. "I read an old quote by you that dismissed Runyon's claims."

Copeman nods.

I continue, but a bit more hesitant. "You accused her of, uh . . . chasing fame and fortune. Is that how you felt?"

The professor drops her chin slowly, thinking through her next words. "No. But I refused to tell the truth publicly because I was selfish."

"Ma, *stop*," Jodie cuts in. "Go easy on yourself."

"I was thinking about my reputation," Copeman retorts.

Jodie sighs, directing her words at me. "My mom is and always has been *brilliant*—a leader for women in psychology, alongside Runyon. She was in the first wave of female students at Princeton, for God's sake. Isn't that right, Ma?"

Copeman remains silent.

"That's where they met, then," I think aloud, recalling an earlier chapter of the book. "Their freshman year in college."

"Exactly. So, no, it wasn't just about her *reputation*," Jodie continues. "Can you imagine the reaction, had she told the world she'd gotten Trapped in a time loop? Well, I guess you can, since you know what happened to Dr. Runyon. Her life's work would have been spoiled, not to mention she would lost have her job—the income our family relied on."

"Rebecca was willing to give it all up, knowing it would help countless others," Copeman says. "I should have been willing, too."

"Well, Dr. Runyon didn't have a husband and kids to feed at home, Ma, so—"

"I should have been willing, too," Copeman says, as forcefully as her lungs allow.

Jodie's hand reaches out from behind the camera and lands on Copeman's wrist. "I know," she says gently. "I know, Ma."

I bet *Trapped in Today* would've been taken much more seriously when it was published, had the professor agreed to back Runyon's claims. I wonder how many others could have been helped. From the regret in Copeman's voice, I'm certain she believes there are many of us.

"What iteration are you in?" Copeman asks. "And who is your Loop Partner?"

"My Loop Partner?" I say, as my palms begin to sweat. "I must not have gotten to that part in the book yet."

"Ma," Jodie says to Copeman. "Loop Partners. Can you explain what they are to Clark?"

"It's who you're Trapped with," Copeman says. "My Loop Partner was Rebecca."

"And before you say it, because Ma's heard it a *hundred* times before," Jodie chimes in, "yes, someone is Trapped with you in your time loop. They have to be."

Beau.

"Why are we Trapped together, though?" I say. "How did it happen?"

"Fate made a mistake," Copeman says as a matter of fact.

"Because . . . fate made a mistake," I repeat to myself. "I'm not following."

"The book goes into much more detail, but here's the gist," Jodie says. "You were supposed to meet your Loop Partner on . . . what's today's date?"

"September nineteenth."

"Right. So you were supposed to meet your Loop Partner on September eighteenth. Yesterday. However, one of you shit the bed."

Copeman cringes at her daughter's cursing.

"Sorry, Ma, but it's the truth."

"One of us messed up?" I ask. "How?"

"You did something that caused fate to make a mistake," Copeman underscores. "And it resulted in the two of you never crossing paths."

So . . . I was supposed to meet Beau last night.

It *had* to have been at The Wrinkles concert.

"How would we know which one of us messed up?" I ask. "And how would one of us figure out the mistake that we made?"

Copeman doesn't respond for a moment as her eyelids begin to close.

"Ma, you okay?" Jodie asks. "You want a break?"

"No," Copeman says, adjusting her robe and sitting up straighter. "I just didn't hear the question."

"I'll take this one," Jodie says. "Technically, the time loop is *one* of yours, even if you're both Trapped together. Whoever's time loop you're in, they're the ones who shit the—*sorry*. They're the ones who messed up."

"Is there a way to figure out whose time loop it is?"

"You've really got to finish the book, Clark, but, yes, there is a way," Jodie sighs. "What time do you wake up every day?"

"Seven fifteen a.m."

"And is that the time you woke up in your original September nineteenth?"

I think about it for a moment. "It had to have been. Because that's the time my alarm goes off for school."

"It's your time loop, then," Copeman confirms, even though she appears to get sleepier by the second. "Your repeating day would begin at your Loop Partner's original waking time if you were in their time loop."

My stomach flips. "What if both Loop Partners woke up at the same time, though?"

"Rebecca's research never found an answer to that," Copeman says.

It wouldn't matter in my situation, anyway. Because when I ran into Beau in Day 346 outside Splendid Cinemas, he said he wakes up at 7:15 a.m., too—fifteen minutes before his alarm went off in his original September 19. Somehow, I got us both stuck.

Somehow, this is all my fault.

"It sounds like you're the one who caused fate to make a mistake, Clark," Jodie says. "Don't be hard on yourself. It happens. What time does your day end?"

"Eleven sixteen p.m."

"And do you know where you were supposed to meet your Loop Partner on September eighteenth?"

I'm not sure if Lakeview Live is a good enough answer. "Sort of?" I say, exhaling. "I'm confident I know the general vicinity, but—"

"You have to figure out the specific spot," Jodie says. "It's critical."

"Why?"

"Because you've got to find your Loop Partner and take them there at eleven sixteen p.m. That's when and where the universe wanted you two to meet on September eighteenth."

My heart flutters.

"But if we were supposed to meet yesterday, then why are we Trapped in *today*?" I ask. "Wouldn't it make more sense to be Trapped in the day you're supposed to meet your Loop Partner?"

"Did you just say, make more *sense*?" Jodie laughs. "Love, you're Trapped in a time loop. Does anything make sense? Besides"—her arm reaches into the frame with a pitcher of juice and refills Copeman's glass—"Runyon speculated about this, too, I believe in Chapter Twenty-Seven. She referred to the day you're Trapped as the *time gap grace period*. The universe is allowing you an additional day to fix your wrong—and make it right."

"And is that how I get to tomorrow?" I ask, chills dancing across my skin. "Is that how we *both* get to tomorrow?"

"Yes," Jodie says. "Get your Loop Partner to the place you were supposed to meet them at eleven sixteen p.m., and I promise—you'll be in September twentieth before you know it. Ma, you down for the count?"

Copeman, whose eyes have been closed for at least a full minute, strains to stay awake. But the attempt fails, and she's out of consciousness again.

Jodie picks up the phone and turns the camera on herself. "The medication makes her drowsy. We may need to call it quits."

"Okay."

"Are you at least feeling better?"

The most honest answer is that I'm drowning in the waterfall of revelations that's been dumped on me the past few minutes. But still, I'm feeling good. Spectacular, even.

For the first time, I have a trustworthy plan to get to tomorrow.

"I'm, uh . . . *very* overwhelmed," I say, grinning.

"That's to be expected."

"But I feel great. You've been so helpful. Thank you so—"

"I panicked," Copeman speaks up.

Jodie turns the camera back on Copeman. "What was that, Ma?"

I strain to hear the professor's weakened voice, bringing my phone even closer to my ear.

"I panicked," the professor repeats. "That's why we got Trapped. I was the one who caused fate to make a mistake." Her eyes begin to open again. "There was just a small handful of women on campus back then, and lots of men didn't want us around."

"Idiots," Jodie breathes.

"I'd heard that I was the only girl in my introductory psych course and became scared," Copeman continues. "I skipped the first class and promised myself that I needed to drop the course altogether. Little did I know, I wasn't the only girl in that class. Once me and Rebecca figured out a hundred and nineteen iterations in that both of us were meant to be in that course, *together*, we got to tomorrow." Dimples appear in Copeman's cheeks, as if she's remembering a wonderful memory. "We became best friends."

One hundred and nineteen iterations?

I'm not sure what that could mean, but Jodie starts to speak before I can ask.

"They were two peas in a pod, those two," she says to me. "Runyon introduced my mom to my dad. One of my mom's connections made Runyon's most consequential study possible. I can't imagine how different both their lives would have been had they never met on January 13, 1970." Jodie turns the camera back on herself as her mom drifts off again. "That should inspire you to keep fighting, huh?" she says. "Whoever you're supposed to meet out there, whoever your Loop Partner is, the universe has big plans for the two of you."

The universe has plans for me and Beau.

I'm filled with gratitude, watching Copeman drift in and out of sleep on the screen in front of me. She may have caused fate to make a mistake with Dr. Runyon and hindered the impact of *Trapped in Today* all those years ago. But she also just rescued me and Beau.

And, from the sounds of it, our future together.

"Thank you, Professor Copeman," I say, although I'm certain she can't hear me.

Jodie begins walking back into the house. "I've got to get Chad to practice, but before I let you go," she says, propping her phone up on the kitchen counter again, "I'm glad Ma mentioned that she and Dr. Runyon were Trapped for a hundred and nineteen iterations. Do you have any idea what number you're on? I've heard it's easy to lose track. Hell, Dr. Runyon even wrote that many people she interviewed didn't have a clue what iteration they escaped on. But even a rough idea?"

"I'm not sure what an iteration is."

Jodie wipes down her cutting board. "I keep forgetting you still need to finish the book. So iterations are the number of days, so to speak, that you've been Trapped. The number of cycles you've been through the same day."

"Oh," I say. "In that case, yeah, I've counted every one. I'm at Day 348."

She freezes. "348?"

I nod.

She sighs in thought, hand landing on her hip. "Okay . . ."

I feel the heat rising in my face and neck. "Why, is that bad?"

"No."

"Because you reacted as if that were bad."

"Mom, we're going to be late!" I hear a boy shout from another room.

"I know, hold on!" Jodie leans closer toward the phone. "What I'm going to tell you may sound dire, Clark, but I don't want you to panic. All right?"

Now the heat is *really* rising in my face and neck. "I feel like that's what people say when someone should start panicking."

"Runyon theorized that . . ." She pauses, thinking. "Well, I guess there's no easy way to say this. You may only have three hundred and sixty-five iterations to escape, love."

"Well . . . what happens if I don't?"

She purses her lips. "Runyon was never quite sure."

I climb back onto the bench as a pit in my stomach grows. "What do you mean?"

"Of the hundreds of people she interviewed, Runyon never found someone who'd been Trapped past three hundred and sixty-five iterations. But statistically speaking? She should have." Jodie shrugs. "Three hundred and sixty-four iterations? A woman in Lisbon made it out. Three hundred and sixty-five? A guy in Sacramento got to July 6, 1999, just fine. But three hundred and sixty-six?" Runyon shakes her head. "All of them—every interviewee—escaped on or before three hundred and sixty-five. You understand what I'm trying to say, right, Clark?"

I can feel my heartbeat hammering against my rib cage. "So, if I don't escape in three hundred and sixty-five iterations, I'll . . . die?"

"No! *No*," Jodie says emphatically. She pauses. "Well . . ."

I stand as a rush of nerves flood my body. "But that means I only have a handful of todays left to escape."

"Runyon could have been wrong," Jodie attempts to assure me. "She emphasized in the book that she's not sure *what* happens exactly, and much more research is needed. Do people die? Do they float away into the abyss? Do they just . . . *disappear?*"

"This," I say, hardly able to breath, "is not helping."

"My point is—"

"Mom! Let's go!"

"Hold your horses!" Jodie bellows over her shoulder before looking directly into the camera. "My point is, Clark, no one knows for sure. And you still have time to figure it out. Maybe not much. But you can do it."

She smiles.

But I don't find it helpful.

"Mom!"

"I really have to go," she says. "Good luck, Clark."

Before I can respond, Jodie disappears.

I pocket my phone and collapse back down onto the bench.

I'm in Day 348. My 348th iteration.

That means, if Dr. Runyon is correct, I have just seventeen more todays to figure out when and where I was supposed to meet Beau on September 18—and then convince him that I hold his fate in my hands.

CHAPTER 22

SEVENTEEN ITERATIONS. THAT'S IT.

That's all I have left.

I'm no Mr. Zebb, but I did figure out that, with each of my Trapped days lasting just sixteen hours and one minute, that means I only have about 272 hours to escape. That may sound like a lot of time, but figuring out how to convince Beau that some soulmate theory he believes to be true is, in fact, *garbage*, and that he needs me just as much as I need him to get to tomorrow will not be an easy feat.

I blast into the apartment after booking it back from the university, doused in a thick layer of salty sweat and existential dread.

"*Whoa!*" Mom bellows as I fly through the family room like a tornado. "I ordered pizza for us, and it'll be here in about—"

"Be right back!" I yell, racing into my bedroom and swinging the door shut.

"I'm telling you," I hear Blair say through the paper-thin drywall. "He's losing it, Mom."

I lean my back against the door and close my eyes, trying (and failing) to slow the avalanche of anxious thoughts racing through my brain. Copeman and Jodie gave me critical information about Dr. Runyon's theory, but there's still a lot I don't know about how me and Beau fit into it.

So what *do* I know for sure?

I was at The Wrinkles concert last night at Lakeview Live. So were Beau, Dee, and Sadie's neighborhood friends. I didn't see Beau, but, according to him, he saw me.

If Dr. Runyon's theory is correct, I made a mistake sometime before or at 11:16 p.m.—the time according to fate I was supposed to meet Beau. The time neither of us can get past on September 19.

But where was I at exactly 11:16 p.m.? I think back to yesterday's timeline, but it's difficult to know for sure. And who's to say where I was is where I should have been if I'd caused fate to make a mistake at some point on Sunday?

I open my phone and start tapping through any and all evidence I have from last night that has a time stamp and could point me in the right direction. I didn't text anyone during the concert, except for a few intoxicated, heart-emoji-filled variations of "miss you" to Sadie at 9:47 p.m. and 10:02 p.m. That's not helpful.

I go into my email inbox and find my concert ticket. If they were on time, The Wrinkles went onstage at about 9:30 p.m. I went to get fresh air outside the venue with a few songs left. So, estimating that The Wrinkles played for about an hour or so in total, I was probably outside Lakeview Live from around 10:15 p.m. to 10:30 p.m., when Truman and the rest of the group joined me. They crossed the street and made their way toward The Honeycomb tunnel, but I ordered a car home instead. So, if that all checks out—and it's kind of a big if—I was drunk in a back seat on my way back to the suburbs at the time I was supposed to meet Beau.

It's no use. I need him to fit the final puzzle pieces together. And I'm willing to do just about anything to do it.

I dash out to the family room with a wild (if not completely unhinged) idea, inspired by Mom.

"How do you file a missing person's report?" I ask her.

She's getting our pizza at the front door.

"What?" she breathes, face scrunched. "Who's missing?" She swings the door closed.

"One of my friends at school."

"One of your friends at school is missing," Mom repeats my words to herself, confused, as she heads to the dining room with our pizzas. "What are you talking about, Clark?"

"That's impossible," Blair shouts from her bedroom. "You don't have any friends at school, so how could you have a friend who's gone miss—"

"Hey!" Mom yells toward the hallway.

"*Jeez*, I'm just kidding," Blair follows up. "Also, what are you baking for my party tomorrow, Clark?"

Mom sets the pizza boxes down and turns to me, skin glistening with sweat. "Talk to me. What's going on?"

"I told you: one of my friends is missing. His name is Beau."

"Have I met him?"

"No."

"How long has Beau been missing?"

"A couple hours."

Mom gives me her *you can't be serious* look.

"Or maybe it's been a few days, I don't know!" I follow up quickly, before I lose her. "All I *do* know is that he's gone and no one can find him. Do missing persons reports get broadcast everywhere? Like, all over Chicago?"

"Blair, come eat!" Mom yells, moseying around the kitchen.

"What toppings did you get me?" Blair asks.

"Pepperoni-sausage."

"Do you really not care that one of my friends is *missing*?" I ask, following her as she preps for dinner. "He could be anywhere with anyone right now."

"I don't know what's gotten into you today, but—" She freezes, paper plates in hand, before turning to me. "I thought you were sick and didn't even go to school. Where did you just come home from?"

"I felt better, so I went to therapy."

"But if you went to therapy"—she glances at the clock above the sink—"you're home too early. Are you lying?"

"No."

"*Clark.*"

"It doesn't matter right now."

"It absolutely does matter right now," Mom says as a look of disappointment creeps into her face. "I thought you were liking your sessions with Ms. Hazel? At least more than you were liking Dr. Oregon and Mr. Rample—"

"I didn't skip; we just ended early."

"That doesn't make sense, Clark, you don't just *end* therapy early because you—"

"Forget it." I march back into my bedroom and slam the door closed.

Well, that couldn't have gone worse.

I don't have time to wait for another chance encounter with Beau at the cinemas, bakery, or ballroom again. Who knows how long he'll hold out hoping to avoid me? I'd probably have better luck standing outside the John Hancock building and screaming his name than setting up shop at Ben's.

Maybe I could try tracking down his grandparents? There can't be too many old people with the last name Dupont in West

Edgemont, after all. But a few minutes and several fruitless searches later, I remember that his grandparents are his *mom's* parents, so their last name could be anything (and likely not Dupont).

Could I find someone to help me hack into Lakeview Live's website? I think I had to put in my contact information when I bought a ticket for The Wrinkles show, which means Beau likely had to do the same. But what are the chances I could find someone with not only the IT know-how but the criminal mindset to help me pull off such a feat in a single iteration? Slim to none, probably.

Maybe I could hijack an evening news report and plead for Beau to meet me at one of our errand locations? (Okay, that's an even more irrational idea than filing a missing person's report.)

I drop onto my mattress and continue mining my brain for any and all clues Beau may have mentioned in the limited time we've spent together.

There's a reason he came to Mr. Zebb's class in Day 310. Although I really can't imagine why Beau would think mocking a teacher and jumping from desk to desk could help him win back an alleged soul mate, I'm sure his ex had something to do with his being there.

Oh. Wait a minute.

I feel stupid for just now realizing that there's a chance Beau's soul mate goes to Rosedore. Is that why he was there in Day 310? I've asked dozens of Rosedore students about Beau before without any luck, but . . . I haven't asked everyone in Mr. Zebb's class yet.

So that's it. I know what my next best option is.

I'm buzzing like an anxious bumblebee in Day 349. Instead of waiting until trig for answers, I decide to seek them out on my own, since time is now at a premium. I track down as many kids in that class as I can before last period.

"Beau *who*?" Sara Marino says, popping her bubble gum in my face before second period.

"Dupont," I repeat, heart pounding. "Does the name mean anything to you?"

"Nah," she says, slamming her locker shut. "Sounds like a French tennis player or some shit."

Amanda Hyde is somehow even less help, explaining to me with all the certainty in the world that "Beau Dupont is that one gross sophomore who won the hot wings–eating contest" during last year's homecoming pep rally. I don't get an answer out of Justine Garcia, who shrugs and tells me that I need to get a life. And Greg Shumaker, of course, finds a way to inject some douchebaggery into our interaction when I approach him after lunch. "Why do you ask, Clark?" he says with a smirk, chocolate milk stains all down his shirt. "You trying to get some D? I support that."

By the time last period rolls around, I've made exactly zero progress toward finding anyone who can tell me a single useful thing about Beau. So I'm going to have to do it.

The bell rings. Thom flies into the room and crashes into his desk chair as usual. "Do you think Mr. Zebb noticed?" he whispers breathlessly.

I shake my head. "You're fine."

"Thank God," Thom says. "I hate trig, but one more tardy and I'm screwed."

"Who hated the homework?" Mr. Zebb asks, dropping down onto his tiny stool. "Don't be ashamed to speak up. I know cosines aren't for everyone."

I raise my hand. "Mr. Zebb?"

He turns my way—along with the rest of the class.

"Yes, Clark?" Mr. Zebb asks.

I clear my throat. "Can I make a quick announcement?"

Mr. Zebb looks just as surprised as everyone else to hear *me* request such a thing.

"It'll be short," I assure him.

"Uh . . ." Mr. Zebb opens and closes his mouth. "Sure."

One perk of being the quiet guy in class is that, when you finally *do* have something to say, people seem especially willing to listen.

I stand, walk down my aisle of desks, and turn to face everyone. It's a view the old me would have absolutely detested: rows of blank faces staring into my soul, waiting for the silence to be filled. Even in a time loop—where no one will remember this when I wake up in the next iteration—it's a bit unnerving. But I've broken out of my comfort zone enough times since Day 310 to know that I got this.

I inhale. "Does anyone know who Beau Dupont is?"

The room stays still.

After an agonizing few seconds of silence, Greg Shumaker cuts in. "Dude," he says, smirking in the first row. "Why are you so obsessed with this guy?"

"Clark's been asking everyone about him all day long," Sara Marino explains to a confused Mr. Zebb. She looks back at me. "It's getting weird as hell, Clark."

Several people laugh.

"I know, it's strange, and I hope it'll make sense to all of you at some point," I say with a smile, attempting to normalize a very abnormal situation. "But I need to find Beau. ASAP."

"Is he a Rosedore student?" Mr. Zebb asks.

"No," Justine Garcia answers for me, "which makes it even weirder that you're freaking out, Clark."

"Really?" I say, scanning faces to find someone who looks anything other than amused or bored to death. "No one knows Beau?"

This can't be right. Someone in here *has* to know more than they're letting on.

Why would Beau come in here on Day 310?

"What's this actually about, Clark?" Mr. Zebb asks.

I start to turn red.

"Sounds like someone has a crush," Amanda Hyde adds. "*Real* bad."

More people laugh and I'm starting to wish the ground would swallow me up.

Then Thom stands in the back. "Can I talk with Clark in the hall really quick, Mr. Zebb?" he asks. "I might be able to help him."

The class simmers with whispers and my heart leaps.

Mr. Zebb contemplates. "All right. Do what you need to do. But be fast."

Thom nods. So do I.

"I mean it—*fast*," Mr. Zebb says as the two of us leave.

I follow Thom out of the room. The second the door closes behind us, he turns to me, his typically pasty complexion now fire-engine red.

"What are you doing?" he asks, glancing up and down the hallway for anyone looking.

"What do you mean?" I ask.

He steps forward, closing the gap between us, and lowers his voice to a near-whisper. "Are you messing with me?"

I open and close my mouth, completely disoriented by Thom's defensiveness. "I'm just trying to find Beau. Do you know him?"

Thom stares, unconvinced. "How'd you figure it out? Did he tell you?"

"Figure what out?" My eyes narrow on his. "What would Beau tell me?"

"You promise this isn't a joke?"

I glance at Mr. Zebb's door. "Will you please start talking? We don't have much time."

"I'm okay missing the least relevant subject in a teen's life."

Trig. *The least relevant subject in a teenager's life.*

That's how Beau described it too, when he showed up in class in Day 310. . . .

"I just want to make sure this isn't some practical joke," he says.

"It's not, Thom."

"Clark, I—"

"Thom!" I shout.

He jolts.

My hand lands on his shoulder, as I take a moment to quell my frustration. "I'm sorry, but I'm *not* messing with you. This *isn't* a joke. This is an emergency and I need to find Beau. *Right now.* So please"—I squeeze his shoulder softy—"can you tell me what's going on?"

Thom stares at me, unblinking. His eyes glisten over with tears before he successfully fights them back. "Beau is . . ." His voice is so quiet, I can barely hear him speak. "Brittany."

I don't think I heard him correctly. "Beau is . . . Brittany?"

He nods, swallowing hard. I've never seen Thom this nervous.

I don't know if I've ever seen *anyone* this nervous.

"I don't understand what that means," I say.

"Brittany?" he says, eyes widening. "You know? From last night?"

It's as if someone inserts a blurry, old Polaroid into my brain:

Thom, also pretty drunk, is leaning against a streetlamp next to me outside Lakeview Live.

"Wait a minute . . . ," I mutter, scrambling to access the memory. "You were there. You were at The Wrinkles. Were you with Beau?"

He looks confused. "I knew you were drunk, but I didn't know you were *that* drunk—"

"*Brittany!*" I exclaim.

The name bounces between the lockers, echoing down the empty hallway as it finally registers in my brain.

"Shh!" Thom urges, looking left to right. "Shut up!"

"Brittany is your girlfriend," I recall, lowering my voice.

I'd been alone outside the venue when I went to get fresh air— until Thom stumbled over and joined me for a minute. Or two. *Five?* I can't be sure.

I'd completely forgotten, and it's no wonder why. I see Thom in every today, but he's never referenced Brittany or our conversation in September 19, which probably made the memory fade away faster. Why would he never bring it up?

"You two got into a fight, right?" I ask. Now that the image is there, the conversation starts to come back a little, too.

"Yes, Brittany *was* my girlfriend, and yes, we got into a fight, but I think you've missed the point." Thom's face is now whatever shade of red is redder than a fire engine. "Brittany doesn't exist, Clark. *Beau* is Brittany."

My stomach twists in a hundred knots.

I think I might be sick.

"*You're* Beau's ex-boyfriend?" I say. "*You're* the soul mate?"

His neck yanks his head away in surprise. "I'm definitely not Beau's soul mate."

Overwhelmed, I backtrack. "So, the story you told me about you and your nonexistent girlfriend Brittany not being a good match for each other, it was actually a story about you and . . . Beau?"

He nods.

I wait to speak until an underclassman walking by is safely out of earshot.

I look into his eyes. "I didn't know you liked guys, Thom," I say quietly.

"No one does, except Beau," he says. "And, I mean, now you too. Obviously."

That's why Beau refused to name the boy causing him boy problems; he didn't want to out Thom. And *that's* why Thom freaked out and ran out of the room on Day 310 and acted on Day 311 like he didn't know Beau; he was too deep into the closet to be honest with me.

Thom covers his flushed face with his hands, embarrassed, and a wave of empathy washes away my frustration with having been deceived.

"Hey," I say to him, his hands still cemented against his cheeks. "It's okay."

But he doesn't budge.

I try my hardest to appear calm and smile. "Thom," I repeat, nudging him again.

He peeks out at me between his fingers.

"Don't worry," I say. "Your secret is safe with me."

The classroom door swings open and Mr. Zebb pops his head out. "Finished?"

"Can we have just one more minute?" I ask.

His eyes dart back and forth between the two of us, suspicious, but when he sees Thom's expression they soften. "Just one, okay?"

He disappears, closing the door behind him.

Thom's hands fall to his side. He stands there awkwardly, rocking back and forth, before finding his voice again. "I didn't have a clue you knew Beau. He's never mentioned you before."

"We're not . . . we're just . . . we're new friends."

"Where did you two meet?"

I sigh, thinking about how deranged I'd sound attempting to provide an answer. "I'll tell you someday, but now I have to find him."

"He's missing?" Thom asks. "Is he in danger?"

"He could be," I say. "Have you heard from him today?"

"No."

"Can you call him?"

Thom pulls out his phone, taps the screen a few times, and holds it up to his ear. "It's not ringing," he says. "His phone must be off or dead. That's not like him."

I'm used to Beau avoiding me at this point. But now he's avoiding his supposed soul mate, too?

"I just sent you his number," Thom says.

"Can you text me his grandparents' address?" I say.

He looks at me suspiciously. "Randy and Paula?"

"Sure, yeah," I say.

He stares, increasingly worried, before messaging me that as well. "Seriously, what's going on with Beau?"

I hesitate. "He's missing . . . . sort of."

"He's *sort* of missing?"

Thom asks a follow-up question, but I'm preoccupied with calling Beau from my own phone. It doesn't ring for me either. I hang up and look back at Thom. "I need you to answer some questions as truthfully and accurately as you can about last night, okay?"

He nods.

"What else did we talk about outside the venue?" I ask.

He inhales, staring off in thought. "Well, you complained about your mom. A *lot*."

"I did?"

He lets out a little laugh. "As much as me and Beau butted heads at the concert, it sounded like it was nothing compared to the fight you and your mom got into. You really don't remember telling me about it?"

Yesterday.

The day Mom told me that *she* was the one who'd wanted the divorce. It makes sense that I was carrying that rage at The Wrinkles'. But that doesn't feel super relevant right now.

I shake my head. "Anything else?"

"I assume you remember how our conversation ended, at least." Thom waits for me to confirm that's the case.

I shake my head.

"You don't remember . . . anything? At all?"

"No."

He clears his throat and diverts his eyes. "This is awkward, now that *you* know that Brittany is actually Beau, and now that *I* know you two are actually friends, but . . ." He cringes. "You convinced me to break up with him."

What? "No."

"Uh, yeah. You definitely did."

I bend over, my palms pressed into my knees, and stare at the floor in shock.

"You were pretty riled up about your parents' divorce," he continues, "going on and on about your mom, and how true love doesn't exist, and how it's nothing like Hollywood makes it out to be."

Oh my God.

"And when you heard how irritated I was with Brittany"—he puts air quotes around her name—"you encouraged me to do it. You said I should dump him—or *her*, or whatever. So I did it last night."

I sink lower into a squat position.

In case I pass out, at least the fall to the floor will be shorter.

I'm the reason Beau got dumped.

I guess *I'm* actually the boy who caused his boy problems.

Suddenly, Thom looks mortified. "Do you think that's why he went missing? Because he's upset about you, me, and the breakup?"

"No, not exactly, but—wait." I stand back up straight. "Did you tell him I encouraged you to dump him?"

Thom grimaces.

Fuck.

"I didn't use your name!" He defends himself. "I said that I had a good talk with a guy from school about our relationship. But I'm sure he's figured it out, seeing as he saw us together outside the venue."

"He saw me?"

Thom's eyebrows arch in thought. "Probably. Because he walked out of Lakeview Live right by us with this new girl he met, so he must have seen us talking—"

"New girl?"

He inhales, clearly stressed by incessant questioning. "I didn't catch her name."

"What did she look like?"

Thom thinks some more. "I don't know . . . She was short and cute. It looked like she'd been crying. I liked her dreads."

Dee.

"I'm sorry I told Beau about our conversation, Clark, but I didn't know that you two knew each other." He looks on the verge of tears. "Please don't be mad at me."

I rub his shoulder. "It's not your fault." It's *mine*. "Did Beau and his new friend try to come over and talk to us?" I ask.

Maybe *that* was the moment me and Beau were destined to cross paths.

But no, that can't be right. It couldn't have been 11:16 p.m. yet.

"I don't think so," Thom says. "The show just ended and the sidewalk was getting crowded, so I told you goodbye and left with Beau."

"What about Dee?"

"Dee?"

"The girl he was with."

He shakes his head slowly, trying to place himself outside the venue again. "I think she gave Beau her number and then just . . . walked off, or something? But yeah"—he starts nodding instead—"now I remember her face up close. She'd *definitely* been crying."

My heart melts.

What happened to Dee yesterday?

What is her embarrassing secret?

"Beau and I took a walk into the city and I ended it," he says. "It was tough, but I owe you a thanks."

"Why?"

"We weren't a good fit—at *all*—and you helped me see that. Beau is a great guy, he's just a bit . . ." He squints, trying to find the right words. "Too much?"

I cock my head. "How so?"

Thom glances down the hallway to make sure we're still alone. "I'm still in the closet, which is not a great place to have a boyfriend who's so *out there*. You know?"

"Not really. You mean like, he's bold?"

"It's more than that," he explains. "Beau is a big personality. He grabs the attention of every room he's in; just says whatever comes to his mind. He's so impetuous, too. Like, he'll drop everything and race go-karts all afternoon or spend a Saturday blowing his paycheck at an arcade without a second thought. He's all over the place."

"I mean, I don't know," I say, trying to be understanding while also being honest. "Go-karts and arcades sound . . . sort of great?"

"Sure," he says, "but when you're in my position, when you're not out, you need someone more subtle. More chill vibes, less impulsivity—impul*stupidity*."

My stomach twists. "He told you about that?"

"His family's word to describe his dumb, rash decision-making?" He smirks. "Yeah. He hates it, but if the shoes fits . . ."

Whatever empathy I had for Thom washes away, replaced with anger simmering in the pit of my stomach. "I can't say that I agree with that—"

"The worst part was," Thom barrels on, "he'd get even *more* unhinged whenever we'd fight. He'd make these over-the-top gestures to try to impress me, or make amends, or whatever. It never worked, obviously."

"You mean over-the-top, like, he'd jump around on desks in order to bring some fun to the most boring, least relevant class in a teenager's life?"

Thom stares. "Huh?"

"Never mind." I take a deep breath, trying to refocus. "I get that you two just broke up, but maybe now isn't the best time to shit-talk Beau."

"You're right." I can tell he's embarrassed. His smirk fades.

"So after you two left Dee, went for a walk, and broke up, what happened next?"

"Nothing."

"Nothing?"

"Yeah. I went home. And I assume Beau went to his grandparents'."

"What time did that happen?"

Thom puffs his cheeks out, thinking. "Probably like eleven thirty-ish, maybe?"

Where was I supposed to meet Beau at 11:16 p.m., then?

I pace back and forth for a minute, racking my brain.

"Mr. Zebb is going to be pissed," Thom mutters, glancing toward the classroom door, "if he even remembers we're out here at this point."

I pause my pacing in front of him. "This question is going to sound strange, but . . . you can't think of any reason why I would have run into Beau last night, but for whatever reason, never did. Can you?"

He stares at the floor in thought. "I mean, you did run into him, though. He saw us outside the venue together."

"Yeah, but we didn't talk. I didn't see him," I say. "Had you planned on last night being your coming out? Had you wanted to introduce Beau to kids from school or anything like that?"

He lets out a laugh. "The exact opposite. I was terrified, knowing other groups from Rosedore were going to be there. When Truman texted and invited me to The Honeycomb I—"

"Truman?" I cut in. "I went to the concert with Truman."

The Honeycomb.

I jump into the air. Thom jolts backward.

"You two were planning on going to The Honeycomb?" I confirm.

"Yeah, to meet up with Truman, Cynthia, and Ron—and, apparently, you too," he says. "But we never went, obviously. Truman said they had to take the long route there to avoid security—the park is technically closed that late—and I was tired. Plus, I had some breaking up to do."

"What time were you planning to get there?"

"Let's see what I texted Truman . . ." He pulls out his phone and taps into his messages before reading aloud: "'Cool, I'll see you there about eleven, eleven fifteen. Heads up that I'm bringing a friend from West Edgemont.'" He looks up at me. "What does any of this have to do with finding Beau?"

I put my hands on the back of my head and exhale. "Pretty much everything."

I was supposed to meet Beau under The Honeycomb at 11:16 p.m. But I allowed my anger with Mom to bleed over into my conversation with Thom, resulting in their breakup and me taking a ride home. I'm the one who derailed the universe's plans for us.

I'm the one who caused fate to make a mistake.

And now I have to fix it.

"Thom," I say, staring into his eyes as I start to drift off down the hallway. "If there's a part of you that somehow remembers any of this tomorrow, please come out to me, okay? I'll be there for you."

He stares back as if I've officially lost it. "Where are you going?"

I turn and sprint away.

CHAPTER 23

NO WONDER BEAU'S BEEN AVOIDING ME. NO WONder he refuses to be found. He thinks I'm the one responsible for this whole mess, and he's right in believing so—just for the wrong reason.

I know that the school will have gotten ahold of Mom in the next few minutes to explain that I basically harassed my class about a kid named Beau and then disappeared out the door. So the last place I want to be is at her apartment, trying to explain away what the heck just happened.

Instead, I sprint away from the school as fast and as far as my legs can carry me, until I collapse into the shade of a willow tree near downtown Rosedore, where hopefully no one will be looking for me. There, I can finally let Thom's revelations sink in.

I may have caused the breakup, but he's Trapped because we never met at The Honeycomb; not because my actions tore his soul mate away. In fact, after talking with Thom, I'm more convinced than ever that their relationship was destined to be a dumpster fire from the start. Thom needs someone subtle? He wants less spontaneity? I can't imagine a less suitable boyfriend for him than Beau.

But it doesn't matter if my thinking they're a bad match was correct. I didn't encourage Thom to dump *Brittany* because I was being honest; I encouraged him to call it off because Mom's divorce soured my thoughts on relationships and I was pissed at her. And now that me and Beau are both Trapped in Day 349, I have sixteen iterations left to save us from . . . whatever comes after Day 365.

I stand, wipe the wetness from my eyes, and think through my options as I work to steady my breath. I can't waste another iteration in this hellhole of a time loop shedding tears and wishing I had been better.

I can be better now.

If Dr. Runyon is right, the only way I'll be able to escape today is to get us both to The Honeycomb at 11:16 p.m. To do that, I have to convince Beau that I'm not the person he witnessed encouraging his boyfriend to dump him on Sunday night, tossing his life into a time-warping blender. Not the *real* me, at least. I messed up, sure, but I can save us.

I try calling Beau again. Still no answer.

I shoot him a text, too, but I don't expect a response.

I order a rideshare and take it to the address Thom gave me for Beau's grandparents on the off chance he's home. The car pulls up next to a tiny, one-story brick house with a sprinkler drowning its brown front yard. An American flag that feels way too big for a house this size is billowing on the front porch. I hop out of the car, climb the steps, and knock on the door.

A few seconds later, Beau's grandpa appears.

"Randy?" I say, feeling awkward referring to an old man by his first name.

He opens the screen door. "Who's asking?"

Randy's got a glistening bald head, jeans belted halfway up his stomach, and nose hair so unkempt that they look like the front lines of the White Walker army.

"Is Beau around?" I say.

"No." He moves to close the door.

My hand stops it from slamming in my face. "Do you know where he is?"

"In class." He hisses, "Where you should be, I suppose."

I can pretty much guarantee Beau's not at school, but I don't tell that to Randy.

"Who are you?" he asks.

"I'm Beau's friend, Clark."

He looks me up and down. "Try back tomorrow."

I wish I could.

Randy starts to close the door again.

But I stop him. Again. "Could I peek in his bedroom, by chance? He borrowed something from me a few days ago and I'd like to get it back." Maybe there's something in there that could help me find him. And, I won't lie, I'm curious to see what Beau's bedroom looks like.

Randy's bushy white brows scrunch together, giving me an answer to my request.

"Can I at least leave you with my phone number in case he—"

This time, I'm not fast enough, and the door slams in my face. No wonder Beau hates living here with grandparents who don't appreciate his true self; grandparents who mock his so-called impul*stupidity, just like his mom had.* I'd want to escape it too.

I sigh, wipe the sweat from my forehead, and make sure to kick over one of Randy's lawn gnomes as I walk off.

I spend the rest of Day 349 avoiding a constant flow of calls from my family and Sadie while wandering around West Edgemont thinking through what I can do with my final fifteen iterations— possibly the last todays I'll ever exist.

And I wake up in Day 350 with a plan.

Now that I know Beau's ex is Thom, it's clear what my strategy needs to be: don't let Thom out of my sight. Beau will surely continue to track him down, just like he did in Mr. Zebb's class. I bet he'll express his love with some off-the-wall antic, just like in Day 310. And when he does, I'll be there to tell him that he's got it all wrong—that it's not Thom he needs to escape today. It's me.

Instead of following my normal schedule at school, I tiptoe around Thom's—waiting outside his classes when no one is around, sitting nearby in the cafeteria with a watchful eye. I even follow him on his walk home after last period, assuming Beau will be paying a visit there at some point in the evening. But he doesn't. He never shows. Beau, as continues to be the case, is nowhere to be found.

He doesn't try to find Thom in Day 351, either. Or Day 352. And each time I drop by his grandparents' house, Randy seems to be even less helpful than the previous today.

Where could Beau be?

And why isn't he still trying to win back the soul mate he believes he needs to escape?

I can't justify following Thom all day a fourth time without a single piece of evidence that Beau has any plans to show up. There's just not enough time to keep trying at a failed strategy.

My next best bet is doing whatever I can to get *Trapped in Today* into Beau's hands—and I'll need a little assistance from Otto, Dee, and Emery to make that happen. I have no idea if Beau will run one of our errands between now and Day 365, but I might as well give it a shot.

I wake up in Day 353 and head straight to the University of Chicago. Kelly is yawning, large coffee in hand, when I bolt into the office.

She jumps. "You scared me—"

"I'm Trapped in today," I say, "and I'll need three copies of Professor Copeman's book."

She blinks for a moment, sunburnt face frozen in indifference. "I need a new job," she mutters, swiveling in her chair to retrieve the books.

With three copies of *Trapped in Today* in hand, I dart off to the campus library, where I snag a computer in a secluded corner. If my plan has a shot at working, I know that Beau needs to understand how we got here and how we can get out. He needs to believe his escaping today has nothing to do with Thom. And he needs to know that our lives—now inextricably linked, for better or worse—are slipping away with every tick of the clock.

I type it all out, explaining the most important points in the clearest way possible: why I'd been so angry at my mom for causing the divorce; how I'd inadvertently channeled that rage into persuading Thom to break up with him; how, if it hadn't been for me, we would have met under The Honeycomb at 11:16 p.m. and our lives would have gone on as intended. Maybe even . . . together.

I print three copies of my letter, each with the same identical message in extra bold, all-caps words across the top:

MEET ME UNDER THE HONEYCOMB TONIGHT.

Who knows if this will work?

But at this point, it's my only hope.

I slip the letters into each copy of *Trapped in Today* and then race to Ben's Everything Blue Bakery first. It's bustling, as usual, when I walk in and sneak up to the register.

"Hi, Otto," I say breathlessly. "I need your help."

A confused Otto wipes his brow. "Have we met?"

"Yes and no."

"It looks like you've cut Betty in line, who needs three butter-scotch cookies for her nieces and nephew. Can this wait a moment?"

"No, it can't," I say. I turn to Betty behind me and mouth *I'm sorry!* before rotating back to Otto. "This has to do with Beau."

Otto freezes. "Beau?"

I nod.

"Is he okay?"

I hesitate. "Possibly. I have to run, but if you happen to see him today, please, *please*, give him this." I hand him a copy of the book. "It's important."

Otto takes it, scanning the cover. "*Trapped in Today?*"

"I don't have time to explain," I say, backing away from the counter. "But Beau needs to read it. Can I trust you'll give it to him?"

Otto looks up from the cover with a bemused expression planted on his face. "Will do—what's your name?"

"Clark."

"Will do, Clark," he says, and goes back to serving Betty. I run off.

Next up is Splendid Cinemas.

I'm standing outside the entrance when Emery finally appears, unsettled by my waiting there. He pulls out his headphones—I briefly hear "Avery," before he hits pause—and clears his throat. "Hey, we don't open for another—"

"I need your help, Emery," I say.

He glances down at the spot where his name tag would normally be, but it isn't on yet. "How'd you know my—"

"You don't know me, but my friend, Beau, might stop in here later today, and he really, *really* needs to get this." I hand him the second copy of *Trapped in Today*, one of my letters tucked inside. "Will you give it to him?"

Emery takes the book, eyes wide. "Um . . . I guess?"

"Thank you," I say, before explaining what Beau looks like. "You're a lifesaver, Emery. And don't give up on your acting—you're going to make it big someday."

His face twists in confusion as I dart off.

I contemplate leaving the final copy of *Trapped in Today* outside the doors of the Aragon Ballroom when I get there but decide it's too risky. So I start pounding on the doors instead, every minute or so yelling Dee's name in hopes that she's wandering around inside within earshot. Finally, after twenty minutes of being a nuisance, I see her silhouette approaching on the other side of the glass.

"We're closed!" she yells, agitated, looking at me like I'm a weirdo.

"Dee, I'm friends with Beau," I say. "He needs your help."

She glances over her shoulder, into the lobby. "What's your name?"

"Clark," I say, taking a step away to seem less hostile. "You don't know who I am, I know, but this is important."

She contemplates giving me the time of day but not before unlocking the door and cracking it just wide enough for the spine of the book to fit through.

"This is *Trapped in Today*," I say, pushing it into her palm. "Beau told me he may stop in later. If he does, will you give this to him?"

She thinks. "Are you a stalker or something?"

"No."

"A serial killer?"

"Definitely no."

She thinks some more. "Okay."

I can tell she's not entirely convinced I'm neither of those things, but Dee hasn't had any reservations putting me in my place in the prior todays that she's deemed me untrustworthy. So I'm confident the book would have already been thrown back in my face if she didn't intend to follow through on my behalf.

"I really, *really* appreciate it, Dee," I say. "Thank you."

She nods, lips curled into a small, brief smile, before the door slams shut. I let out an exhausted sigh and head to my final destination in Day 353.

The Honeycomb.

I'm eager to leave the asphalt and blinding sun behind and take a shaded path into the heart of Lincoln Park. I'm sure it was a noisy, dark trek last night when Truman and the others drunkenly stumbled their way toward The Honeycomb from Lakeview Live, but today it's bright and calm. Birds are chirping, the soft hum of the breeze helps put me at ease, and the sounds of city life slowly fade, blending into comforting white noise.

I glance at the map on my phone and realize that The Honeycomb will come into view as soon as I make one last turn through a patch of trees near the Lincoln Park Zoo. I doubt he'll be there already, happily waiting for me in the tunnel, as if we're in the closing scene of *When Clark Met Beau*. So it's not entirely devastating when I round the corner and see that Beau's nowhere in sight.

I approach The Honeycomb and stand beneath its towering twists and turns. It's obvious how the art installation got its name. Its sandy wooden structure is molded into mesmerizing, oval cells practically straight out of a beehive. Wedding photographers go bananas here, Sadie told me once, and it makes sense: it's a cozy spot, planted in a pristine area of the park, with Chicago's skyline gracing the clouds to the south and an endless Lake Michigan to the east.

It would have been a magical place to meet someone as special as Beau. If I just hadn't gotten in my own way.

I sit crossed-legged in The Honeycomb's tunnel. And then I wait. I have nowhere to be, no responsibilities to see through, except to ensure I can escape September 19 for good with my Loop Partner at my side.

The sky gets darker as the sun falls lower in the sky. Both tourists and locals trickle through—snapping selfies, laughing at one another's jokes, admiring the structure's beauty against a canvas of blues and greens. I hide behind a patch of bushes to avoid a security guard on the prowl after the park has officially closed.

But Beau never comes.

I wait and I wait. I pace and I pace. And as blackness begins to blanket Chicago, the city's artificial lights dotting the horizon, a sinking feeling of defeat begins to settle in.

I open the digital clock app and watch as another today draws to a close.

11:15:31 p.m., 11:15:32 p.m. . . .

What did Beau do today? Did he go on any of our errands?

11:15:44 p.m., 11:15:45 p.m. . . .

What if he did and still chose not to meet me at The Honeycomb?

11:15:52 p.m., 11:15:53 p.m. . . .

What if I've lost him for good?

11:15:59 p.m.—

My white wooden nightstand is staring back at me. Day 354.

I sigh, flip over in bed, and prepare to repeat my strategy for a second time.

I go to the university, get my copies of *Trapped in Today*, and print out my three letters. I drop off the books at our errand spots before heading to The Honeycomb to wait for Beau. The sun rises and falls. Excited tourists and locals scoot through. I hide from the same security guard. And as I watch the clock tick closer to 11:16 p.m., it's confirmed that I've lost another iteration and have nothing to show for it.

In Day 355, I do it all over again.

Beau doesn't come.

Has something happened to him? Is he still avoiding our errands solely to avoid me—the only person who can help him escape?

Day 356. Day 357.

Lather, rinse, repeat.

After I drop off the books in Day 359, my desperation leads me to go door to door in his grandparents' neighborhood, hoping someone, *anyone*, can point me in a helpful direction. No one can.

Since I memorized his number after Thom sent it to me, I've been calling and texting Beau in every today, too. But I take it even further in Day 361. I recruit any stranger on the street willing to help me call Beau, hoping he'll pick up an unknown number. That plan fails too.

My panic reaches new heights in Day 363. Inspired by Beau's trip to Rosedore in Day 310, I sneak into West Edgemont High as a pretend transfer student to see if his classmates have seen him around. I'm hardly there for ten minutes before a suspicious custodian starts berating me with questions and I book it before they can throw me out.

My loneliness shifts from bad to worse—and then to downright unbearable.

And still, nothing.

No Beau.

It's a powerless thing to experience, knowing my life is slipping away like loose sand between my fingertips, as the rest of the world ticks away, business as usual.

Despite my best efforts, I know my chances of escaping today are next to nothing at this point. Whether or not Beau shows up under The Honeycomb is out of my control. One thing I *can* find hope in, though? Ms. Hazel's homework assignment. I don't know if it's possible to defeat loneliness in a time loop. But I did it in at least one of my todays: Day 310. And it was listening to Ms. Hazel's advice that allowed it to happen.

The time loop may take me out all alone, but I refuse to go out lonely.

In Day 364, I decide to go to therapy after dropping off the books and letters at our errand locations.

"Clark," Ms. Hazel says, setting a mug onto the coffee table and checking the time. She pops up to her feet, surprised to see me. "I wasn't sure if you'd make it."

"Why not?" I say, walking in. "We have a session today, don't we?"

"Yes, but your mother called just a bit ago wondering if I'd heard from you. She said you were home sick today and that she's had trouble reaching you."

"Oh."

"You should call her right away," Ms. Hazel urges, concerned. "She's worried."

"I just talked with her," I lie. "I told her my food poisoning cleared up."

"You did?"

"Yes."

She eyes me suspiciously.

I stare back.

"Okay," she says, gesturing to my chair. "Have a seat."

I do. "I'd like to cut right to the chase—past all the *how was your day* bullshit—if you don't mind."

Ms. Hazel's eyes grow wide, taken aback by my straightforwardness. (I was never quite *this* blunt, prior to September 19.) "Well, all right, then, Clark. Go right ahead."

I breathe. "I'm lonely, Ms. Hazel."

She grins sympathetically, snagging a caramel out of the candy dish. "I'm proud of you for telling me."

"Thank you." I fold my arms against my chest. "I remember you mentioning a while ago that you have four tips to beating loneliness?"

Ms. Hazel pauses. "Did I?"

"Yes, but I can't remember all four tips," I fib, finding a way into the topic.

She ponders. "That's odd."

"Why?"

"I don't recall us discussing my four tips, is all," she says, crossing her legs. "But clearly, my memory is failing me. Yes, Clark, I have a four-part homework challenge that I often ask patients to try in their attempts to feel more connected. I've found it can be a great benefit to those who take it seriously." She smiles. "Would you like to give it a go?"

I nod, smiling in return. "Yes."

Ms. Hazel stands, heads to her desk, and starts shuffling through odds and ends until she finds the notepad and pen she was looking for. "Now, this four-part challenge may seem like a lot to take on at once—especially for someone like yourself, who has said they're a bit on the shyer side. That's perfectly fine." She starts writing. "You can take your time. It's much more important to give these a shot than to do them quickly or perfectly. It's the long-term *effort* that counts, is what I'm getting at, Clark—it's the *effort* itself that will reap the benefits." She rips the paper from the notepad and returns to my side of the room, extending her arm so I can see.

I take the notepad paper and glance down, recalling each numbered point as I read them:

Clark's 4 tips to beating loneliness:
Try to make a new friend.
Help someone who could use it.
Be vulnerable so others can be too.
Do the thing that scares you.

"Hm," I mutter, mulling them over and pretending they're new to me.

It's not like my attempts to cross off tips two, three, and four were complete failures. I helped Otto with the bakery's afternoon rush, I tried being vulnerable with Dee even though I never did learn her secret, and I agreed to take acting classes with Emery, even if it terrifies me.

But still.

The tips don't seem . . . complete.

"I can see your wheels spinning," Ms. Hazel says to me, standing by my side with a grin. "What's going on in that head of yours, Clark?"

"I have three people in mind to try these out on," I explain. "But I have to figure out the best way to do it."

"The best way?"

"Yeah," I say. "I know it's the effort that matters most. But I still want to help someone—*truly* help them—and be vulnerable in a way that's infectious, and dig deep enough to find the thing that actually scares me most." I shrug. "You know?"

Ms. Hazel is beaming. "Well, first of all, Clark, the fact you've even brought this up shows me how much you've grown since we first met." She smiles. "Would you like a piece of advice?"

I nod. "Please."

"I present the homework as four separate parts because I've found that it's easier for many patients to put them into practice that way," she says. "But for you, it might be beneficial to think about the tips as a whole—not individual boxes to check off." She bends closer to the notes. "You see, oftentimes it's a very scary thing to be vulnerable"—her finger moves between tips three and four—"but when we are, our openness helps others in profound ways"—it glides up to number two—"and that may very well lead to a beautiful friendship."

It lands on number one.

"They're all interconnected, Clark," Ms. Hazel concludes. "And when we keep them all in mind, we have the best shot at defeating our loneliness—and helping others defeat theirs, too."

I look back at the notes and think for a moment as ideas begin to surface.

"I think it's clicking, Ms. Hazel," I say, standing.

I head to the door.

"Where are you going?" Ms. Hazel asks, standing as well. "Our session just started."

"I need to run a few errands," I explain. "If I don't see you again, though, thank you, Ms. Hazel." I smile.

"Why wouldn't I see you again?" The lines on her forehead deepen with concern. "Clark, you're scaring me."

"I'm going to be fine." I smile wider to assure her that I'm telling the truth. "You've been my favorite therapist, Ms. Hazel. By far. And I've loved our sessions."

I swing the door open and dash away before she can stop me.

CHAPTER 24

I TAKE A LONGER ROUTE THROUGH ROSEDORE AFTER leaving my session with Ms. Hazel, hoping the fresh air will help me think through how I can best make my last attempt at her list count. Even though I've never been overly fond of this place, I feel surprisingly sentimental taking in my hometown for what may be the last time. When I pass through the city park, I'm reminded of the person whose voice I'd be absolutely thrilled to hear right now.

"Hey," Sadie says, answering my FaceTime. She's twirling spaghetti on a fork, sitting at the counter in her family's new kitchen. It's quickly apparent that she's not as cheery as she usually is, though. "Where the hell are you?"

"I love you." I get it out without wasting another second.

"Is everything all right?"

"What do you mean?"

She gives me a *you should know what I mean* look. "Your mom and dad called a bit ago wondering if I've heard from you. They said you were out sick from school but that you're not at home and won't call them back. And now you're calling to tell me that you love me?" She sets down the fork. "Something's up."

Sadie's graying, bespectacled dad appears in the corner of the frame. "Hi, Clark."

"Hi, Mr. Green," I say with a nod. "How's Austin?"

"Too hot. How's Chicago?"

"Also too hot."

"Terrific," he says, raising a glass of red wine to his lips. "What's this I hear about your mom and dad not being able to get ahold of you?"

Sadie stands and begins migrating somewhere more private, bowl of pasta in hand. "Can you please stop eavesdropping, Dad?"

"Call your parents, Clark!" Mr. Green calls out in the distance. "Or I will!"

"Okay, Mr. Green."

The screen blurs as Sadie climbs a staircase and hides away in her bedroom before shutting the door. "My dad's annoying, but he's got a point," she says, falling onto her orange comforter and pillows. "You need to call your parents."

"I know."

"Like, yesterday."

"I know, I will."

"But also," she says, twirling more spaghetti. "You flaked on our FaceTime date before school, which rarely happens, and then didn't text me back all day, which *never* happens."

Sadie's clearly upset, and she's got a right to be. This seems like one of the rare moments where *I* need to be the one who's there for *her* and not the other way—

I need you.

Sadie's text from Day 310 lights up in my memory and my stomach churns with guilt. I've been so consumed with finding Beau, running errands, and attempting to escape today that I'd forgotten about it. I open my mouth to ask how she's been doing, but Sadie speaks up first.

"Really, though, where are you?" she asks. She lowers her voice.

"I get scared when you start dropping earnest *I love you*s, Clark."

I raise my phone high above my head so she can see where I'm at.

"Look familiar?" I say.

She squints at her screen for a few seconds before realizing. Her lips curl up into a small smile. "The swings in the Rosedore City Park."

"Where we became friends in middle school."

"And where we promised to have amazing senior years—"

"—even if we couldn't spend them together."

We stare at the rectangles in our hands, wishing more than anything the real versions of ourselves were face-to-face instead.

"I'm sorry I've been so out of it today," I begin. "It's been *such* a Monday, to put it mildly, and I . . . Sadie?"

Her eyes are filled with tears.

"Wait, wait, stop," I say, immediately feeling guilty. "Don't cry! I'm sorry, I didn't mean to go MIA and flake on your texts—"

"It's not that," she says. "I mean, that's *part* of it. But now, seeing you by the swings, *our* swings . . ." She trails off. "I don't have a bunch of new friends down here, Clark. I don't have any."

I adjust my earbuds to make sure I heard her correctly. "You haven't made new friends in Texas?"

"No," she says, dabbing at her eyes.

"But . . ." I stare at the phone, confused. "You're always talking about all these new people in your life."

"Yeah. It's called faking it."

"But . . . " I repeat again, trying to process this revelation. "What about the girls in the Podcast Club? Or that guy you like in your first period? The one girl with a pet ferret who tried out for the football team—"

"I've been exaggerating." She swallows hard. "They're all real people I'm *friendly* with, but they're hardly my *friends*." She drops her voice yet again to barely above a whisper. "I haven't been invited to a single thing outside of school by a single person. Not by the Podcast Club, not Chris in first period, not Sydney with the ferret." She sniffles. "I'm not Ms. Outgoing down here, Clark. I'm Ms. Invisible."

This is why Sadie needed me in Day 310. Something about the ripple effects of my deviations that today must have caused her to reach out to me for help. And I didn't text back.

But it's not just Day 310. She's needed me in every September 19, regardless of if she sent a text or not.

And to think, I've spent every today in this time loop so consumed by my *own* loneliness, it blinded me from spotting it in my very best friend.

"Why didn't you tell me about this?" I ask, rattled with guilt. "You know you could have told me the truth, Sadie."

She shrugs. "I know I should have. I've been doing the same thing to my parents, too. It's just, I know how you all see me. Like I'm this fun-loving, happy-go-lucky girl who can take any curveball that's thrown at me in stride."

"Moving across the country the summer before our senior year is a *massive* curveball, though," I say.

One of her tears makes it all the way to her chin. "It's been hard to find my people here, Clark. *So* hard. You don't know the FOMO I had last night knowing you and Truman and that whole crew were together seeing The Wrinkles."

I've never seen Sadie like this before. I take a moment to think about what I want to say, especially knowing that it may be the last time I'll get to say it.

"I'm just . . . I'm so, *so* sorry," I say. "I should have been a better friend to you, Sadie. I should have checked in more."

"It's okay."

"But it's not. I've been struggling, too, but you've helped me navigate this year without you, and I just assumed you didn't need the same from me."

She shrugs and smiles, eyes still watery.

"It's been lonely up here without you."

She smiles. "It's lonely down here without you, too."

"We'll get through this together, from here on out," I assure her. "We have each other."

"We'll spend next summer together," Sadie dreams aloud, even though we both know that's not happening. "I'll come back up to the Midwest."

"And I'll bake stuff for us every day," I add.

"And we'll *finally* meet guys who are worth our time."

"And we'll never live more than, like, ten miles apart. Ever again."

"*Ever*. Again."

It grows quiet a third time.

"Thanks for telling me the truth," I say. "I'm proud of you."

"I'm proud of you too," Sadie says. "God, it's been an emotional couple days, huh?"

"What do you mean?"

"The fight with your mom yesterday? It sounded awful."

I sigh. "Yeah."

"How's your dad taking the divorce, since she's the one who wanted it?"

"He's fine, I guess." Then it dawns on me.

Is he though?

"I'd be a wreck if I were him," Sadie says. "I'm glad he's keeping it together."

But I have no idea if he is.

I've seen so little of Dad in the time loop because of his job and our separate Monday schedules, I haven't even talked to him about what Mom told me. I need to, though. Right now.

I'm not sure how many other chances I'll get.

I look beyond the city park to my left; the direction of our old subdivision.

"Sadie, can I let you go?" I ask. "Your question reminded me of something I have to do with my dad."

She smiles sweetly. "For sure. Thank you for listening to me."

The sadness starts to become overwhelming, as it truly sinks in that this may be one of the last times—if not *the* last time—I'll get to see my best friend's face; get to hear her voice, get to laugh at our inside jokes. It's Day 364, and mere hours separate me and . . . whatever is going to happen after Day 365.

There's a million things we could talk about, and a million more things she deserves to know, if this is it. But I decide to keep it simple and to the point.

"I love you," I tell her, meaning it more than I did even a few minutes ago, more than I ever have before. "You are, and always will be, my best friend."

I know it's impossible that she would understand why this moment means so much. But the sparkle in her eyes makes me wonder if, deep down, she somehow gets it. "I love you too." She swallows hard. "Always."

And then her smiley, tear-stricken face disappears.

CHAPTER 25

APPROACH THE HOUSE THAT, UP UNTIL JUST A FEW weeks ago, had been our family home.

It's not unique or impressive. With its yellow shutters and green bushes lining the front deck, it looks like any other house you'd drive by in the suburbs without giving it a second thought. But it's still special to me.

I approach the front door and gather my thoughts before I walk in.

Dad's bearded face—white as a ghost, with his cell phone pressed firmly against his cheek—collapses into relief when he sees me. He stops pacing. "He just walked in," he tells whoever's on the other end of the conversation. "I'll call you back in a bit." He hangs up and gives me a disapproving look.

A wave of guilt washes over me. "I'm sorry, Dad."

For everything.

But he thinks I'm only apologizing for going off the radar this afternoon.

"Where have you been?" he says, exhausted. "I came home early from work to figure out where you are. Does Mom know you're here, C?"

"Yeah," I lie.

He asks another question, but I don't really hear it. I cross the carpeted living room and fall into his chest, my cheek pressed against his yellow duck tie.

Dad holds me tight. "What's wrong?"

I'm not sure what I want to say just yet, so I just hold on. He starts rubbing my back and repeats the question.

But, still, I can't find the right words.

We stay like this for another few seconds—or maybe a whole minute (being Trapped has truly messed with my sense of time)—until I pull away. In the real world, Dad saw me just a few days ago, but it's felt like ages for me.

"C," he says, this time softer and less hostile. We're nearly the same height—maybe I would have been taller than him by now if I'd been able to get to eighteen—but he still needs to look down to see into my eyes. "Talk to me."

"You and Mom," I say.

"Yeah?"

I hesitate, questioning how direct I should be.

On the one hand, this conversation can't turn into a dogpile on Mom. I'm still bitter that she broke our family apart for no good reason, but my time with her is limited as well, and revisiting my anger over the divorce with Dad right now will make it too hard to have the goodbye I want to have with Mom soon. When I misdirected that anger before, it caused fate to make a mistake and got me Trapped in a time loop. Why would I want to go down that road again?

I need to find a way to forgive Mom, just like Sadie chose to forgive me.

On the other hand, Dad deserves to have this conversation with me. He needs to understand that I know the divorce was Mom's idea and destroying our family wasn't on him. I know it probably won't matter, seeing as today will restart in a few hours, but on the slim chance that a September 20 will exist out there in a multiverse succeeding Day 365, Dad will know that *I* know it's not his fault.

"I'm sorry she did that to you," I blurt. "I'm sorry she did that to us."

"What are you talking about, C?"

"I get that every couple has problems and you two fought sometimes and no family is perfect, but still." My voice is unsteady, but I need to get it out. "She didn't need to do that."

"Get a divorce?"

"Yes."

He exhales. I get a whiff of the minty mouthwash he uses, a scent I never thought I'd grow to miss. "You must be hungry."

"I'm not."

"Thirsty?"

I hesitate.

"C'mon," he says, walking away. "I've got your favorite."

I follow him into the kitchen.

I forgot how much messier the house has become compared to when we all lived here, which you wouldn't think to be the case. A family of four eats more food, has more stuff, and causes way more chaos than one single guy. But Dad's proving to be the exception.

His laptop is out on the counter next to his planner, a pile of tangled phone chargers, and an array of pantry items he hasn't put away (which would drive Mom up a wall if she still lived here). The dining room table in the adjacent room is covered in what I can only hope is clean laundry—although I can't be certain—and there's a mountain of dirty dishes piling up near the sink.

Dad pushes his laptop to the side, making more room for me to take a seat. He searches the fridge for a second and returns with a bright orange can, which he opens with a *pop* and slides my way.

"I'm glad we can talk about this," he says, standing by my side. He hunches over, resting his forearms against the countertop.

I take a sip, aware that this will probably be the last time I get to savor the euphoric feeling of whatever artificial concoction creates the orange flavor rushing down my throat.

"I don't want you to be upset with your mom," he says. The seriousness in his tone surprises me. "She told me about your chat yesterday."

"You mean our fight?" I say, eyes watery.

"Yes."

"What did she say about it?"

Dad's typically intentional with his words, but I can tell he's being even more so now. "She said she told you that she wanted the divorce, and that you didn't take it too well."

"And that she was the one that wanted to move out, too," I add. "Because that's fucked up."

Damn it.

I didn't want my anger to bubble over, but I can feel it happening right now.

"What's fucked up?" Dad says. "And don't say 'fuck.'"

"It's *messed* up," I continue, "that she not only forced the divorce on us, but then made me and Blair move in with her too. How selfish can you be?" I take another sip of pop. "Yeah, she promised that we'll only be there for a few months, until we can find a nicer place, but still. You've been in that tiny apartment. It's awful."

"It's more complicated than that, C," he says, "but I can't argue with that apartment being small."

"The water barely drips out of the showerhead, the place smells like cigarettes from the last person who lived there, and the walls are paper thin," I explain. "I'm forced to listen to Blair's seventh-grade bullshit, whether I want to or not."

Dad smiles.

"Why aren't you angrier?" I push back.

He stares at the counter. "It's not that simple—"

"I feel like I'm the only one who's saying anything about how messed up this whole situation is. I know Blair is hurt, she just masks it by being a little brat, but you—out of all of us—should be the angriest. Why aren't you as pissed as I am?"

"C, I get it, but your—"

"If it weren't for Mom, we'd all still be living here, Dad. Don't you miss us being around? My senior year wouldn't have been turned upside down, you wouldn't be spending every night in this quiet house all alone, and—"

"I had an affair, C."

I *think* I heard what he said, but . . . that can't be right.

"Huh?"

He pauses, breathes, and licks his lips. "I cheated on your mom."

My mind goes blank.

I don't think a single thought. Or feel a single feeling. I just stare into his eyes, confused by the words that just came tumbling out of his mouth.

But then I spring up from my seat on autopilot and take a step away from the counter.

"You . . . had an affair," I say aloud.

He nods, his eyes avoiding mine. "Yes."

"You cheated on Mom."

"I did."

I swallow hard. "How . . . how could you do that?"

The kitchen gets quiet. I don't know what to say, and—even though I can tell he has a *lot* to say—Dad is choosing to stay silent.

"It wasn't a one-time thing," he admits, barely above a whisper. The shame in his words is so tangible, it feels like hands gripping my throat. "We agreed not to tell you and your sister for now because we wanted to protect the both of you. But . . ." He pauses. "I think you deserve to know—especially now, seeing how upset you are at Mom. That's not right."

I feel numb.

"That's why Mom wanted a divorce," he says, surrendering to the truth. "And that's why I thought it was fair that you two live with her, even though she was insistent on moving out of the house. Because *I* was the one who messed up. *I* caused this mess." He pauses. "She couldn't keep going, and I can't fault her for that. Neither should you."

"You had an affair," I repeat, the impact of his words beginning to sink in. "Who was it with?"

"It doesn't matter."

"But it does," I say. I can feel my numbness shifting into rage. "Do I know this person?"

"No," he says sheepishly. "She doesn't live around here. It was a stupid mistake."

"You mean stupid *mistakes*, right?" I say. "Because, like you said, it wasn't a one-time thing? You messed up several times?"

He drops his head, fists planted firmly against the counter.

"I should go," I say.

"Please don't. Let's talk."

"I don't have anything else to talk to you about."

"Can we at least talk about your mom?" he says. "You can be angry at me all you want. I deserve it. I know that I'm not going to convince you otherwise right now, and that's fair." His eyes get watery. "But you shouldn't be upset with her, okay? She doesn't deserve it. She should get to have the best version of you."

I move toward the front door.

"Can you at least promise me that, C?" Dad calls after me. "Can you promise you'll be there for her?"

I struggle to unlock our finicky front door and swing it open.

What if I hadn't come over here? What if I never got Trapped in today? Would they have *ever* told me the truth?

Would I have been bitter toward Mom until the end?

"This whole thing's been a nightmare for you and Blair, and it's my fault," Dad says. "Your mom's been lonely, Clark. And I want you to be there for her because I can't be."

I freeze in place, staring out over the front yard that used to be all of ours.

Lonely.

"You and Blair are her everything, C," he says, voice shattering into a million pieces. "Her whole entire world."

I want to run from him, as far and as fast as I can. *There's not a single reason why I shouldn't,* I think—except for the fact this is Day 364. And as irate and exhausted and confused as I am, this can't be our ending. I won't let that happen.

I turn around, cross the carpet, and fall into his arms again—maybe for the final time. "I love you," I whisper.

"Love you more, C." He squeezes me tighter. "Can we talk again tomorrow?"

I hope so. "Yeah."

"Can I tell your mom that you know about everything before you mention it to her?" he asks softly. "But it's okay if you'd rather talk to her about it tonight."

"It's fine, Dad. I won't say anything." I don't even know *how* to talk about it yet.

Just as it did before, time seems to freeze. I'm not sure how many seconds or minutes tick by, but the next thing I know, I'm walking out the door, crossing the front yard, and headed back to the tiny, not-so-terrible apartment that I'm now proud to call my home.

The tears finally arrive as I pick up the pace, angry with myself for being so awful to Mom, for taking my misplaced rage and letting it persuade Thom to break up with Beau, for getting us Trapped and ruining everything.

I burst inside.

Mom runs into the family room, hands crossed against her chest. "Clark," she breathes, "why haven't you—"

I pull her into a hug as my tears, salty and warm, continue to fall. They roll down my cheeks and onto her bare, tanned shoulders.

"It's okay," she whispers into my ear. "I'm here."

"I'm so sorry," I whisper back. "For fighting with you yesterday, and for being so upset about the stuff with you and Dad."

"Clark, it's okay," she repeats. "I'm here."

"I don't want you to feel alone, okay?" I say, sniffling. I can smell her shampoo. *This may be the last time I ever smell her shampoo.* "I don't want you to ever feel alone."

Whether or not Mom caused the divorce never should have stopped me from talking to her about it. If I'd let out my own feelings sooner, maybe I would have been more perceptive of everyone else's. Maybe I would've checked in on Sadie before getting Trapped; maybe I would've had a candid conversation with Dad about his affair; maybe I would've let Mom help me bake after pizza one night, where I could've talked about why I was still upset. I could've helped her feel less alone.

I hear Blair's footsteps bolting into the room. "Dude! Where have you been?" Although I can't see her, I feel her arms wrap around my middle as well. "You were supposed to bake for my birthday tonight!"

Mom sighs. "Can you give your brother and me a minute, please?"

"It's okay," I say, peeling away from the both of them. I blink away my remaining tears and wipe the wetness from my face. "I'll get started while we talk. How does blue velvet brownies sound?"

Blair's eyes pop open. *"Blue?"*

"I'd love some help in the kitchen," I say, smiling at Mom. "Are you two busy?"

CHAPTER 26

BAKING IS EVEN MORE FUN WHEN DONE WITH MY family, I'm realizing far too late.

Mom, spatula in hand, glances between me and the bowl of beaten eggs and brown sugar. "Does this consistency look right to you?"

I pause from greasing the pan and crane my neck to see. "Definitely."

She smiles, proud of herself. I haven't seen her this happy in a long time.

"You're both doing great," I say, smirking, "for amateurs."

"Oh, c'mon," Blair says with a grin, sitting atop the counter. She's assessing our ingredient list. "At least we're trying."

It's so pleasantly strange to see Blair helping with a bake and not blasting off snarky comments from behind her phone. I remember when I was in that rare good mood making Ben's brownies last time and it resulted in her thanking me outside the apartment door.

You're a great big brother and I love you.

I saw how much my attitude toward Mom affected her day, too (even if she'd never admit that to me), but I still didn't do anything to stop it, until now.

"Hey, maybe this can be our new thing?" Mom proposes to us, circling the bowl with her spatula. She looks between me and Blair, beaming. "Monday night baking?"

My heart aches.

I want to tell her the truth; that my time is limited and that there's a good chance I won't be around for week two of Monday night bakes. But, just as I decided with my last talk with Sadie, Mom shouldn't hear the whole truth right now.

"Monday night baking sounds like a plan," I say.

She wipes her hands on her apron and turns to Blair. "What about you?"

Blair glances up from the ingredient list to consider it. "Maybe. As long as we avoid cake, I'm in." She hops down off the counter. "I'm taking a quick break—"

"From the arduous task of reading ingredients?" Mom pokes fun. I lock eyes with her for a second, and we grin.

"*Yes*," Blair retorts, smiling, as she falls onto the family room couch with her phone. "But I still want to drop in the blue dye when it's time."

I finish up greasing and flouring the pan and then check the oven temperature, but it's still got a ways to go (unlike the sparkly new appliances at Ben's, our apartment oven is ancient and takes forever to preheat). I start to help Mom clean up while we have a few minutes between tasks, but she nudges me away.

"Don't worry about this," she says. "I got it."

"You sure?"

"Yes." She leans toward me and whispers, "Why don't you go spend some time with your sister? Please distract her from that horrible video guy I know she's always secretly watching—even if she thinks she's being sneaky."

I stifle a laugh, also lowering my voice. "Derek Dopamine?"

"That's the one."

For a moment, I let my mind wander.

What was Beau thinking when it came to Derek Dopamine and his time loop theory anyway? *Could* he have been trolling, urging me to spend time seeking out a serious video by a not-so-serious influencer who got famous off viral fart jokes? It doesn't seem like Beau. But if he thinks I'm in large part to blame for his breakup, I guess it wouldn't be out of the question.

I can't let my last evening with Mom and Blair get derailed by my train of thought trying to understand Beau's, though. Before I head into the family room, I turn to Mom. "Hey, can I tell you something?"

"Anything."

Butterflies fill my stomach.

"I've been . . ." I hesitate, but decide to commit. "I've been lonely, Mom."

She sets down a washcloth and gives me her full attention. "Yeah?"

"Yeah."

She smiles sadly, eyes glistening.

"But this is a *good* thing," I emphasize. "Well, good that I'm telling you."

"I agree."

"I was thinking about what I've learned with Ms. Hazel, and also about the fight we had yesterday, and I just . . . I wish I'd been better at talking to you about this stuff," I explain. "Just like I should have been better talking through my feelings about the divorce, I should be better about opening up about the other stuff, too. So . . . yeah. I want to be honest."

Mom steps toward me. After one of her blinks disperses a tear, she lifts a hand to pat my chest. "I'm glad you can be honest with me, Clark."

I feel myself turning pink.

"I get lonely, too, sometimes," she adds. "This divorce has been tough on all of us. And I know Sadie moving away has been difficult. But we'll get through it. *Together.*" She ruffles my hair before her arm drops to the side. "Thank you for telling me what's going on inside."

I nod with a smile and pop the brownies into the oven, feeling like the weight of the world has been lifted, before going to see Blair.

"Hey, brat," I say, falling onto the sofa next to her. "What is Derek Dopamine doing this time?"

"*Shh,*" she scolds, looking up to see if Mom heard me and lowering her voice. "She doesn't know I'm watching him. Why do you think the volume's low and the subtitles are on?"

I try not to smile. "Sorry."

I look down and see the obnoxious internet star on Blair's phone, his hair styled in a towering purple mohawk. The video she's watching is titled "The REAL Reason My Dog Hates Mayonnaise!" and I'm not sure that I can stomach this, even for the sake of our sibling relationship.

"What *is* the real reason his dog hates mayonnaise?" I ask anyway.

She snorts. "As if you actually care."

I frown in thought before caving. "You're right. I don't. But I like that his videos make you happy."

She hits pause and whips her head in my direction. "Okay, what is up with you today?"

"What?"

"'I like that his videos make you happy'?" she repeats with a giggle, suspicious of me. "You came home all emotional, crying and hugging Mom and stuff. Then you want to bake with us, which was actually a lot of fun and I'm glad we'll be doing it more, but, like . . . where's this new you coming from?"

I sit there for a second, thinking of how I could answer the question. "I know that I've acted strange today."

"Understatement."

"And it's probably been a little weird to see me like this."

"Understatement two."

I smile. "It's because I talked to Dad earlier," I say, barely above a whisper so that Mom won't hear. "I dropped by the house."

"Just to say hi?"

I think for a second before shrugging. "I wanted to see him. We had a good talk."

"Is he doing okay?"

"Yeah." I pause, reminding myself that I shouldn't bring up the affair. "I mean, maybe he's not doing okay right now, but he will be. Talking to him made me realize how much Mom and Dad both need us right now. You know? Because even though it hurts us, they're the ones who don't have each other anymore, but we still have them both."

She nods.

"And we still have each other. I want to be better at being a good brother for you, too. Okay?"

She nods again.

"This whole situation has been tough on us," I say. "I realized it's okay to admit that sometimes."

She rests her head on my shoulder. "I know."

"I love you."

"Love you too."

"Now can we please get back to whatever dumb Derek Dopamine video you're watching?"

She lifts her head away from me with a devilish grin on her face and taps play. I pull a pillow out from one of the moving boxes and onto my lap, and Blair sinks farther into the sofa, as we watch this twentysomething-year-old clown explain his dog's relationship with condiments. I'm smiling on the outside and cringing on the inside.

When the video wraps, another auto-plays. It's called "I Dressed Up As A Witch To Scare My Old Neighbor And OMG!" Miraculously, I'm able to stomach the whole video as I feel Blair vibrating with laughter next to me. The next one is titled "The Time I Went On A Date With A FREAKING COCKROACH." It's after the fourth video—"Wait, Are Rainbows LITERALLY Gay?"—that I decide that enough is enough.

"I'm impressed you sat here as long as you did," Blair says, clapping for me as I stand.

As I take a bow, I spot the title of the next video that's about to start playing: "Yes, You CAN Get Stuck In Time!"

I crash back down next to her. "What's that next one?"

"Oh." Blair taps out of the browser and tosses her phone aside. "That's an old and *especially* stupid one. You'd hate it."

"What was it about?"

"He interviewed some guy who believes in time travel or something."

"Time loops?"

"Yeah, maybe that was it." She rolls her eyes, the topic of time loops seemingly too farfetched for even this off-the-wall internet personality's biggest fan. She looks at me, as though she is suspicious of my curiosity. "Why do you care?"

I concoct a story on the fly. "I was just talking to Sadie about movies with multiverses and she mentioned there was a Derek Dopamine video sort of on a similar topic."

"Sadie watches Derek?" Blair says, surprised. "But, yeah, it was probably that video."

"The thing is," I say, now genuinely confused, "I tried googling it a bunch and nothing came up."

Blair smirks. "You were using Mom's laptop, huh?"

I nod. "You know the screen cracked on mine. Why does it matter?"

She cranes her neck to make sure Mom isn't eavesdropping on us. "When we had remote learning and I had to use her laptop for school, she changed something in her search settings to block Derek's videos from showing up so I wouldn't get distracted." She smiles mischievously. "Mom didn't think I'd notice, but *obviously* I did. She never changed the settings back, I bet."

Oh my God.

Well that explains it. Blair watches me start to drift off awkwardly to my room, trying to keep my cool.

"You . . . okay?" she asks.

"Yeah, of course. Be right back."

I shut my door and pull out my phone. "Derek Dopamine time loop," I mutter, typing the search term into my browser.

"Yes, You CAN Get Stuck In Time!" is the first result.

"Damn," I say. It has over eleven million views.

I wish I would have known that Mom's hatred of an annoying vlogger was hindering my ability to uncover what I'm sure is one of the more prominent internet theories this whole time. But here we are.

I hit play.

"Hey, you! Yes, *you!*" Derek Dopamine begins with his go-to line. With a much smaller mohawk and rounder face, the vlogger looks younger than he did in the videos I watched with Blair. I notice that it was uploaded six years ago.

"This week I made a different kind of video for all you Dope Kids out there. Don't fret, though. I still get pretty silly—especially in the last half of the video! But you guys"—Derek grins and leans toward the camera before whispering—"I got to interview a relationship expert about, of all things, how time isn't as straight a line as we think it is. It was *bonkers.*"

"What are you doing in there?" Mom calls for me from the kitchen. "Want to check on the brownies for us?"

"Just some homework!" I yell, popping in my earbuds so that Mom and Blair don't get any nosier. "Be right back!"

"Can you imagine repeating the same day over and over again?" the vlogger continues. "As it turns out, that's not just a thing in the movies. Nope! It actually happens to *real* people, in the *real* world. And, you guys"—Derek leans forward again to whisper at me—"this dude, Mr. Thunderburnt, is legit. He even has his own fandom." Derek laughs. "I've got you *Dope Kids*; Mr. Thunderburnt has his *Thunderbolts.*"

Thunderbolts.

Jodie asked to make sure I wasn't one of them before I talked to Professor Copeman, but I had no idea what she meant.

"He thinks that a person can get stuck in a time loop in order to win back their soul mate," Derek continues, "and, as *insane* as it sounds, he's got the evidence to back it up!"

The video cuts to the interview between Derek and an elderly Mr. Thunderburnt sitting across from each other in what looks like a library. Mr. Thunderburnt, dressed in a classic suit and tie, has silver-white bangs floating above the greenest eyes I've ever seen. Derek, on the other hand, is wearing a bright yellow jumpsuit and, for whatever reason, has a Chihuahua sleeping on his lap.

"So, doc," Derek begins, stroking the pup's ears.

"To be clear, I'm not a doctor," Mr. Thunderburnt clarifies in a high, raspy voice.

Derek ignores him. "Tell me about your expertise—what you did *before* discovering the existence of time loops."

"I was a relationship counselor for twenty years," Mr. Thunderburnt answers. "Every type of couple you can imagine walked into my office at one point or another. I've seen it all."

"*All?* We talkin' cross-species stuff?" Derek asks, cringing. "That kind of freaky—?" The video bleeps out a curse word.

Mr. Thunderburnt pauses, unsure how to respond.

"I'm kidding, doc, I'm *kidding*," the vlogger follows up, tickled with himself.

I really can't understand how Blair enjoys this idiot.

"But for real," Derek continues. "How the heck did chatting with *couples* about their problems in the bedroom lead to discovering *time loops?*" His eyes pop wide open.

"After helping as many people as I had, you start to pick up on patterns," Mr. Thunderburnt explains, "even the most subtle ones. One particularly interesting pattern began to jump out at me and—"

Derek jumps up in his chair with a squeal, thinking he's clever.

Mr. Thunderburnt jolts.

"I'm sorry, doc, I'm *sorry*," Derek laughs, holding his belly.

"I couldn't help it. Please, continue, *continue* . . ."

Mr. Thunderburnt sighs and swallows hard, attempting to get comfortable in his seat again. "Throughout my career, I had a small number of clients admit to me that they'd experienced déjà vu."

"Don't we all, though?" Derek asks. "I just did this morning while I was ordering hash browns from the drive-thru lady."

"That sounds like it was a normal déjà-vu experience," Mr. Thunderburnt says. "That wasn't the case with my patients, who reported long-term and incredibly *intense* experiences with the sensation. These patients claimed to be reliving the same moments— and in some instances, entire days—over and over again. The one common denominator that I was able to pinpoint between them all was that they had survived these surreal experiences immediately after their true loves, their soul mates, had broken up with them—"

A loud farting noise erupts, cutting off Mr. Thunderburnt.

"Oh my *God*," Derek howls. The camera pans to see the crew filming the interview, and it becomes clear that someone put a whoopie cushion to use behind the scenes. "I can't handle you, Brett!" Derek yells, pointing off camera, now crying from laughter. "Was that you? Did you think of that idea? Get his reaction, *get his reaction!*" Derek orders a camera operator.

I click out of the video.

Blair might be able to stomach that clown, but I can't.

Instead, I search *Mr. Thunderburnt time loops.* Virtually all the results are associated with the vlogger—*Derek Dopamine Profiles Time Loop Expert; Dope Kids React To Thunderburnt's Wild Claims*—which explains why I hadn't run into this theory while researching on Mom's laptop before.

I stand and start pacing, hating the fact that I'm just *now*, in Day 364, able to learn more about the theory Beau believes to be true.

Seven pages deep into the search results, I finally find a trustworthy report about Mr. Thunderburnt that doesn't seem to have any overt connection to Derek Dopamine. (Thank God.)

The article, "Local Relationship Expert's Claims About Time Gain Traction," was published in a small San Francisco newspaper several years ago.

The article begins:

> Louis Thunderburnt, 71, has had a long career helping couples sort out their relationship woes. But he's now faced with a problem he didn't foresee being part of his work in counseling: figuring out how to convince the world that, for some of us, time isn't linear.
> Allegedly.

"Clark!" Blair yells. "I . . . don't think the brownies look right. Are they supposed to be purple?"

I exhale, trying to be patient. "I promise, it's just the oven light giving them that hue!"

I skim the article, passing by the facts I already learned from Derek's video.

> According to Thunderburnt, several of his patients have reportedly been, as he describes it, "frozen in time"—reliving the same hours, days, or weeks with no end in sight.
> "The experience had only happened to those who'd recently been abandoned by their one true love, oddly enough," the relationship counselor explains, citing twenty-two patients who've lived through disturbingly similar experiences. "I realize twenty-two people over the course of many years doesn't seem like much. But of the folks I

spoke to, their experiences were strikingly similar."

Twenty-two people.

My heart begins to race.

Thunderburnt's right; twenty-two isn't a lot. But still. It's not nothing. And unlike the plethora of other time loop theories I've discovered since getting Trapped, this one has something important in common with Dr. Runyon's; it's not based off one ridiculous, singular anecdote from an anonymous troll online. It's happened to multiple people.

And their experiences were supposedly the same.

None of Thunderburnt's patients were in a state of mental or cognitive distress that would have deemed them incapable of separating reality from fiction, he noted—they were all perfectly stable.
When asked to provide proof of his claims, the San Francisco native gave *The Bay Times* records from past decades that document nearly identical reports from people with various genders and sexual orientations. They all allegedly got stuck in what one patient characterized as "infinite time loops" after their partners ended the relationship. *The Bay Times* confirmed the authenticity of Thunderburnt's records.

A legitimate newspaper fact-checked Thunderburnt's materials and confirmed he's not full of it? His theory has another thing in common with Dr. Runyon's: credible data.

I continue reading:

For nearly all of the patients Thunderburnt spoke to, convincing their ex-partner to take them back is what ended their so-called infinite time loop.

What does winning a partner back entail?

"It could require lots of different things, depending on the situation," Thunderburnt said. "A few patients said it involved changing their in-laws's opinions of them. Some patients said they had to steal back their partner from a third party—their partner's new significant other. Others had to prove to their soul mates that they've changed—became kinder, more attentive, those sorts of things."

Prove to their soul mates that they've changed.

No wonder Beau thinks he needs to change who he is in order to win Thom back.

"I know what you're thinking," Thunderburnt said. "Could my patients have imagined this? Could the trauma from being left by your soul mate spark some sort of altered, dreamlike fantasy? Well, sure, maybe," the relationship expert admits before concluding, "but after hearing their stories firsthand and seeing how undeniably consistent their experiences have been, I doubt that's the case."

I toss my phone onto a blanket.

Could Thunderburnt's theory be right?

It relies on empirical evidence to back up his claims—claims that a news source corroborated. And even though, to me, Beau and Thom feel more like a match made in hell rather than heaven, I'm a relationship novice in every sense of the term. Can I really know, without a doubt, they *aren't* meant to be?

I either need Beau to meet me under The Honeycomb at 11:16 p.m., or Beau needs to forget about me and win Thom back. Now I'm not so sure which one of us is right.

CHAPTER 27

T HERE IT IS, GREETING ME FOR WHAT'S LIKELY THE very last time. My white wooden nightstand.

It's my three hundred and sixty-fifth day of being Trapped.

Three-hundred and sixty-five iterations of mushroom-ham pizza, birthday bakes, and cosines. Three-hundred and sixty-five iterations of Greg's spilt chocolate milk, Sadie FaceTimes, and caramel candies cracking between Ms. Hazel's teeth. If Dr. Runyon is correct, today may be it—the last today that I'm alive. If Mr. Thunderburnt is, it'll take Thom choosing to take back Beau for Beau to get to tomorrow.

And if *that* ends up happening, I have no idea what will happen to me.

I roll out of bed and stretch near the window, taking in the not-so-terrible view of the trees swaying in the breeze—a scene I wish I'd appreciated before this moment. I head to the bathroom and wash my face, reminding myself to breathe, *just breathe*, while standing in front of the mirror, permanently seventeen-year-old me staring back. My olive skin, wavy brown curls, steel-blue eyes.

At this point, I'm not sure how to feel about Mr. Thunderburnt's theory. Beau's confidence in it has to be the reason he's avoided meeting me under The Honeycomb. But what can I do about that now?

Nothing. *Absolutely nothing.*

So, I can't focus on where I'll be sixteen hours from now. I refuse to spend my final hours alone with my loneliness. And with my new strategy to complete Ms. Hazel's homework in mind since our last session together, I think I have a shot.

I may be able to spend Day 365 as un-lonely as I'd been in Day 310. But it'll take running my errands very differently than I've ever run them before.

First, I head to the University of Chicago. I grab my copies of *Trapped in Today* from Kelly and type out and print my final letters to Beau. Except this time, I include that I've learned about Thunderburnt's theory, along with an extra personal note.

A note that truly scares me. But I do it anyway.

Then I head to my first errand for the last time: Splendid Cinemas.

"Oh," Emery says—as always, surprised to see another soul. I wave and he plucks his earbuds out—I hear "Avery," by The Wrinkles playing as usual—and tosses his lines to the side. "Before you ask—no, I can't tell you how *fresh* our soda is."

I stride across the room. "I don't think pop can even . . . *be* fresh?"

He shrugs. "Well, that hasn't stopped customers from asking."

I pretend to look up at the showings for the cinema's one and only theater, as if I don't know the schedule by heart.

"Any of them seem enticing?" Emery fills the silence.

I sigh. "Honestly? No."

He laughs.

"But I do have an odd favor to ask of you," I say.

Emery cocks his head. "Okay . . . ?"

"I haven't been able to find my friend this morning, but I know he comes in here a lot," I say before pulling out a copy of the book and explaining what Beau looks like. "Would you mind giving this to him if he happens to drop by?"

Emery takes it from me, staring at the cover. "*Trapped in Today*. Sounds interesting."

"It is," I say, a bit nervous. "There's a personal note for him in there that you might notice, so if you wouldn't mind, please don't . . . read it?"

"What, are you like, professing your love to him or something?" Emery laughs.

I turn pink.

"Oh . . . shit," he says. "Really? I didn't realize—"

"It's okay."

"That's awesome!"

"Yeah?"

"Yes!" He raises his hand for a fist bump above the counter.

I oblige, feeling the heat still rising in my cheeks. "Thanks."

"Are you nervous?" he asks giddily. "And why this book?"

I breathe deep. "It'd take me all afternoon to explain the book, but, yes, I am definitely nervous." I smile. "I was recently given the advice by a very smart person to do the thing that scares me. So"—I nod at *Trapped in Today*—"I'm doing just that."

"Shooting your shot," Emery says, shaking his head in disbelief. He pauses. "It's very strange that you came in here today."

"Why is that?"

"I was thinking about doing something that scares me tomorrow, too."

I glance down at his papers. "I thought those looked like lines. Have a big audition?"

He looks down at the papers as well. "Oh. Yeah, I do. My very first one, actually." He exhales. "But that's not it. A first audition, as terrifying as it is, *definitely* isn't as scary as telling your best friend that you're in love with her."

My jaw drops. Emery brought up liking a girl in a previous today, but failed to mention that it was his best friend—and that he has plans to tell her *tomorrow*.

"That's amazing," I say. "Well, I vote that you go to that audition *and* tell this lucky person how you feel—even if they both scare the absolute crap out of you."

He nods slowly, thinking it through. "You know what? You're right." He pounds his fist on the countertop (in the case, a pack of M&Ms falls to floor). "I'm going to do it."

I laugh. "Incredible."

"This is so wild," he says, looking at me in wonder. "I was feeling iffy about telling her, but you're like a sign from the universe right now."

"Thanks?" I shrug awkwardly, before nodding at his lines. "I should come in here and help you run lines sometime—only if you'd like the help, of course."

His face lights up. "Really?"

I nod. "Why not?"

"Are you an actor? Because I've been wanting to sign up for these acting classes, and they're cheaper if you bring a friend—"

I hold up a hand to pause him, smiling. "I'm not an actor. And as much as those classes sound interesting, they're just not for me."

He laughs. "Fair."

"I mean it about helping you run lines, though," I say, holding out my hand. "I'm Clark."

Emery shakes it. "Emery."

We exchange numbers.

"I should get going," I say. "But I—"

Emery launches himself over the concession stand, belly pressed against the glass, and wraps me up in his arms. His polo smells of stale buttery popcorn and cologne that's too strong for its own good, but this hug still feels wonderful and long overdue.

"I really needed this today," Emery says. "Thank you, Clark."

I leave Splendid Cinemas imagining an updated version of Ms. Hazel's tip list in my head:

Clark's 4 tips to beating loneliness:

~~Try to make a new friend. (BEAU)~~

Help someone who could use it. (OTTO)

Be vulnerable so others can be too. (DEE)

~~Do the thing that scares you. (EMERY)~~

CHAPTER 28

NORMALLY, I'D HEAD TO BEN'S EVERYTHING BLUE Bakery to help Otto during the afternoon rush. But running to the university this morning and then seeing Emery in the afternoon pushed my schedule back. The Aragon's not too far from Splendid Cinemas, anyway, so I head to meet Dee as she leaves work instead.

Shortly after the clock strikes 6:00 p.m., she comes firing out the front doors.

"Hello?" I say, following in her footsteps. "Are you—"

"No," she cuts me off.

"But you—"

"Whatever it is you're selling, bro, I don't have the time, energy, or patience to deal with it." She plows forward with exactly zero intention of giving me the time of day.

"I'm not selling anything, I'm just—"

"*Still*, no," she hisses. "I'm not interested in going on a date with you, hooking up with you, or doing *literally anything* with you."

"I know Beau."

"What?"

"I'm friends with Beau—the guy you met at the concert last night."

She stops and turns. Her face, tear-stricken and puffy, scans me up and down. "Who are you?"

"Clark," I explain, slightly out of breath, "and I'm sorry Beau didn't text you today."

She squints. "Did Beau *send* you here? Like you're his personal assistant or something?" She looks even more suspicious. "Does he not know how to use a phone?"

"He's had a rough day," I say, which is probably the truth.

Just like in most of my todays, she's not sure what to think of me.

"I promise that I'm not trying to hit on you, or sleep with you, or sell anything to you," I continue. "I'm sorry, but since I'm here . . . it looks like you could use an ear to vent to. I was planning to grab dinner at the diner on the corner up there." I nod toward the intersection straight ahead. "Want to join?"

She sighs, considering it. "Sure."

"Yeah?"

She thinks it over a bit more. "Yeah."

We walk in silence as I remind myself that I shouldn't overstep—especially when it comes to a secret as important and personal as Dee's seems to be.

We walk into the diner, and my nostrils immediately fill with the now familiar concoction of bleach and sizzling meat as we find our seats.

"Hey, hon, what can I—*oh my God*," Sandy gasps seeing Dee's face. "What happened?"

Dee laughs. "Today has been a *a day*." She nods at me. "Sandy, this is . . . what's your name again?"

"Clark," I reply, smiling at Sandy. "How's it going?"

But Sandy is too distracted by Dee's despair to care about me. She lowers her voice and points a finger in my direction, eyes still glued on Dee. "Is he legit?"

"Yes."

"You sure?"

"Well"—Dee glances at me—"I hope so. Maybe keep an eye on him?"

Sandy nods, sliding plastic menus in front of us, and straightening back up. "The usual?"

Dee gives her a thumbs-up. "Make it two."

She slips away to put in our order.

"So," Dee exhales, wiping at her face. "What's got Beau bent out of shape today?"

I think through how I want to navigate this. "I should probably let him tell you," I answer. "But let's just say, his September nineteenth has sucked."

She lets out a sharp laugh. "Welp"—she gestures at her blood-shot eyes while rolling them—"that makes two of us."

"Make it three."

That gets another laugh out of her.

"I had one small victory though," I say, fidgeting in my seat, preparing myself for the conversation I want to have.

"Yeah?" Dee says, staring out the window, her mind clearly somewhere else. "Let's hear about your win, Clark."

I swallow hard, remembering Ms. Hazel's tip.

"I'm lonely," I start with, "and I finally told my mom and my therapist."

Her eyes shift back to mine, surprised by my revelation.

"Was that too much to say to a stranger?" I ask.

She shakes her head. "Not at all." She smiles.

I smile, too. "I've been lonely for a long time—a *really* long time. And it felt nice to tell someone."

Dee folds her arms on the tabletop. "You see a therapist?"

"Yes."

"Does it help?"

I nod.

"But it took me a while to find a therapist I liked," I explain. "The first two were awful—I mean, I probably shouldn't say that. They were awful for *me*. Ms. Hazel, who I see now, is amazing. I feel like I'm actually getting somewhere with her after the divorce and Sadie's move."

"Who's Sadie?"

"My best friend. She moved to Texas. *That*, layered on top of my parents' divorce, put me in a bad place."

I pause, reflecting on my loneliness in the time loop. "It's weird," I say, "because I used to blame my loneliness on something else entirely. I was in denial. I mean, that other thing may have *exacerbated* it, but it wasn't the root cause. Ms. Hazel helped me to realize that."

"That's good," Dee says. "Denial doesn't get you anywhere." She stops, letting her own words sink in. "I, of all people, need to understand that."

I smile. "Do you go?"

"To therapy?"

I nod.

Dee shakes her head. "I've thought about it. I probably should." She laughs, gesturing to her teary face again. "*Clearly*, I'd have a lot to talk about."

Sandy appears once more with our milkshakes and sets them down in front of us.

Dee raises hers to the middle of the table. "Well, cheers to you, Clark, for taking on your loneliness—and being brave enough to tell me about it."

I smile, raising my glass to *clink* with hers.

"How long have you worked at the Aragon?" I ask.

And our conversation flows from there.

I try not to steer it in any particular direction, which is harder than it sounds when you know much more about a person than they know about you. But Dee discloses her love of live music and lists off each member of her big family and even bigger group of friends. Through a mouthful of BLT, Dee advises me on the best Chicago neighborhoods for food (Pilsen, she notes, is the most underrated), and updates me on her plans to rid the oceans of plastics one day as an environmental engineer.

I'm so enthralled listening to her explain why the collapse of marine ecosystems will be a disaster for humans that I'm just as surprised as she is when Dee's phone starts vibrating on the table.

"Hey, you," she says, answering it. Her face lights up. "Oh my God, that's right! I'll be there in like, one minute, okay? Okay, okay, bye!"

She starts scooching out the booth.

"You've got to run?" I ask.

"I'm so sorry," she says, throwing cash on the table. "I forgot that my friend was picking me up after my shift."

"It's okay," I say.

"Tell Sandy bye for me?" Dee asks.

"Will do."

I open my mouth to say a more sincere goodbye, but she's gone before I can.

I sigh, feel surprisingly okay about our last dinner of BLTs and chocolate milkshakes. Sure, I may be a bit bummed that Dee didn't finally open up about her embarrassing secret from last night.

But maybe she was never supposed to. Maybe she's supposed to tell someone else; a close friend or family member, who's already earned her trust.

As I pull out my wallet, I hear the bell on the diner door ring again.

It's Dee, walking back toward our table, a nervous smile on her face. She stays standing, but leans against her side of the booth. "Hey," she says.

I smile back. "Hey."

"My friend can wait a minute or two," she says. "I just . . . thank you for this."

I feel my face getting hot. "Of course."

"Thank you for eating with me, and for listening to me," she says, "but also, for telling me what you told me about being lonely and seeing a therapist and . . . yeah. I think it's good that I heard that. I think it inspired me to think about some things."

"You're very welcome."

"I never did tell you the reason why you found me basically *sobbing* on the sidewalk," she says, pulling the straps of her purse higher on her shoulder.

"Do you want to?"

She hesitates for a moment before dropping back down into the booth.

My heart is racing.

"It's *so* mortifying," she says. "I haven't told anyone."

"No one?"

She shakes her head.

"Well," I say, "your secret is safe with me."

She inhales deeply, staring unblinkingly. "I'm . . . in love."

A big smile spreads across my face, even though I'm confused. "Congrats! That's—"

"—*with my best friend.*"

She face-plants into the table, barely missing her sandwich.

I move her plate so that ketchup doesn't get in her hair. "How is that mortifying? That's great! I mean, unless your best friend sucks. Then maybe not so great."

"No," she says, her voice muffled in a napkin, "that's not the mortifying part. I had big plans to tell him last night, at this concert I went to."

"But . . . you chickened out, I take it?"

"*Well,*" she says, straightening back up again, "not exactly. I got confirmation that he doesn't feel the same way about me."

"Why do you think that?"

"We were supposed to see The Wrinkles together but he bailed. Apparently, his younger sister"—she uses air quotes—"*got sick* at the very last minute."

Wait a minute.

"He said his younger sister got sick?" I repeat her words, jogging my memory.

"Yes," she says. "But I bet he suspected that I was up to something and freaked out because he doesn't feel the same way about me."

"Well, were you up to something?"

She face-plants again.

"C'mon," I say. "It couldn't have been that bad. . . . Right?"

She swings her torso upright. "The Wrinkles are his favorite band. And I know their lead singer, Mae Monroe, from when they played the Aragon. *So,*" she sighs, "I asked Mae if she could swap out some of the lyrics to his favorite song, 'Avery,' and replace them with *his* name onstage since it sounds similar."

Oh my God.

Dee's phone rings. "I know, I *know*, I'm sorry, I'm coming! Just give me one more minute, all right?" She hangs up.

I try my best to contain the excitement flooding my entire body. It's not easy. "What's his name?"

"Emery."

I nod thoughtfully, trying to keep my cool, even though my insides are exploding.

"You know—*Avery, Emery?*" she continues. "It'd be a super-easy swap."

I clear my throat to help my voice stay steady. "But it didn't happen, I take it?"

Dee tries to face-plant a third time, but I catch her forehead with my palm and lift her head back up. "I relayed a message to the backstage crew letting Mae know that Emery wasn't there. I was hopeful it'd get to her, too, because it was one of the last songs The Wrinkles played; there was plenty of time for her to be notified. But . . . she wasn't."

"That's okay, right?" I try finding a silver lining. "I bet no one even noticed because their names sound so similar."

I mean, I know *I* didn't notice. But then again, I don't remember The Wrinkles performing "Avery" at all, so my opinion doesn't hold much weight.

Dee breathes, shaking her head. "At the end of the song, we'd planned for a spotlight—an actual, *literal* spotlight—to land on us in the crowd. I'd tell Emery how I truly feel; how I've been in love with him for a long, long time."

"Oh boy."

"The spotlight found me and the crowd cheered"—she face-plants again, and this time I can't stop her—"until they realized I was all alone, no Emery in sight. Then, all you could hear was awkward silence. Emphasis on the awkward. And I bolted to the bathroom."

Even with a terrible memory of last night, I probably *would* have remembered something so cringeworthy happening. But I had already left the venue.

"Thank God for Beau," she says.

"Why?" I ask, practically holding my breath.

"He saw me all alone by the bathrooms and asked if I was okay. I could tell he was upset, too. You've probably heard about his issues with his boyfriend . . . what's his name again?"

"Thom."

"*Thom.* That's right." She rubs her face. "Anyway. So, yeah, that's that. The first person I fell in love with, who happens to be my childhood best friend, flatly rejected me last night and an entire arena saw."

"Dee," I say, beaming. "I promise, you were *not* rejected."

She drops her chin, unconvinced. "Oh yeah?"

"Yeah."

"And what makes you so confident about that?"

"Is this Emery guy the kind of person who'd lie about his sister getting sick?" I've only spent September 19th with him, and even *I* know the answer is no.

She thinks. "I guess not."

"And would he really flake out on seeing his favorite band—at the very last minute, no less—just because he got a vague hunch that you might be up to something?"

She shakes her head. "Well . . . I guess when you put it like that . . ." Her phone starts ringing again. She answers—"*Okay*, I'm coming right now, I swear"—before hanging up.

"Listen." I steal a fry off of her plate. "I know it must sting to feel rejected. And what happened to you last night? You're right—that's pure nightmare fuel."

She grins.

"But you can't let that stop you from telling Emery how you feel for real," I say. "I bet you'll be surprised by his reaction. And even if I'm wrong—even if he doesn't share the same feelings—you won't regret being honest with him."

"You think?"

"I *know*. Believe me. I'm in a similar . . . *ish* boat," I say, choosing not to name Beau. "I expressed to someone how I really felt. I put it in a letter. I have no idea how he'll take it. But either way, I can at least know that I gave it my all."

"Yeah." She smiles. "I think you're right."

A car honks directly outside the diner. Dee waves at them, agitated, before springing up and gathering her things.

"Oh!" I remember the two remaining copies of *Trapped in Today* in my bag.

Dee pauses next to the table. "Yeah?"

But . . . what are the chances she'll somehow, *miraculously*, see Beau tonight? What are the chances he'd even care enough to show up at The Honeycomb—assuming Dr. Runyon's theory is even the correct one?

What are the chances I have even the tiniest shot at getting to tomorrow?

"It's okay," I say, gesturing for her to go. "Never mind."

"Are you sure?"

"Yes, go, *go*."

"Thank you, Clark," she says. "Get my number from Beau, okay?"

"I will."

"And you're right, by the way," she says. "I spent all today convincing myself that it wasn't meant to be with Emery. I never really tell anyone how I feel and I thought this was a sign that I was right and it was a huge mistake. But you know what?" She throws cash on the table. "I think sometimes fate can make a mistake."

My insides tingle.

No. I need to do whatever I can to escape today—with Beau at my side. "Could you do me a favor?"

Dee nods.

Feeling reinspired, I pull out a copy of Dr. Runyon's book. "This is a longshot, but if Beau finds you later tonight to say hi, would you mind giving this to him?"

Dee takes the book, reading the cover: "*Trapped in Today*. What's it about?"

I hesitate. "It's . . . a *very* long story."

She tucks it under her arm. "You can tell it to me when we hang out together with Beau soon, all right?"

"Of course. And, hey, maybe Emery will be joining us as well." I smile.

Dee grins, waves goodbye, and leaves.

I close my eyes and imagine crossing another item off Ms. Hazel's list.

Clark's 4 tips to beating loneliness:

~~Try to make a new friend. (BEAU)~~

Help someone who could use it. (OTTO)

~~Be vulnerable so others can be too. (DEE)~~

~~Do the thing that scares you. (EMERY)~~

I get our bill for the BLTs and milkshakes, leave Sandy a 500 percent tip along with Dee's cash, and head out to run my last errand of Day 365.

CHAPTER 29

HELP SOMEONE WHO COULD USE IT. I KNOW SOME-
one who will appreciate the last item on Ms. Hazel's tip list.

I haven't been to Ben's Everything Blue Bakery after
sunset, but it looks as blue and inviting as it does in broad daylight. The storefront is visible from blocks away, warm lights setting
the brick exterior aglow, and it appears far less busy than it is in
the afternoons, with no stream of guests flowing in and out of the
entrance.

I swing the door open and, to my surprise, there's not another
soul inside.

This, I'm not used to.

The navy tile floor is spotless after having just been mopped.
The turquoise ceiling fans, usually spinning on high above, rest
motionless instead. And the royal-blue tables and chairs, typically
pushed and pulled in all sorts of configurations throughout the day
to meet guests' needs, are lined perfectly along the walls to my right
and left.

"Hello?" I say to the emptiness.

I hear a jolt of movement from the kitchen.

"Hi!" I hear Otto's voice—booming, but more strained than
normal—from the back. "We closed at eight! My apologies; I forgot
to lock the door."

I check my phone: 8:02 p.m.

"Shoot," I breathe, lingering near the entrance. "No more blue velvet brownies I can take for the road?"

The room falls silent.

"I'm sorry, sir," Otto says. "We open at seven a.m., though, bright and early."

Dang it.

A pit forms in my stomach. I've grown increasingly terrible at staying cognizant of the time while being Trapped, but I should have known better to stay on top of it in Day 365, of all my todays. I may have just lost my last chance to see Otto.

I stand there, running through various excuses I could try to stick around, before realizing how selfish I'd be in doing so— especially on a day as long at Otto's surely was.

Especially on Ben's birthday.

"I'll be in tomorrow if I can swing it," I say, turning to leave. "Thank you—"

"Wait, wait, *wait*," he calls after me.

I hear more movement from the kitchen before the baker pushes through the swinging, silver doors, looking absolutely haggard. His eyes, sunken and dark, are uncharacteristically lifeless, and his gingery beard—never not collected in a tight hair net—is dangling, unkempt, against his chest. He looks more than tired; Otto looks defeated.

"I'm sorry for being short with you," he says sheepishly, glancing down at his apron, which is covered in various hues of blue. He uses one arm to lean against the display case and extends the other in my direction, a plastic container housing my blue velvet brownie in his palm. "Here you go, pal."

I cross the bakery and take it from him. "Thank you."

It takes an effort, but he's able to smile.

"What do I owe you?" I ask.

He waves his hand, declining the question.

"No, I feel awful," I say, reaching into my pocket. "How much?" (*I* know that it's $2.50, but it'd be weird for a new customer to.)

"I already closed the register," he says, shaking his head. "It's no problem. Tell a friend about Ben's Everything Blue Bakery and we'll call it even."

The room gets still, and I know that that's my cue to leave. I want to stay to complete the final item of Ms. Hazel's homework, but there's probably nothing Otto wants to do less right now than deal with a customer overstaying their welcome after the bakery's closed.

So, as much as I'd rather do otherwise, I nod in gratitude one last time and head for the exit, feeling my eyes swell with tears.

Goodbye, Otto.

My hand lands on the door when he speaks up.

"Hold on," he says. "Have we met before?"

I freeze, questioning how I should answer, before turning around.

I shake my head.

"You look familiar," he continues, squinting across the room. "But I can't place a name with your face—and I'm usually *very* good at placing names with familiar faces."

I grin. "I've never been to this bakery before today, but who knows?" I say. "Maybe we met in another life."

His tired face cracks into a smile. "Maybe so. I'm Otto."

"Hey, Otto," I say. "I'm Clark."

The lines across his face deepen. "I know what it is. You remind me of one of my regulars. A *former* regular, actually."

I take a step forward, back into the bakery. "Really? Who?"

He shakes his head, as if it's unimportant. "A fellow about your age who used to stop in quite a bit to see me."

I tense up.

"I don't have a clue why you remind me of Beau," he says, more to himself than me, seemingly confused by the association. "But you do."

I gulp and try to keep it together. "Yeah?"

"Truth be told, the two of you look nothing alike," he continues, "and I can't speak to your personalities, having only met you a moment ago. But . . ." He stares, as if I'm a mystery he can't crack, before giving up with a shrug. "I don't know. Maybe it's because Beau's been on my mind today. I'm not making much sense, am I?" He chuckles. "Long day. Long, *long* day."

I suspected that Otto was concealing his sadness, but I didn't expect him to be *this* dejected. Has he been this upset every night in the time loop? Has he spent Ben's birthday waiting on customers with a smile all day, before finally allowing the pain to surface once the bakery doors were locked?

Has he spent every tonight alone with his loneliness, too?

"I get it," I say, taking another step toward him. "Sometimes people have energies that just seem to . . . *click*. There's no good way to describe it."

He nods.

Despite the obvious exhaustion draped across his face and the fact that it's past closing time, I get the sense that Otto doesn't want to be by himself anymore. And neither do I.

I take another step forward, adjusting the straps of my bag. "Now I'm curious," I say, "why did this Beau stop coming into the bakery?"

The baker laughs. "Do you want to hear the long story or the short one?"

I smile. "Long."

Otto exhales, taking a beat to think through where to start. "I messed up, Clark."

"How so?"

"My son, Ben, got sick many years ago. I got into the habit of bringing his favorite treat"—he nods at the container in my hand—"my homemade blue velvet brownies, into the hospital to cheer him up." Otto smiles, staring at the floor, remembering. "One day, I offered a brownie to one of Ben's nurses. She *loved* it. The next day, another nurse heard my brownies were good, so I let him try one, too. Before I knew it, I was bringing in dozens each week for the hospital staff and other families I'd see around in the cafeteria. I may have been breaking the hospital's food safety rules, but everyone loved the brownies too much to make a fuss. That's how I met Beau."

Otto leans against the counter and shifts his weight off his bad knee with a slight grimace.

"Beau was a patient at the hospital?" I ask.

"No, but his father was," Otto says. "I'd see Beau in the cafeteria all the time. This was . . . let's see . . . eight years ago, so he was *young* to be hanging around a hospital by himself. It always caught my attention. Beau's mom—" He freezes. "Let's just say she wasn't winning any parenting awards, that's for sure. So with his dad being sick and his mom being who the hell knows, Beau got the next best thing." Otto laughs with a shrug. "Me."

I feel my eyes well with tears.

"Anyway, Beau loved my blue velvet brownies—*loved* them,"

Otto continues. "So I made sure he got some every week. The two of us, we'd hang out in the cafeteria a lot. Especially when Ben was resting and Beau's dad was asleep. Then, the worst days of our lives came in the same week. Beau lost his dad and I lost my Ben."

It feels like someone punched me in the gut. "I'm so sorry."

"Hey, that's life." He clears his throat and tries standing taller. "I may have lost Ben, but I gained a new type of son, you know?"

I try to pretend as though I'm listening to a story about two strangers, even though they both feel like family to me.

"We'd have a lot of fun together, me and Beau," Otto says. "I'd take him to Cubs games, the arcade, those sorts of things. It helped me to have Beau around, and I think the reverse was true, too. After I opened the bakery—right around the same time his mom went off the radar and Beau moved in with his grandparents—this place became his second home."

"He came in here a lot, then?"

"Oh, every single day," Otto says. "He'd find a way to trek into the city from West Edgemont, rain or shine. Before school, after school, often all weekend. I can still imagine him doing his home-work at the desk in the kitchen as if it were yesterday."

"I'm sure he really appreciated having this bakery to call home," I say.

"Maybe so," he says, "but then I opened my big mouth and ruined it." The baker pauses, staring at the floor in thought.

I wait for him to continue, but he doesn't.

"We don't have to talk about it," I say. "I know I've already overstayed my welcome anyway—"

"It's all right," he says, shaking his head. "You're fine. It's just . . . I don't like his boyfriend much, is all."

"How come?"

"They're not a good match," Otto says. "Beau is a free spirit. And he's certainly no wallflower. He thinks big, goes big, and, at six-foot-whatever tall, literally *is* big." Otto chuckles to himself.

"I feel like this other fellow held him back, though. Between you and me"—Otto gets quieter, despite the fact we're the only ones here—"his boyfriend isn't out of the closet, at least to the best of my knowledge. Which, hey, who am I to judge? But it became an issue between them. Beau felt like he was a secret. And this other fellow kept pressuring him to change—to shrink himself down, to compromise who he is—if Beau expected them to be together." Otto sighs, shaking his head. "Anywho. One afternoon, I made an off-the-cuff, stupid remark to Beau noting that I thought he deserved better."

"I'm guessing he didn't appreciate that?"

"Not one bit," Otto says, smiling sadly. "I should have been the adult in the conversation, but instead, I let the whole thing snowball, and he got pretty upset with me. That was a few months ago. Beau hasn't been back in here since."

Otto hangs his head.

"I shouldn't have said anything," he says. "It wasn't my place. But my dad instincts kicked in and I couldn't bite my tongue." He strokes his long, wiry beard. "If I had known it would hurt him so badly—that Beau wouldn't want to speak to me again—I never would have uttered a damn word." Otto gestures at his disheveled self. "And look at me now, a complete mess, missing both of my sons on Ben's birthday."

The bakery grows quiet.

I shift my weight, hoping I can say the right words in the right way. "Well," I begin, "I can't speak for Beau but it sounds like you were there for him when he needed someone the most," I say. "And if we are actually anything alike, I doubt he'll ever forget that."

Otto stands up straight, his eyes glistening with tears.

"I wouldn't worry about why he hasn't been in to see you," I add. "I bet he'll be back in before you know it."

Otto blinks a few times.

"I also wanted to tell you, and I hope this doesn't come across as strange, seeing as we haven't met before today," I say, remembering Ms. Hazel's second homework tip. "I'm a baker and a big fan of Ben's on Instagram."

"Oh, really?"

"Yeah. And I read your post this morning, and I . . ."

I tense up.

Otto waits for me to continue, but my throat has gone completely dry.

I've wanted to mention Ben so many times working in the bakery, and I promised myself that I'd do it now, before it's too late. Before I never have the chance again.

The words have left me, though. My mind is blank. I'm standing here, frozen like the blue ice cream in back, completely speechless.

Instead, tears just start to fall.

"Oh no," Otto says, circling the display case and moving toward me. "You don't have to say a word, Clark, I know. I know."

His tree trunks for arms pull me in. My cheek presses into his apron, and the remnants of a day's worth of buttery, blue concoctions fill my nostrils.

"I know you don't know me, but I know Ben would be proud

of you, Otto," I mumble through my tears, finally able to say it out loud. "I know that he'll never leave your side."

Just like, regardless of where I end up at 11:16 p.m., I won't leave Sadie's, or Blair's, or Mom or Dad's sides. I'm forever stuck with them, and they're forever stuck with me. Just like Otto and Ben.

Because, if there's one thing I've learned while being Trapped, it's that time may be able to warp many things, but it can never destroy the life I've shared with the people I love—regardless if I shared all seventeen years, or just a single afternoon of running errands.

The time loop may have tried, but it couldn't conquer me. Not really. In the end, I found my way back to them.

We pull away from each other. I hope that I've paved the way for Otto to have a better, less lonely tomorrow, regardless if I make it there or not. And if Beau's theory is correct and he gets to escape one of these todays, I hope he comes back to Ben's. I hope he and Otto can make it right.

"I should get going," I say, dropping the blue velvet brownie into my bag. "Thanks for staying open late for me."

"Any time," he says. "I hope you'll come back to see me soon, Clark."

So do I.

That reminds me. "Oh, you aren't hiring, are you? I'd love to work afternoons, if you think you could use the help."

CHAPTER 30

I T'S A LONG WALK ACROSS CHICAGO FROM BEN'S Everything Blue Bakery to The Honeycomb—a distance I'd never even dream about enduring under any normal circumstances—but I want to see, breathe, and hear as much of the city as I can before it's too late.

I notice the most mundane things on my way—a woman happily bobbing her head to the beat with her earbuds in, an old guy enjoying soup in the window of a Chinese restaurant, two friends hugging before they go their separate ways—and am reminded of the repetitions I'd relive on my commute home from my sessions with Ms. Hazel. The squirrel fight that breaks out on the corner of Eighth and North Streets, the yappy Yorkshire Terrier that barks at passersby, the ancient tree branch that creaks in the breeze. They used to gnaw at my sanity, but now I'd give anything to experience them again, one final time.

Instead, I reach the edge of Lincoln Park.

I pause, the wide, gray sidewalk beneath my feet transforming into a narrow dirt path ahead. I take a deep breath and pull out my phone, ignoring the dozens of missed notifications that have piled up throughout the day. As heartbreaking as they are to see, I made peace with my goodbyes to Mom, Dad, Blair, and Sadie in Day 364 and I don't think I can go through it again. So, instead, I tap into the time app.

11:00:53 p.m., 11:00:54 p.m. . . .

My stomach churns.

If Dr. Runyon is correct, fifteen minutes remain between me and . . . well, Whatever Comes Next.

I wish I never would have caused fate to make a mistake. I wish so many things could have gone differently. But they didn't. And now I'm here, staring into the darkness of Lincoln Park, as the seconds tick away before my flawed fate is sealed.

I'm glad I went out the right way, though, defeating my loneliness in Day 365.

I did the thing that scares me most and expressed how I *really* feel to Beau in the note I left for him at Splendid Cinemas. I opened up to Dee so she'd feel confident being vulnerable enough to tell me her secret, securing another love story's fairy-tale ending in the process. And I just helped an exhausted baker feel a little less alone when he needed it the most.

I may be terrified about what the next fifteen minutes will bring, but at least my heart is fuller than it's ever been before.

I imagine Ms. Hazel's four-part challenge one last time.

Clark's 4 tips to beating loneliness:
~~Try to make a new friend. (BEAU)~~
~~Help someone who could use it. (OTTO)~~
~~Be vulnerable so others can be too. (DEE)~~
~~Do the thing that scares you. (EMERY)~~

I take a deep breath and venture ahead, not lonely anymore.

Just like every other today I walked to The Honeycomb, the distinct sounds of the city slowly fade, replaced by the whispers of rustling leaves and humming insects.

I approach the last bend in the path—the final turn before The Honeycomb comes into view. Normally, in all the other iterations that I had left copies of *Trapped in Today* for Beau to find, this was a crucial moment. My entire day's work would lead to this turn, the anxious butterflies in my stomach flapping away incessantly, as my eyes search for his long, lean silhouette around the bend. But I've been crushed too many times to be hopeful that he'll be standing there tonight. So I veer left and rip off the Band-Aid, and when I look up—

I'm validated once again.

Beau isn't under The Honeycomb.

I imagine he's pursuing Thom in hopes of getting to their tomorrow. And who am I to blame him? Maybe I've just been a bottleneck in someone else's love story this whole time. Maybe I'm the villain in their fairy tale.

I follow the path up to the curved structure, soaking in its beauty, which—even having done this so many times before—hasn't gotten old. Of all the places where I could disappear into oblivion, I guess this spot isn't so bad.

After checking to make sure no security guard is in sight, I stand in the direct center of the tunnel and raise my hands into the air, admiring how the warm glow of The Honeycomb's lights bathe my limbs in orange. I take a breath, remembering that I have a blue velvet brownie in my bag. I might as well disappear with the tastiest thing that's ever been created in my mouth, huh?

I crack open the container and have a taste before glancing down at my phone. *11:09:42 p.m., 11:09:43 p.m. . . .*

Shit.

Shit.

Just a few minutes left.

I start to panic.

I thought I had this. I thought I could get to 11:16 p.m. without spiraling into a meltdown. But I don't know if I can.

My pulse picks up. I can feel my heartbeat in my fingertips. I'm light-headed, chest heaving up and down, *up and down*, as my lungs begin begging my body for more air and—

"Is that a blue velvet brownie?"

I jump.

I don't have to turn around to know that it's him. His voice—deep, raspy, and comforting like the same crackling bonfire I heard in Day 310—rattles me to my core. But I'm almost afraid I'm dreaming it. I look over my shoulder and see the unmistakable outline of his frame just beyond The Honeycomb. He takes a few steps forward, and the structure's light falls onto his face; his lips are spread into a small smile, and his amber eyes are staring back at me.

Beau.

A copy of *Trapped in Today* hangs at his side. "Hi," he says.

I exhale, beginning to tremble.

From nerves? From relief? I can't be sure. All I know is that my whole body starts practically convulsing, and it won't stop.

Beau strides forward and pulls me into him. "It's all right," he says. His skin is soft and smooth, warm to the touch.

I can't be completely sure I'm not hallucinating. Not really. Beau *feels* real in my arms. He sounds and smells real, too. But I've been dreaming of this moment for so long—for so many anxious iterations—that I can't be certain my mind isn't imagining what I want to be true in order to protect me from the inevitable.

I pull away to see his face, hardly able to speak.

We stare into each other for a moment.

"Hi," he says again, composed and sincere, as always.

This is the Beau I met in Day 310.

And I know that I'm not dreaming.

"I'm sorry I didn't trust you sooner, Clark," he says.

"But maybe you shouldn't have," I blurt.

His eyes narrow. "Why not?"

"Mr. Thunderburnt's theory?" I say, voice breaking. "That's what you believe is true, right?"

He grins. "So I take it Derek Dopamine helped you connect the dots."

"What if you're right?" I say, my teeth rattling. "What if you need to be with Thom in order to get out of today?"

"Then I don't want to get out of today."

"What?"

"I said, 'Then I don't want to get out of today.'" Beau gently moves my head onto his shoulder and squeezes me tightly. "Who needs tomorrow, when I've got you right now?"

My heart is racing. Beau's isn't, though.

I can feel it pushing against the inside of his chest, slow and steady.

His words make me want to melt, but my mind is racing as much as my heart. I have to know why.

"Why didn't you try to use me to get Thom back when we met on Day 310?" I ask. Despite the oppressive heat, I can't stop shivering. "I know you didn't tell me he was your ex because he's closeted. But, still, you could have taken advantage of me to win him back, since you believed in Thunderburnt's theory."

Beau stays silent as he rubs my arms. Finally, he exhales. "I need to tell you something, Clark."

I mumble, "Okay," but I'm not sure if he hears it through my trembling jaw.

"I went on our errands before in the time loop—many times," he admits. "I'd go to the bakery and apologize to Otto for avoiding him for so long. I'd go to the place I used to escape into as a kid, Splendid Cinemas, and reintroduce myself to Emery every afternoon. Then I'd go hang out with Dee under the stars because she needed a friend—a shoulder to cry on—after a rough night. I used to run my errands every day."

I want to tell him about Emery and Dee.

But I want to learn about his errands more.

"Why did you do it?" I ask.

"The same reason I imagine you did," Beau says. He stops stroking my back and pulls me in closer. "If I couldn't get out of the loop, I at least wanted to see my friends. I wanted to share my day. I wanted to feel less alone."

Guilt grips my insides, as it dawns on me how much it probably hurt Beau to see me taking over his errands—and, thus, the people and places that brought him at least some happiness—while he was avoiding me after Day 310.

"I'm sorry I denied you the comfort of seeing Otto and Dee and Emery," I say. "I was only trying to find you, Beau, and didn't realize how selfish and harmful it would be for me to be showing up in those spots all the—"

"Don't apologize," he cuts in. "You were trying to do what was best for me *and* you. Besides, running our errands only goes so far in curing loneliness. It starts to be painful, growing closer to people who can't grow closer to you."

I know the feeling.

"So I stopped," he says. "Until I found Thunderburnt's theory. And realized I had to win Thom back."

"So that's why you came to Mr. Zebb's class, then?" I say. "For Thom?"

"Yes. I came by the school a couple times before I met you to convince him we should be together—but he *hated* when I did that," Beau explains. "So, instead, I went to see him at his house, in the evenings. His parents weren't home, so it was fine. At least he despised that less. But it still wasn't working. I couldn't find a way to break through to him. But one day I got this really intense . . . I don't know how to describe it . . . *feeling*."

"In Day 310?"

"It would have been Day 309, the day before I met you. And I remember experiencing the feeling shortly after five p.m., as strange as that sounds, because that's when my grandparents watch this game show they love."

Shortly after 5:00 p.m. in Day 309. I would have been with Ms. Hazel.

That was when I told her that I'm lonely.

"Something told me that I needed to go to his class at the end of the following day and do something over-the-top—like disrupt the class he despises most and whisk him away on my favorite errands across the city. That way, he'd know how much I loved him."

"Did you, though?" I say. "Did you love him?"

"Of course not," he says. "Maybe I convinced myself I did at some point before all this. But I thought he was the key to my escape. So, knowing how much he despised trig, I jumped around the desks in Mr. Zebb's class like an idiot, hoping that, maybe *this* time, he'd be impressed with my boldness and we'd run off together.

I thought maybe that feeling I had was telling me to take him on my errands, because I hadn't tried that yet. Otto didn't think we're a good match, but maybe—if I played my cards right at the bakery—I could show him that Thom wasn't too bad, and maybe that was the key to winning him back. I wanted to take Thom to see Dee, too, so we could lie under the stars. Maybe that was where we'd fall back in love. Then we'd head to Splendid Cinemas, I'd tell him why I like going there so much, ending the night on the rooftop, breathing in the city—but alone, where he'd feel comfortable, still in the closet. Obviously, my plan blew up in spectacular fashion," he laughs, "and thank God it did. Because when I saw you in the parking lot, I felt it again; that *feeling*. So I invited *you* to run errands with me instead. I know now *you* are what drew me to Mr. Zebb's class in Day 310."

He breaks apart from me just enough to look into my eyes.

"It took me a while to realize it, Clark, but it was *you* who I needed to introduce to Otto; it was *you* who I should have been lying under the ballroom stars with; it was *you* who I fell for on the rooftop, overlooking the city." He smiles, his eyes aglow. "I'd already spent hundreds of days desperate to win Thom back, without success. So—to answer your original question with another— why would I ruin the best day of my life by making it about him again?"

I know that the city must be swirling around us still; that its white noise and glowing skyline exist somewhere beyond The Honeycomb. But Beau is all I can see, hear, or touch. Everything else has faded into nothing.

Beau lets out a laugh.

"What?" I say, smiling.

"Can we forget about the next part, though?"

"What part?" I ask.

"The part where I saw you talking with Thom in the hallway at school the next morning? Seeing you both together again brought the memory from yesterday roaring back."

"When you saw us talking outside Lakeview Live . . . ," I mutter to myself.

"I remembered why you looked so familiar, and I panicked," Beau says. "I followed you around that day to confirm you were Trapped. But after that, I knew I needed to say goodbye." He sighs, shaking his head. "It was wrong, but I started avoiding you. Because I knew that I liked you, Clark, and I knew you'd distract me from my goal. I couldn't let the same guy who caused Thom to break up with me to also prevent me from getting back together with him too. I'd never win back the person who I believed to be my soul mate. But I was wrong. *So* incredibly wrong."

Beau lifts my chin and presses his lips into mine. I would stay like this, *just like this*, for as long as he wanted. But a moment later, I'm nestled back into his torso again. And I think I might like this feeling just as much.

"Where have you been in our recent todays, though?" I ask softly. "I followed Thom around everywhere, assuming you'd still be trying to win him back. I went to your grandparents' house. I even pretended to be a new student to sneak into West Edgemont High School—"

Beau laughs. "Really? You took a page out of my book, huh?"

"But you weren't there, either."

I feel his chest rise and fall.

"I've been in a dark place, Clark," he says. "Nothing I tried to be was what Thom wanted and I realized nothing ever would be. And I was still too scared of how I felt about you. I got so lonely being stuck in here with no answers. And I just . . . I didn't know what to do. So I gave up."

"Gave up?"

"I turned off my phone every morning. I found a place where no one could find me—a deserted beach, an empty rooftop, whatever—and just . . . went numb."

My heart aches for him, knowing firsthand that level of loneliness. "I'm sorry, Beau."

"But then, this evening, I decided that I'd had enough," he says. "I had the urge to watch a movie. It's called *When Harry Met Sally*. It's one of my favorite classic rom-coms. Ever heard of it?"

I smile into his chest.

"And that's where a guy named Emery gave me a book called *Trapped in Today*, which came with a note," he says, breaking apart from me. "May I read you some of it?"

I nod, hardly able to comprehend that this is real. That this is *happening*.

He opens the book, takes out the letter, and begins.

"'I'm scared to write this, Beau,'" he reads. "'Terrified, really. But I don't know if I'll be able to tell you this again. If this book's theory is right, this might be our last today. So here it goes.'"

He glances up at me with a grin.

I might melt into the ground.

"'I believe I'm your soul mate,'" he reads. "'I love the way you crave adventure on a whim, even if I'm left holding on for dear life in the passenger seat. I love how lost you become in a cheesy rom-com, even when you know the ending because you've watched it a hundred times before. And I love that you made my world a bigger, brighter, less lonely place to be—even as we're frozen in time.'" He smiles. "'I love you, Beau Dupont, and I hope you love me too.'"

He sticks my letter back into the book and pulls me in once more.

"I owe you my life, Clark Huckleton," he says. "I believe you're my soul mate. And I am head over heels in love with you too."

We kiss again, and just like on Splendid Cinemas's roof, I feel like I might just float away.

An ambulance siren blasts on a nearby street, yanking me back to the ground. My stomach churns as I pull out my phone and peek into the clock app.

11:13:19 p.m., 11:13:20 p.m. . . .

This is it.

These could be my very last moments in existence.

I jump away from him. "I'm not sure that Dr. Runyon was right, though!" I say, panicking. "What if she wasn't? What if we stay Trapped forever, or worse?"

He thinks, cool as a cucumber. "Well, if that's the case, I wouldn't want to be Trapped forever with anyone else but you."

"Even if she *was* right, though," I barrel on, "I'm not sure that this is the exact location. I know we were supposed to meet at 11:16 p.m., and it had to have been in the park, but I'm only somewhat certain that it was right *here*, in this exact spot, under The Hon—"

"Do you remember what I told you in Day 310?" he cuts in, brushing a curl off my forehead. "When we were on the rooftop?"

"What?"

"I told you that I didn't feel lonely that day," he says. "I meant that."

I feel tears cascading down my cheeks. "I meant it too," I say. "I'm not lonely when I'm with you."

"Don't you see? We're in a win-win-*win*, Clark," he says, eyes glistening in the orange glow of The Honeycomb. "It doesn't matter if I'm Trapped in today with you forever, if we wake up tomorrow, hand-in-hand, or if this is my ending and it all fades to black for good." He leans forward, grinning, his forehead gently bumping into mine. "I'm the luckiest because I got to have you, even if it was just sixteen hours."

My breath begins to steady.

My heart finds its beat again.

I check the time.

11:15:03 p.m., 11:15:04 p.m. . . .

Under a minute left.

I'm no longer filled with dread, I realize, even though I should be. I should be terrified, leaving my fate in the hands of a universe that's prone to errors. But I'm not, because, regardless of what 11:16 p.m. brings, I got to share a life—a full, messy, beautiful, sometimes lonely life—with the people I love.

Incredible years with Mom, Dad, Blair, and Sadie.

Delightful days with Dee, Otto, and Emery.

And a time loop with Beau Dupont.

11:15:13 p.m., 11:15:14 p.m. . . .

"What are we going to do tomorrow?" Beau asks softly into my ear. "What errands should we run?"

I close my eyes, imagining what tomorrow could bring. "We'll FaceTime Sadie. I'd love for you to meet her."

"I'd love to meet her too."

"And I want to see Dee."

"Yeah?"

"Yes. Oh my God, Beau, I have so much to tell you about her . . . and Emery."

He laughs. "I can't wait. What else?"

"I want to watch *The Princess Bride* with you," I say. "This time, I'll stay awake."

"Perfect."

I feel our chests rising and falling together.

I never want this feeling to end.

I hope this feeling doesn't end.

"Blair should have blue velvet brownies for her birthday," I say. "So I need to make sure that happens."

"Am I invited to the party?"

"Of course," I say. "And we should visit Otto."

"I was thinking the same thing."

"He needs you, Beau."

He pauses. "I need him too."

I open my eyes and glance at my phone.

11:15:39 p.m., 11:15:40 p.m. . . .

Whatever happens, I've given this my all. Sure, I may have pushed fate to make a mistake. But, with a little help from Ms. Hazel, I also made it right in the end.

11:15:47 p.m. . . .

I made a new friend who happened to be my soul mate.

11:15:50 p.m. . . .

I did a thing that scared me. *Big-time.* And I stayed vulnerable so someone else could be too.

11:15:53 p.m. . . .

I finally found a way to defeat my loneliness.

I fell in love.

And it felt better than I ever thought it could.

11:15:56 p.m. . . .

"I'm looking forward to our tomorrow together, Clark," Beau says gently.

"I am too," I say back.

I close my eyes and hold on to him tight—tighter than I've ever held on to anyone before. I stop counting the seconds—I stop breathing, too—and brace for . . . *something* to happen, preparing to disappear into oblivion, or to see my white nightstand staring back at me.

I'm scared to open my eyes again. But when I finally do, I don't see a white or black void. I see blue. Ben's brownie is in my hand and Beau is still embracing me under The Honeycomb.

And when I glance at my phone, it reads: *11:16:09 p.m.*

ACKNOWLEDGMENTS

What would it be like to get stuck in a repeating day? As the pandemic trapped many of us indoors indefinitely, clearing our calendars and putting our social lives on hold, that question began to feel less like a creative exercise rooted in sci-fi and more like a nightmare come to life. At some point, I began to feel like Bill Murray in 1993's *Groundhog Day*. Would we ever get to tomorrow?

A lot has changed since the pandemic inspired me to write about a lonely, gay teen trapped in a time loop, but one thing that hasn't is my absolute certainty that *If I See You Again Tomorrow* would've been an impossible story to tell without my family, friends, and the powerhouse publishing team behind me.

Endless thanks to:

My editors, Amanda Ramirez and Alexa Pastor, and the rest of the pros at Simon & Schuster Books for Young Readers, who believed in Clark's story and helped make it shine.

BookEnds Literary and my agent, Moe Ferrara, for being a relentless advocate for me and all the other authors on #TeamMoe.

My publicist, Jeffrey Chassen, for always having my back (and knowing all my best angles).

My family in Michigan—Mom, Dad, Melanie, Doug, Carson, Parker, Max, and Hocus—for your unconditional love through rain and shine.

My closest friends, all of whom I wouldn't mind getting stuck in a time loop with (and, yes, I'm putting you all in A-B-C order to avoid implying I have favorites!): Adam S., Armand, Carlee, Christian P., Christian Z., Dan, Franco, Melissa M., Sean, Sebastian, Vitor, and Vy.

The big, beautiful city of Chicago and its wonderful people for inspiring Clark Huckleton and Beau Dupont's magical errands in Day 310.

Anyone—especially young LGBTQ+ people—who've ever felt trapped in their loneliness. Tomorrow will come, and I can't wait to see you there.

ACKNOWLEDGMENTS

What would it be like to get stuck in a repeating day? As the pandemic trapped many of us indoors indefinitely, clearing our calendars and putting our social lives on hold, that question began to feel less like a creative exercise rooted in sci-fi and more like a nightmare come to life. At some point, I began to feel like Bill Murray in 1993's *Groundhog Day*. Would we ever get to tomorrow?

A lot has changed since the pandemic inspired me to write about a lonely, gay teen trapped in a time loop, but one thing that hasn't is my absolute certainty that *If I See You Again Tomorrow* would've been an impossible story to tell without my family, friends, and the powerhouse publishing team behind me.

Endless thanks to:

My editors, Amanda Ramirez and Alexa Pastor, and the rest of the pros at Simon & Schuster Books for Young Readers, who believed in Clark's story and helped make it shine.

BookEnds Literary and my agent, Moe Ferrara, for being a relentless advocate for me and all the other authors on #TeamMoe.

My publicist, Jeffrey Chassen, for always having my back (and knowing all my best angles).

My family in Michigan—Mom, Dad, Melanie, Doug, Carson, Parker, Max, and Hocus—for your unconditional love through rain and shine.

My closest friends, all of whom I wouldn't mind getting stuck

ACKNOWLEDGMENTS

in a time loop with (and, yes, I'm putting you all in A-B-C order to avoid implying I have favorites!): Adam S., Armand, Carlee, Christian P., Christian Z., Dan, Franco, Melissa M., Sean, Sebastian, Vitor, and Vy.

The big, beautiful city of Chicago and its wonderful people for inspiring Clark Huckleton and Beau Dupont's magical errands in Day 310.

Anyone—especially young LGBTQ+ people—who've ever felt trapped in their loneliness. Tomorrow will come, and I can't wait to see you there.